Four Wishes

Christine Nolfi

*This book is dedicated to my daughter Christian,
who dares to color outside the lines*

Acknowledgments

My heartfelt thanks to the brilliant Wendy Reis, who has lovingly edited the entire Liberty Series. Her patience, humor and guidance make the long days of writing a joy.

Special thanks to Linda Weber for reading early drafts and the final manuscript with an unerring eye. I'd also like to thank Loreen Smith, Karla Nodorft Heller, Joan Maholtz, Deborah Blanchard and Franziska Schneider for their thoughtful suggestions.

No acknowledgement would be complete without expressing my gratitude to Renaissance woman and award-winning author and graphic designer Kathleen Valentine of Valentine-Design.com. Kathleen, I not only appreciate your unique art direction; I value your friendship as well.

Chapter 1

Whatever tragedies had visited the girl, they didn't stop her from seeking the refuge of sleep.

After the bursts of tears quieted and she drifted off, a strange energy sizzled in the air. It altered the physics of the servants' quarters, as if supercharged atoms of sadness and despair were colliding. They seemed to snap and pop in a dismal dance.

Banishing the odd notion, Meade Williams stepped away from the bed.

The jarring truth had yet to set in. A stranger—a girl barely on the brink of womanhood—was here, asleep in a portion of the mansion no longer in use.

Not that the lack of occupants in the servants' quarters could alter the habits of Meade's housekeeper and friend, Reenie. Year in and year out, Reenie vacuumed and dusted each room with unstinting devotion. She took simple pleasure in keeping the floors gleaming, and freshening the beds at the onset of each season. Spring, summer, autumn, winter—she perfumed the air with the scent of fresh linens as if readying the environs for a staff to rival the number of maids, butlers and cooks employed during the mansion's glory days.

There was no sense in dissuading Reenie from her habits. They were as ingrained as the lines on her face.

The housekeeper smoothed the blankets around the sleeping girl. She took care not to brush her fingertips against fluttering eyelashes or soft skin. A moan drifted from the girl's lips. Her shoulders flexed and Reenie pressed her palms down as if calming a child fleeing danger. The instinct was a good one. The girl sank deeper into dreams.

With relief Meade left the room.

She hurried down the hallway past the row of empty bedrooms. A flood of memories accompanied her: The timid maid who'd taught her how to jump rope when she was five years old, and the cook, a moon-faced woman who'd shown Meade photographs of the family left behind in Ireland. The rooms housing the butlers, valet, and her father's chauffeur had been off limits, but the women servants had allowed the lonely child to rummage through drawers and fondle the keepsakes positioned on dressers. To this day, Meade missed them all.

The heels of her Italian pumps clicked as she climbed the stairs to the first floor. Shadows churned in the kitchen like spirits writhing in a panorama of ash grey and black. Outside a flash of bluish light erupted. Thunder followed, a booming gong that silenced, for the briefest moment, the rain tapping on the windows.

In the foyer's echoing spaces, Meade paused at a side table and flicked on a lamp. A golden glow spilled across the ocean of ivory marble beneath her feet. On instinct she glanced up the curving staircase. Stained glass windows cradled the stairwell's landing. Behind them, another blue flash lit the sky. The thunder rolled off, and she listened for movement on the second floor.

A reassuring silence greeted her ears. With luck her father had taken a sleeping pill. Reenie may have given him one while helping him to bed, before her evening was interrupted by the appearance of the girl tucked in downstairs.

To release tension, Meade rolled her neck. As she collected her thoughts, she was faintly aware of the ache in her hand. She glanced down at her fingers clenching the briefcase in a white-knuckle grip. She set the case down.

The day had been long, with a shipment of perfumes from Paris delayed and several members of her staff up in arms about the increase in next week's hours. During the afternoon an order of cosmetics from a supplier in Avignon went missing in the warehouse. Pandemonium ensued as several employees cornered a young man, recently hired. He'd logged the shipment incorrectly then stacked the packages in the wrong place.

May was always a busy month, with unexpected orders from shops purchasing for summer and the larger department stores making last-minute additions to Mother's Day inventory. On the long drive home, Meade was stiff with tension.

Now she had a girl asleep downstairs—a girl who was little more than a child, really. What was she *doing* here? And what was her relationship to Reenie?

In the library, she went directly to the bar. Imbibing during the workweek wasn't typical, but today warranted the exception.

She was finishing the last of a very dry martini when Reenie announced her arrival with a subtle clearing of her throat. Her eyes were inked with worry.

"Who is she?" Meade asked.

The question sent a tremble up the housekeeper's spine.

"Glade Wilson. She's the daughter of my niece."

"Is your niece aware she's here? Perhaps we should call."

"Oh, I don't think it'll do much good."

"You don't? Why not?"

"Glade is terribly independent. She wouldn't have the sense to tell anyone she was coming to Ohio. Certainly not her mother—or me, for that matter." Reenie worked her hands with jerky movements. Finding a measure of composure, she added, "A while back, in West Virginia? She dropped out of high school and ran off. The police brought her home, but she ran off again."

"How difficult for your niece."

"There wasn't much she could do. She tried the usual things. She asked the police to talk to Glade. They gave her a good talking to in hopes she'd change her ways. A social worker was brought in, but she wasn't able to settle the girl down. Some kids have a wild streak running through them like a fever."

"What happened after she ran away the second time?"

"No one in the family has seen Glade for quite some time." The housekeeper lowered her eyes. "Until now."

The explanation was disheartening. Struggling for calm, Meade pinched the skin between her brows. Her sister's wedding was less than a week away. The preparations had already taxed the last of her energy. Add in her chronically depressed father, and the situation couldn't be more problematic. Even in the best of times his depression made unpleasant changes a burden on his fragile nerves. If the girl stayed, even for a few days, how would he respond to the intrusion? The Williams mansion was a broken kingdom. Reenie was all that was left of a brilliant era.

With a look of apology, the housekeeper stepped into the library. She continued working her hands at risk of rubbing them raw. Yet her tall, slender frame hid a resolute character.

During the worst years of her employer's depression, she'd remained steadfast. Reenie coordinated the basic maintenance of the mansion around an emotionally unpredictable man's visits into Liberty and the rare vacations he took at Meade's insistence. Gardeners to prune the topiary, a flurry of maids brought in periodically to air out musty rooms, the servicemen who stomped through the house checking the furnace or the air conditioning—she orchestrated the completion of a thousand tasks during the spare hours when her employer left the estate. A lesser woman would have quit long ago.

Taking pity, Meade poured Reenie's favorite drink. Handing over the brandy snifter, she asked, "Where's Melbourne?" Usually her beloved toy poodle waited with ears perked for the sound of her car.

"We gave him a good, long walk this afternoon. He trotted off to bed with your father."

"More bribery with biscuits? If I didn't know better, I'd think my father was trying to steal Melbourne's allegiance. He's grown fond of my dog." They shared a smile then Meade steered the conversation back on track. "Did Glade arrive by taxi? I didn't see a car."

"She walked from the bus station in Liberty."

"In the rain? She walked all the way?"

"Folks in West Virginia are used to it. She wouldn't think twice about a ten-mile trek."

The information melted the temper festering inside Meade. She'd returned home to the shocking scene of Reenie calming the sobbing girl she'd bundled into bed. No luggage in evidence, and the girl's coat was flung across a chair. Little more than a rag, it smelled of grease and something else, a woodsy scent reminiscent of the camping trips Meade had enjoyed with her father during childhood.

Apparently the scent had arrived all the way from the Appalachian Mountains, a region as graced with beauty as it was mired in poverty. The trailers where Reenie's extended family lived were crammed together in isolated hollows, the children underfed and skittish. Privately Meade understood *why* her father insisted on paying the housekeeper an outlandishly generous wage. Much of the cash, sealed in envelopes, was mailed south each month.

Now one of those relatives was in trouble, a girl with feverish independence.

Why else make the journey all the way to northeast Ohio? Given the other pressures filling Meade's days, she didn't need another problem to untangle.

She sank onto the sofa and patted the cushion to her left.

"Reenie, please sit down," she said, glad when the suggestion brought the housekeeper forward. "I'm not angry, truly. It's safe to say we're both surprised by Glade's appearance. It's late. We can sort out the particulars in the morning. My father . . . he was asleep?"

"Oh, yes. He didn't hear the doorbell. As soon as I saw who it was, I brought Glade down to the servants' quarters." Perched on the cushion's edge, Reenie took a grateful sip of brandy. "She was crying buckets of tears. Hard to understand anything coming out of her mouth."

She patted the housekeeper's knee. "How awful. For you, and her."

"Every time she tried to explain, she started sobbing again. Something happened to scare her nearly out of her bones."

"A man?" An impetuous romance followed by a devastating break-up—was there anything more common?

"From what I gathered, she broke it off."

"Did you get his name?"

"She won't say. Mind you, I didn't press. It didn't seem worth the trouble."

"She's overwrought. A full night's sleep will help. Get to the bottom of it tomorrow." Meade sent a glance toward the ceiling. "I'm not sure how to explain any of this to my father. You know how he is about strangers."

11

The comment bowed the housekeeper's back. "I'd never want to upset him. He's been in such a good mood, what with the excitement surrounding your sister's wedding. You know what happened yesterday? He asked me to deliver his tux to the cleaners. I just about dropped my jaw to the floor."

"Why does he care about an old tux? I bought him a suit for Birdie's wedding." The ceremony would be held in Liberty Square's center green. "Most of the women will wear floor-length gowns, but the men will be in suits."

"Don't bother trying to talk him out of his choice. Wearing the tux reminds him of your mother. Doesn't matter how long she's been in heaven, he'll always miss her."

It was doubtful her mother had earned a place among the angels. Keeping the dreary assessment to herself, she said, "You're right, of course. The tux brings back fond memories. Let's do this. Find a seamstress in Liberty who can work on short notice. It's been so long since he's worn the tux, it's too large. If Daddy thinks formalwear is perfect for the wedding, who are we to disagree?"

Despite her best efforts to ward off the emotion, her heart throbbed. Many of her most cherished memories were of clinging to Reenie's knees, hidden from the crowds in the ballroom, as her parents glided past their adoring guests in a swish of red satin and elegant black.

Now the ballroom was yet another area of the mansion blanketed in bitter memories, the chandeliers threaded with cobwebs and the air redolent of expensive perfume. A cleaning crew would arrive in the morning to air out the massive room for the wedding reception.

Was it foolhardy to think they'd host hundreds of guests without stirring up memories best forgotten? Dispelling the thought, Meade asked, "What do you think of the flowers? I need a second opinion. I promised the florist we'd get back to her on the final arrangements."

The library boasted two walls of floor-to-ceiling bookcases. Between them, a bank of windows, during daylight hours, gave an arresting view of the manicured grounds. The long table situated before the windows was bedecked with a dozen floral bouquets, everything from creamy tea roses to fragrant sprays of freesia.

"I can't decide which I like best," Reenie admitted. Appraising the bouquets, she added, "Which one do you think your sister will choose?"

"Birdie, choose wedding flowers? Don't hold your breath." Releasing a soft wave of laughter, Meade slipped off her pumps. "She doesn't know the first thing about planning a wedding and this is all terribly rushed."

"I suppose she couldn't have organized a wedding in three weeks' time without you."

"Which is why she's leaving most of the decisions to me."

"Even the choice of flowers?" Reenie asked with faint disapproval. "Do you mind?"

"No more than I mind taking care of the invitations, band selection and a million other odds and ends. Daddy and I paid the wedding planner double her usual wage. The caterer took some bribing, but we're on his schedule." Taking charge was an instinct, one she relied upon.

Birdie, on the other hand, was still resisting simple lessons like how to use a checkbook or keep a proper schedule.

"Putting together a wedding this quickly isn't Birdie's forté. At least she's going through with it and making Hugh an honest man. He's been so patient. I will say this—she walked right into a wedding gown. No alterations, nothing. Even the hem is the perfect length. She should've been a model."

"Did you help her pick out the gown?"

It was more accurate to say she'd dragged Birdie into the boutique after a ridiculous argument about *why* it wasn't appropriate to recite wedding vows in a sundress. If Birdie had won the argument, she probably would've walked down the aisle in flip-flops. Meade's younger sister had a quick comeback ready for any conversation; she also had no respect for ceremony.

"We shopped earlier this week," Meade explained. "The gown is beautiful. Nothing but my sister's flawless skin until you get to the silk organza bodice and the yards of sherbet tulle. Hugh will faint when he sees her. I should pack smelling salts. Or you should. I'll be too busy orchestrating the event."

The lighthearted joke didn't reach its mark. If anything, the stab at humor deepened the frown lines framing Reenie's mouth.

She downed the last of her brandy. Placing the glass on the coffee table, she stared straight ahead.

Meade pressed her palm to Reenie's back. "Now what's wrong?" Physical affection wasn't her strong suit, but the housekeeper's distress was palpable.

"I've never seen your father this happy. Going on about the wedding, talking to anyone who'll listen. He's more apt to stare out a window brooding. When the florist dropped off the flower samples, he talked her ear off."

"That's news." Usually he stalked off to a shadowy room until the mansion was restored to an unhappy silence.

"He was a regular chatterbox. Birdie this and Birdie that, and wasn't it something how she and Hugh Schaeffer were making the *Liberty Post* into the finest newspaper in the county. Oh, I don't mean he loves your half-sister more than you. Of course he doesn't. He's always been proud of your achievements, running your own company and all those employees—you're cut from the same cloth. When your father was your age, he was one of the most respected bankers in Ohio. Now you're making your own mark. Birdie, why, she isn't like either of you."

"She had a difficult childhood." An understatement. The horrors she'd known as the daughter of the notorious grifter Wish Kaminsky were hard to imagine.

Reenie nodded vigorously. "Oh, yes. Such a pity to have a criminal for a mother. Conning people out of their money, taking advantage of decent folks like your father—Wish Kaminsky is the worst sort. She never deserved a daughter as nice as Birdie. Thank goodness *your* mother, rest her soul, never learned of the affair or your father's illegitimate child." The housekeeper cut off, her cheeks quivering. Clearly she thought she'd gone too far. On a nervous laugh, she added, "Everything worked out, didn't it? You've discovered the younger sister you didn't know you had, and your father has found his missing daughter. I doubt he imagined Birdie would make Liberty her home, let alone turn the *Post* into a success and marry Hugh in the bargain."

Her father *was* happy—ebullient. A wedding couldn't eradicate his depression, but he was filled with a zest for life he hadn't displayed in recent memory.

"A wedding is exactly what our family needs. My mother has

been gone for a long time, and this old house could use grandchildren running around. And Birdie's mother can no longer cause harm. From what I gather, she's back in Mexico."

"She ought to be in jail."

Meade couldn't agree more. Wish Kaminsky was a criminal who'd scammed people across the U.S.

"She'd better hide in Mexico. If she tries to return to the States, she'll do prison time," she assured the housekeeper. "Hugh's best man, Hector Levendakis? He has friends keeping tabs on her."

"I like Hector. He always has something nice to say. Your father will miss him when he leaves."

"So will Hugh." She declined to add that Hector was too flighty for her liking, a man approaching middle age without a clear direction. It seemed miraculous that someone so groundless *had* driven Wish away. "Thanks to him, she'll never hurt my father or Birdie again."

"They both deserve happiness, your father especially. He's such a good man."

"He is."

Reenie knotted her hands. "I don't want to hang a cloud over him," she whispered. "I don't know what to do."

"I don't understand." A lie. Meade's powers of perception were honing in on a problem too uncomfortable to contemplate.

She was circling the truth when Reenie said, "It's Glade. I can't turn her out, not until I find her somewhere safe to live. Glade's mother, my niece? She has three other kids under her roof and she's divorced. She's got her hands full."

Meade's compassion for the housekeeper warred against her responsibility to her long-suffering father. "You're asking if Glade can stay for an extended visit?"

"The timing couldn't be worse, but I can't ask her to leave. Not in her condition."

Meade's throat was unbearably dry. Another martini? She was sure she'd need it as Reenie pulled to her feet and began pacing.

"Glade didn't just drop out of school." Reenie's eyes seemed to beg for mercy. "She was drinking and carrying on with the worst sort of boys, the type that'll use an impressionable girl

15

without thinking twice about it. How can I let her down? I'm the only relative she trusts. Please don't ask me to disappoint her."

Meade grappled for a sense of calm. When she'd found it, she asked, "When is the baby due?"

From across the shop, the bubble–gum-popping Delia Molek tossed another leering glance.

On principle Hector wasn't against women staring at him like sirloin sizzling on the grill. He was a man after all, and the sexual sparks Delia threw his way gave his ego a boost. But he was also a man with decency bred to the bone, and warning bells clanged in his head.

Money or looks—women hunted for one or the other.

A guy might have nose hair long enough to braid and the social skills of a chimp, but the gentler sex, picking up the scent of greenbacks, would trail him in droves.

Hector couldn't boast much in the way of material success. Since wrapping up the job as a bounty hunter, he was out of work. Clearly his lack of prospects didn't matter. The way Delia was staring at him, he nursed the sinking suspicion she'd mentally stripped him down to his skivvies.

Or worse.

Increasing the distance between them, he strode up the row of tables. The number of place settings the caterer had laid out for Hugh's inspection was mind-boggling, everything from simple stuff for a picnic to place settings befitting royalty. The groom was leaning toward a high-end look. Hugh nodded approvingly at the Baccarat goblets and china rimmed in gold.

Hector dragged him away from the spread, and out of earshot.

"Why did she tag along?" he demanded. Together they appraised Delia, blowing another bright pink bubble. "She's not in the wedding party. She shouldn't be here."

Hugh smirked. "Don't play dumb. You know why Theodora brought her along."

He did, but that wasn't the point. "Tell Theodora I'm not in high school looking for a date for the prom. I'm an adult. I don't like meddlers."

"I'll get right to it," Hugh remarked dryly. He regarded Liberty's town matriarch, grilling the caterer at the front of the store. The caterer, shriveled in her chair, couldn't get a word past Theodora's barrage of questions. "Think she's packin' her Saturday Night Special? I don't want to get my head blown off right before the wedding."

"Your fetching bride is related to her, right? That makes Theodora family and therefore *your* problem. Get her off my back. If I'm desperate for a date, I'll use an online dating site."

"Theodora believes finding the right woman will keep you in Liberty. She doesn't want to lose you to Philly."

Did Delia think the same? In one of those tactical maneuvers women used to overrun the battlefield, she drew in a long breath. Pert breasts strained beneath her knit top.

His pulse scuttled. This much incoming he could do without.

Severing the connection, he followed Hugh to the back of the store. "Delia's just a kid," he whispered, coming to a halt behind a rack of tablecloths.

"Not true. She's in her twenties."

"Early twenties. Even if she *were* old enough to date, I'm leaving after you get back from your honeymoon. Not that I know how to run a newspaper while you're gone, but I'll manage."

"You don't have to run it. I'll videoconference with the staff every morning. Just keep them on a tight leash. Don't let anyone near petty cash, and no travel without my approval. I don't want problems. The *Liberty Post* hasn't even celebrated its six month anniversary yet."

"That'll make the rag about the average age of the newbies you hired." Not to mention Delia.

"What did you think? I'd find experienced reporters willing to work for slave wages? I'm building a daily newspaper from the ground up. Who doesn't scare up cheap labor by scouring colleges for recent grads?"

"You have other options. Your bride-to-be has a large inheritance tucked away at the bank. Come to think of it, you should hire an experienced office manager."

"I'm making a go of the newspaper without Birdie's inheritance."

"Great. You're a guy with honor. All the same, I need to get back to Philly." He didn't add how much he'd miss the people of Liberty once he returned to the City of Brotherly Love.

A month ago he'd joined the team of bounty hunters Theodora hired to track down Birdie's mother, Wish Kaminsky. He'd been down on his luck after stock market losses pummeled his dreams. His sense of duty had compelled him to find a way to repay the losses of his two ex-wives—and those of his enraged ex-fiancé. Thanks to the payout for ridding the town of Wish, he'd restored the women to financial solvency. He'd also earned the personal satisfaction of driving Wish from the town of Liberty forever.

How to top the recent success?

The future was murky. His sister was a successful accountant in Philadelphia, and she'd promised to help him craft a resume. Five years from forty, Hector was still looking to board the ship to success. He enjoyed working with people, which meant a job in sales wasn't out of the question. Or something in marketing. He'd always been able to think on his feet, spinning ideas like cotton candy in his frothy brain.

Theodora brought his reverie to a halt. The petite titan strode forward at an impressive gait for a woman her age. Her raisin-skinned face was scrunched with concentration or irritation. It was hard to tell. Odds were it was the latter.

She regarded Hugh. "Well? Did you choose a setting?"

Hugh pointed at the Baccarat. "This one."

"You're sure? I fancy the picnic dishes."

Hector peered over her shoulder at her choice. The dishes were bright yellow with tiny cowboys riding the rim. "You're kidding, right? This stuff is for a kid's birthday party."

"I like it."

Hugh took the plate from her grasp. "If the reception were in your backyard, they'd work. Not at the Williams' estate."

"Why the hell not?"

"The mansion screams 'elegance.' Landon is bringing in a crew to get the ballroom up to snuff. I hope we have enough guests to fill it."

Theodora *harrumphed* with disbelief. "Meade invited hundreds of guests. We'll fill the ballroom."

"How many people? I never saw the final list."

"If you start fretting, I'll lose my mind. Birdie's nerves are all I can take. And how did I lose the argument about where to hold the reception? Hell and damnation, who needs a ballroom? I'd picked out nice big tents for my backyard." She shimmied her shoulders in a burst of irritation.

Hector wiped the sheepish grin from his face. He couldn't help but like the raging wildfire of Theodora's personality. Life beat most people down, leaving them cynics or too exhausted to give a damn. Not so with the elderly woman before him.

He was still privately singing her praises when she diminished herself in his eyes. Snapping her fingers, she drew an eager Delia from across the store.

"I like the fancy dinnerware too," Delia said in a breezy voice that revealed her exceptional skills at eavesdropping. She sashayed up to Hector. "What do you think? Fancy place settings or something simple?"

"I'm with Hugh. I haven't seen Landon's estate, but I've heard the ballroom is a sight to behold. It's got to be elegant dinnerware." People talked about the mansion like it was a mysterious palace outside town. From what he'd gathered, there hadn't been a party at the estate since the death of Landon's wife years ago. "A formal reception will be a nice switch from the wedding in Liberty Square. Casual to elegant." To Hugh, he said, "I'll bet the *Liberty Post* runs photos on the front page."

"Already scheduled," Hugh said. "One of my newbies will accompany the wedding photographer to Landon's estate. Don't tell Birdie. It's a surprise."

Delia fluttered long lashes. "I can't wait for the reception," she said. "I've bought the perfect dress."

Theodora gave Hector a meaningful glance. "I'm sure Hector can't wait to see it." With the subtlety of a Jewish matchmaker, she added, "He'll be waiting to ask for a dance. I hear Landon picked out a fine band."

"Oh, I can't wait!"

Hector suffered the itchy desire to flee. The bright-cheeked waitress swayed an inch, pressing her overheated flesh into his side. If she dropped her head to his shoulder, Theodora would host a cowboy-themed wedding. Something with balloons and a rodeo.

Only he wasn't ready for the hitching post. Not with a girl so young.

Hugh rode in to the rescue. "Don't you have another appointment?" he asked Hector with ill-concealed mirth. "Something with Landon? If he needs help with the ballroom, lend a hand. He may be in over his head."

With relief, Hector moved off. "I'm on it," he said.

Chapter 2

The spring morning transformed Glade Wilson.

Gone was the sobbing girl from last night. She beamed happiness as Reenie set a banquet of food before her; a poached egg in a silver holder as ornate as a chalice, red strawberries sparkling beneath a dash of sugar, a warm croissant, three varieties of jam, and links of maple sausage still hot from the frying pan. Her face was round and plain, but the curiosity sparkling in her bottle green eyes lent an attractive quality as she canvassed the kitchen's generous spaces. She seemed astonished by the rich surroundings, her eyes lingering on the overlong center island before moving closer, to take in the miles of wainscoting surrounding the table.

Meade, smartly dressed in a wool crepe suit, had already received three calls from the office. No matter how detailed her instructions, her wholesale cosmetics company *Vivid* didn't function without her on the premises. A shipment of perfumes was trapped at the airport. Pouring a cup of Reenie's cinnamon-scented coffee, she made a mental note to check into it on the drive to work.

Noticing her, the housekeeper left the table and busied herself at the sink. Taking the cue, Meade went to the table.

"Good morning, Glade."

The greeting sent the ripe strawberry aimed for the girl's mouth back into the bowl. With an air of desperation, she glanced at the sink. Reenie, dunking her hands in suds, kept her attention studiously on the task.

"Feeling better this morning? Reenie said you had quite a trip."

"Yeah, it was something." At last she looked up, adding, "You sure have a nice house. This place is like a hotel."

"It's my father's home, actually."

"Don't you live here? This is too much room not to share with family."

A hint of accusation rimmed the question, raising Meade's defenses. "I keep an apartment in Beachwood, but I usually stay here," she agreed. The girl meant no harm. Curiosity was natural, especially for someone of limited means. In a warmer voice, she added, "My father is getting on in years. I stay to keep him company. He doesn't get out much."

"Does your husband mind when you stay here? Or does he come with you?"

"I've never married. I own a company."

Confusion clouded the girl's eyes. "That's okay," she said, as if granting approval. "Lots of older ladies don't settle down. Owning your own company sounds great."

"It is."

"I didn't know houses came this big. I mean, I've seen stuff in movies but it's pretend. Do you have lots of friends come over? If I were you, I'd have a million slumber parties. I'd invite everyone I know."

The ramble wound into an awkward silence, leaving Meade unnerved. Evidently the proprieties of common etiquette were beyond the girl. As was the ability to select flattering clothing—she wore a sweatshirt large enough for a man. It all but hid her voluptuous body. She was on the heavy side with brown hair blooming in a frizzy swirl around her shoulders. Was she four months pregnant? Five? Impossible to tell.

"Reenie says you're from West Virginia," Meade said at last.

"Not anymore. I like Ohio. It's real nice here."

No surprise there. A lucky fate had dropped her onto a country estate. Why wouldn't she think it was nice? Good manners precluded asking about the length of her stay. Instead Meade said, "How was your trip?"

Considering, the girl succumbed to temptation and selected

a strawberry. "It was okay. The bus was smelly but I fell asleep." She popped it into her mouth.

"I'm glad you made it in one piece."

"Can I ask you something?"

Meade took a lingering sip of coffee. "Of course," she said with false cheer.

"What's it like to be rich? Do you buy stuff without checking the price? Just buy it because you want it? I used to clip coupons for Mom every Sunday after we got back from church. She wouldn't go to a store without coupons. You're pretty too. I bet you've never *seen* hand-me-downs. I'm going to be rich someday. I'll never shop in Goodwill again."

Meade rattled the teacup back into its saucer. Drumming up a polite response proved impossible.

At the sink Reenie ejected her hands from the soapy water. Suds plopped on the floor.

She sent Meade a look of apology. To her imprudent relative, she said, "Glade, why don't you finish your breakfast? Miss Williams doesn't have time to chat. She has a guest waiting in the sunroom."

Meade allowed the housekeeper to remove the cup from her hand. Together they went into the foyer.

"I have a guest?" Meade asked.

"He's waiting for your father. I couldn't think of a better way to extradite you from the kitchen."

"You're intrepid, Reenie." The tinkling of bells on her miniature poodle's collar sent her attention up the stairwell. After Melbourne trotted down and leapt into her arms, she added, "What would I do without you?"

"Encounter fewer embarrassing questions. Glade means well. She's a country girl, and rather overwhelmed."

"Who's waiting in the sunroom?"

"Hector. Your father asked him to stop by."

"I can't imagine why Daddy asked to see Hector." There was no sense prodding the housekeeper. Chances were, she wouldn't know the reason for the visit.

She freed the squirming poodle from her grasp. He trotted toward the kitchen. Glade's squeal of delight was followed by Melbourne's *yip, yip, yip* of canine excitement.

23

"Do you mind if Glade gives Melbourne a walk around the grounds?" Reenie asked. "I have a busy morning ahead of me. It'll keep her out of my hair for at least half an hour."

"It's a perfect idea. Tell Glade she'd be doing you a service if she gives Melbourne a good run. If you can keep her out of sight, it's best. I'll mention her to my father tonight after work."

"Thank you, Meade."

"It's nothing. Now, stop worrying. Everything will work out."

Excusing herself, she went to the sunroom.

Hector was casting appreciative glances at the jungle of plants trailing from baskets and placed on every available surface. Unlike the other rooms in the mansion, the sun-washed space had returned to life after Meade's father discovered a latent green thumb. The air was moist in here, and thick with the pleasing scents of potting soil and leafy vegetation.

Hector's back was to her, and she hesitated before making her presence known. She wanted to like him. He'd grown close to her younger sister and Hugh. Theodora, who lobbed inflammatory remarks at Meade with regularity, treated him with warmth she usually reserved only for Birdie. Even Meade's father, whose only close friend was Theodora, seemed to enjoy his company.

More laughter from the kitchen, and Hector turned around. His inquisitive gaze found Meade's.

"Is that your housekeeper?" he asked. "Sounds like she's won the lottery."

"No, Reenie isn't laughing."

"Who then?"

"I'd rather not go into it."

"Why not?" he persisted. "State secret?"

Glade was a troubling issue better forgotten until tonight. Contrary to the assurance she'd given her housekeeper, she was *not* looking forward to discussing the girl's visit with her father. Nor would she bring Hector into her confidence.

With a tight smile, she said, "It's none of your business."

He approached, his eyes sparkling. "Don't hold back. I applaud honesty in women."

A backhanded compliment, but she wasn't impressed. "Do

you always pry into other people's lives?"

"Depends. If they're tight-lipped, I can't resist."

She started over. "Fine. If you must know, my housekeeper has a relative visiting." Hector's brows rose, prodding her on, and she added, "Reenie didn't know she was coming. Glade's from West Virginia."

"It's good to have time with family."

"Depends," she said, mimicking his playful tone. "Reenie's a nervous wreck about the visit." She paused a beat. "Her young relative is pregnant."

This got his full attention. "West Virginia isn't ten minutes away. Is her husband with her? A pregnant woman shouldn't travel alone."

Count on Hector to cast a positive assumption on a difficult situation. No wonder she felt ambivalent toward him—the unabashed optimism. It paired nicely with his inability to settle into a career. Given his Greek heritage, his striking features and ebony hair seemed his birthright. If he were a woman he would've landed a Sugar Daddy by now, someone enthralled by his effervescent personality and easy sexuality. He'd spend his days shopping and planning dinner parties.

Or slumber parties like the ones Glade dreamed of hosting. Like her houseguest, there was something adolescent in his personality, something she mistrusted.

"There's no husband," she revealed. "If I had to guess, Glade is seventeen years old. Eighteen, tops. She has a history of wild behavior and a mother in the Appalachian Mountains too busy raising the rest of her brood to take this one in hand. I have no idea how long she plans to stay."

"And she's pregnant? How many months?"

"She's wearing a man's sweatshirt. I can't tell."

The peevish response lowered Hector's brows. "Meade, take her to a doctor. I don't care if the kid is twelve years old. If she's pregnant, she needs guidance on appropriate prenatal care."

Heat climbed her cheeks. If her father had chastised her, she couldn't have felt more embarrassed. Why was she treating the girl's arrival like an invasion? So they'd have an additional guest at Birdie's wedding reception. Undoubtedly Glade ran away from home because she was tired of clipping coupons and shopping at

Goodwill.

"Forgive me." Meade offered a whisper of a smile. "Of course you're correct. What's the matter with me?" Poor, uneducated, pregnant—Glade deserved compassion. "I'm behaving dreadfully."

"It's understandable. You've got a lot on your plate with Birdie's wedding. You weren't expecting a houseguest."

"You're too kind."

"Usually."

She let his bravado pass. "I don't know the first thing about teenagers," she admitted. "Do they always bash you with questions? I wasn't expecting a Q&A first thing this morning."

"Kids are naturally curious, if that's what you mean."

Her thoughts exactly, and the comment sent her attention back to his eyes. Their gazes meshed for an electric moment. Sexual energy charged the air with potency impossible to dispel. His tight appraisal heightened her senses, making her acutely aware of her shallow breaths and the increasing tempo of her pulse. Men rarely had such an effect on her. She didn't relish the sensation. She wasn't in control of her emotions—or the situation.

No wonder she preferred to dislike him. It was safer.

"Reenie never married, which makes her no help whatsoever," she said in a conversational tone that belied the effect he was having on her. "She's no more experienced at dealing with teenagers than I. How my father will react when he discovers a pregnant girl wandering around the house is another worry. He's very private."

"He's not the only one," Hector replied. "You are too."

She was, but the observation bothered her.

What's it like to be rich? Do you buy stuff without checking the price? The girl's brutal inquisitiveness had nearly brought on Meade's temper, the ungovernable emotion she despised.

What was it like? Lonely.

She'd spent her childhood on the fringes of her mother's celebrity, the great philanthropist Cat Seavers. A trophy child, Meade was shuttled among a forgettable series of nannies with only the stalwart Reenie as a playmate. She'd built a company on her own and was just beginning to enjoy the first taste of success when her mother, during one of her more narcissistic tantrums—and over her frightened daughter's objections— piloted her motorboat into Lake Erie. Cat drowned, and the ensuing publicity captivated Ohioans. News reports about her affairs and Meade's father's longstanding association with Wish Kaminsky continued to pop up for months after.

Meade then spent the following years tending to a father grieving the loss of his wife and his reputation. His spirit was fully broken when Birdie's mother took her child and disappeared.

The smartphone tucked in Meade's suit gave off a hum, rousing her from the sad reverie.

"I'm late for work." She pivoted toward the door then paused for a parting shot. "Why *are* you here to see my father? I wasn't aware you had an appointment."

The rude query filled Hector's eyes with merriment. "None of your business," he said, throwing down a gauntlet of his own.

Near the end of Landon's impromptu tour of the estate, a truck laden with tables and chairs pulled into the circular driveway with a grind of shifting gears. It rolled to a stop behind the cleaning service's three vans.

The cleaners were already at work, the whine of floor polishers and vacuums spilling from windows opened to let in the spring air. Evidently the noise rattled Landon Williams. He steered his guest in the opposite direction, away from the chaos descending upon his magnificent home.

Contrary to what Hector led Meade to believe, the reason for the invitation wasn't clear.

Only a few days ago he'd met her father at the *Liberty Post.* The retired banker had stopped by to discuss his younger daughter's wedding with her excited groom. Hector spoke to Landon briefly. He came away with a positive impression of the man whose wealth, according to local gossip, was rivaled only by Theodora's.

Now, as they moved farther from the house, Landon took him by the arm like a trusted confidante. It struck Hector that his quiet, introspective companion possessed the bearing of a man who'd walked the corridors of power with confidence and ease. He was a genteel host, providing snippets of conversation as they strolled stone paths away from the mansion. With relish he pointed out dogwood trees in bloom and the cutting garden his housekeeper Reenie favored. He was enjoying himself, and Hector waited patiently for him to reveal the reason for the visit.

The journey took them all the way to a boathouse wrought of silvery granite. Ivy of an intense emerald green laced the rough-hewn walls. The quaint structure's east side faced the sun, allowing the roses clinging to its surface to fan the air with pink blooms. The luscious scent had just reached Hector when he paused to take in the private stretch of beach and the dock thrusting out into Lake Erie. The lazy waters rippled in the sunlight.

Evidently tired by their walk, Landon motioned to a bench at the water's edge. The sun warmed their shoulders as they appreciated the lake.

After long minutes, Landon broke their meditation. "It's about Birdie." He pinned his intelligent gaze on Hector. "I hope you'll forgive me for involving you. Hugh isn't aware we're having this conversation, although I doubt he'd object. You're the first close friend he's had in a long time."

"A kind observation. I'm not sure it's true."

"It is. Before meeting my daughter he led, shall we say, a colorful life. Women, drink, working to secure the types of awards every journalist hopes to win—he was motivated by sensual pleasures and a thirst to get ahead. Friendship wasn't among his ambitions."

"It is now?"

"He trusts you. So does my daughter."

"Your *younger* daughter," Hector corrected. Meade treated him like one of her employees at *Vivid*. Why she despised him was a mystery. "I've only run into Meade once or twice. We've never hit it off. I'm not to her liking."

"You're an acquired taste."

The comment startled him. "Come again?"

"From what Theodora tells me, you've dabbled in everything from the U.S. military to day trading on the stock market. It leaves the impression you're unsettled."

"I wouldn't call a stint in the military 'dabbling' when you were under fire in an Afghani outpost." He was proud he'd done his duty, but it sure hadn't been easy. "Being unsettled . . . okay, I'll give you that one. I'm a work in progress. It doesn't mean I'm irresponsible, although I *have* chucked jobs too quickly. I want to feel driven, the way Hugh is driven to make the newspaper into the biggest daily in northeast Ohio. It's fascinating to watch how he pours his heart and soul into his work. I want to feel the same passion. Problem is, I haven't found the right vehicle to drive myself to success. "

Why was he revealing his deepest fears and aspirations? It seemed self-serving.

He started to apologize but Landon, savoring the explanation, held up his hand. Hell, he looked amused. "I think I understand why Hugh trusts you," he said, and the pleasure reached his eyes. "You're without a shred of artifice. It's refreshing."

"Good to know."

"I'm not trying to embarrass you."

Hector scrubbed his palms across his face. "Got it. Thanks."

There was something fatherly in the way Landon treated him, and he wasn't sure how to react. His own father had died when he was a kid. He didn't have a stash of memories to keep the relationship kindled in his heart.

His parents had spent their brief marriage working from dawn to dusk, hanging on to a middle class life by their fingernails. The only paternal influence Hector received was the one he'd cultivated in his head as he'd tried to protect his mother and sister. That hadn't worked out well, and he'd lost his mother in a traffic accident.

His sister Calista, on the other hand, was doing all right. More than all right. Life in a wheelchair didn't thwart her achieving her goals. Like Meade, she was a successful businesswoman who could buy and sell him many times over. If financial prosperity was the gauge to measure a man, he was coming up short.

The thought was self-defeating. Quashing it, he said, "Now that we've established my friendship with Hugh, may I ask why I'm here? I'm sure you have better things to do with your time."

29

Landon studied him as if appraising his worth. "Birdie is pregnant," he said. "We're keeping the secret until after the wedding."

"Does Theodora know?" She was Birdie's second cousin or third. Whatever their connection, she'd be thrilled.

"She does. She's been helpful although there isn't much she can do about morning sickness. From what Hugh describes, it's debilitating. Birdie is putting up a good front, but she needs to restrict her schedule."

"Who's covering her beat?" She wrote for the human-interest section, the *Post's* lighter and, in Hector's opinion, more interesting stories. "Hugh's training a staff, but they're not ready for prime time. Most were sitting in journalism classes about ten minutes ago."

"Hugh plans to take on the majority of Birdie's work, which leads me to the problem at hand. He needs an office manager, someone for a few months while he brings the *Post* into the black. I want you to consider taking the position."

"I've already promised to watch over the paper while they're on their honeymoon."

"They're putting off the trip to Barbados. He's worried Birdie isn't up to it. She agreed."

"The honeymoon's off? You're sure?"

"It was a hard decision, but for the best. Birdie won't be able to enjoy herself in the shape she's in."

"Sure. There's not much you can do about morning sickness. But if Hugh needs help for the entire summer, why didn't he ask?" Which wasn't what really bothered him. He *did* like Hugh, and should've sensed his worry over Birdie. At the least, he should've noticed she wasn't feeling well. He hadn't. The oversight was inexcusable. "Why are you the one offering the job?"

"You seem eager to get home to Philadelphia. I doubt Hugh wants to stand in your way."

"I do need to get back. Start sending out resumes—land something in sales or marketing. I don't have the skill set to play office manager for months on end. Bookkeeping isn't my strong suit."

"If you run into problems, I'm a phone call away."

There was more to it. Deducing the real issue, Hector said, "You want me to stick around for moral support." He looked off at the lake. "Seeing that Hugh and I are good friends. You think he'll need someone to lean on."

"For several months, that's all. Let them settle into marriage. They've both led precarious lives. With a baby on the way, they'll have more responsibility than anticipated. Oh, I think they'll be marvelous parents once they've warmed to the idea. They're excited about the baby. Nervous too. All perfectly reasonable."

"How is Meade taking the news?" An odd question, but he was curious.

Not that a woman of her caliber needed home and hearth. Given her professional success, she'd done all right. More than all right—the company she owned was a major player in Ohio. Yet the prospect she might feel jealousy, even fleetingly, piqued his interest.

"I don't think Birdie has told her yet. However, I'm sure she'll be happy for them."

"You don't seem positive."

The wrong thing to say, and Landon tensed. "Meade was unaware of Birdie's existence until last year," he replied. "Now she'll become an aunt. Another change, and she's rather inflexible—sadly a trait she inherited from me."

"Tough deal for an only child. I'm not sure how I'd feel if I found out in adulthood I had a half-brother. Confused, probably. Angry too."

"It was a mistake."

"What was?"

"Keeping my children apart." Landon grew still, the contentment on his features seeping away. He looked older then, a man bitterly aware he'd never atone for his sins. "After Wish broke off our affair, I should've tracked her down and fought for custody of Birdie. I let my daughter drift out of my life. I was weak, too much of a coward to allow my deplorable behavior to become public. Meade's mother was a philanthropist, highly regarded. I had Wish while my wife had many . . . dalliances. Our popularity on the social circuit was a ruse—we were both imposters. We were miserable, but the mess we made of our marriage wasn't the real tragedy. Why didn't I consider how my choices would affect my daughters?"

Unsure of how to offer comfort, Hector shifted on the bench. His knowledge of Landon's history consisted of a few offhand remarks by Hugh, none of it pitiful like the revelations just shared.

Searching for something positive to lighten the mood, he said, "Look at it this way. Meade and Birdie are now in each other's lives. I'm not sure how Meade looks at it, but Birdie loves having a big sister. From what I gather, they get along fine. Now Birdie's pregnant. Kids bring families together, right?"

"One would hope."

"Congrats, by the way. I'm sure you're looking forward to becoming a grandfather, and Meade will enjoy being an aunt. I don't have nieces or nephews, but my cousins have lots of kids. I love every one. It's hard to worry about the past when children keep you happily in the here and now."

The sorrow hanging over Landon didn't abate, but he managed to smile. "A baby is exactly what my family needs."

"There you go."

"I have no preference. Boy or girl. Either is a blessing. A healthy mother and child—it's miracle enough."

"You got it."

Landon rose. Hector got to his feet, adding, "I hope the baby inherits Birdie's violet eyes. They're remarkable."

"I'm proud to report the trait is from my side of the family," Landon remarked, strolling to the gently rolling waters. From over his shoulder, he said, "You haven't given an answer."

"About spending the summer masquerading as the office manager of the *Liberty Post?* Let me sleep on it."

"Nonsense. You may lack confidence in your abilities, but you strike me as a man with solid instincts." Landon pinned him with a calculating gaze. "So answer me, Mr. Levendakis. What does your gut tell you to do?"

Chapter 3

Dr. Mary Chance loved her life. Except on the days when she didn't.

Today was proving less than enjoyable. This morning her general practice, located on the second floor of the building housing The Second Chance Grill, had been jam-packed with patients. Kids pulled from school for summer camp physicals, patients from a nursing home suffering a nasty stomach virus, a woman covered in poison ivy after planting her vegetable garden—there hadn't been a break. Bongo drums were having a go at her temples and her feet were on fire. And an afternoon of more patients awaited her.

Now this.

She'd made the short drive home for a 10-minute lunch in relative peace. Which wasn't in the cards.

She hated playing the role of truant officer. Restraining her temper, she stopped in the kitchen doorway to glare at her stepdaughter's back.

"Blossom, why aren't you in school?"

Whirling around, the mischievous preteen sent a slice of bread slathered with peanut butter spinning like a Frisbee. Instantly her golden retriever was airborne. Sweetcakes nabbed the bread before it whirled past.

Leaning against the doorjamb, Mary crossed her arms. Last year she'd married Blossom's father, Anthony Perini, and her parenting skills weren't yet up to snuff. Even so, she did her best to transmit disapproval.

"We've been over this a thousand times. You're not allowed to sneak out of school during lunch period. I can't spend half my life getting an earful from the principal. I'm a doctor. I'm busy."

Blossom ran her fingers through the corkscrew curls tumbling from her head. "What are you doing here?" she asked. "Don't you have patients?"

"Stop changing the subject. I'm waiting."

"Uh . . ."

She snapped up her wrist. "Don't keep me in suspense. I now have nine minutes to dine and get back to the office. I don't have the time for this."

"Mom, I'm sorry. Really."

Mom.

The endearment filled Mary's heart with an emotion as gooey as the peanut butter on Sweetcakes' snout. Was there anything as sweet as the mother-daughter bond they'd already forged? Still, she'd never prove her mettle if she didn't keep Blossom on the straight and narrow.

"Stop snowing me," she said.

"I didn't mean to leave the school. It just happened."

"Nothing just happens."

"You don't understand. I went to the cafeteria like I promised. I got one whiff, and ran for the exit."

"Let me guess. The cafeteria manager is on another binge of Mashed Potato Medley?" The woman was on a roll with nutritious if unpalatable dishes.

"It was the worst. Mashed potatoes with fatty pieces of meat. And there were peas mixed into the glop. *Peas.* Kids were taking off from the cafeteria like it was the end of the world. A seventh grader tried to hide in his locker. The gym teacher pulled him out."

"He's not my problem. *You* are. We had a deal—no more leaving school at lunchtime." She sniffed the air much like Sweetcakes hunting for a tasty morsel. "Where's Snoops?" The girls were inseparable.

"Not a clue. Haven't seen her all day."

"Blossom—"

"Okay, okay. I give up. My *compadre* is heading for the hills.

She saw your car coming down the street."

Mary stalked to the kitchen window. Sure enough, Snoops was hobbling across the backyard with her purple-framed glasses bobbing on her nose. It would've been the perfect escape if she weren't on crutches and her leg in a cast.

Earlier this spring, Birdie's mother Wish Kaminsky had descended upon Liberty. She'd driven Snoops' bicycle off the road during a malicious crime spree. Snoops was healing nicely, and would soon be out of the cast.

Mary retreated from the window. "Oh, for Pete's sake. Go and fetch her. I can't have a kid with a broken leg fleeing across my backyard. What if she breaks her *other* leg?"

Blossom darted into the yard, and Mary went to the refrigerator. She made a salad and poured a glass of iced tea. Sweetcakes ran circles around her. Shooing the dog away, she approached the table. A card was tucked beneath the napkin holder.

Valentine's Day was months past. Not that it mattered to her husband—in late February Anthony had cleared out the drugstore's sale rack. He was sweetly intent on extending the honeymoon phase of their marriage indefinitely. Love cards, tiny boxes of chocolate tucked beneath her pillow, bunches of daisies slipped into her car—every romantic gesture deepened her love for him.

She traced the hearts embossed on the card's thick paper. Marriage was everything she'd hoped for. Anthony showered her with affection. He supported her work as Liberty's only local doctor. And from the start, Blossom, whose mother had taken off when she was a toddler, had welcomed Mary into her life. Sure, they quarreled about skipping school and clothes flung around the house. The arguments were refreshingly typical—Blossom *was* nearly a teenager, and determined to chart her own course. Their bond, newly-formed, withstood each disagreement and came out stronger.

The squeak of the screen door announced the girls. They shuffled into the kitchen. Snoops' black bean eyes took in everything but Mary's disapproving stare. The more confident Blossom stomped to the counter to fix PB&Js. She handed one to her friend.

35

Mary made quick work of her salad. "You have exactly five minutes to eat." After they'd seated themselves at the table, she added, "This is the last time you're ducking out at lunchtime. Give me your word."

"Why should I?" Defiance sparked in Blossom's eyes. "You can't expect me to swear a blood oath if you never keep up your end of the bargain."

"Enough with the melodrama. Who said anything about a blood oath? All I want is a promise."

"Fine. I'll keep my promise if you'll keep yours. No offense, Mom. When it comes to important stuff, you don't keep your end of the bargain."

The comment was made lightly, but Mary detected a note of injury underneath.

Had she done something to hurt Blossom's feelings? Adolescents were thin-skinned. They took offense at the most innocuous remarks. Yesterday at breakfast Anthony made the mistake of asking his daughter if she was tired—her eyes were puffy—and Blossom reacted as if he'd called her ugly. They'd finished breakfast in a silence as frigid as the Arctic.

Needing to get to the bottom of it, she scooted her chair close. "What have I done to break a promise?" She draped her arm across the back of Blossom's chair. "Whatever it is, let's discuss it. Just because I'm angry you skipped Mashed Potato Medley doesn't mean I'm not here if you need me. What's going on?"

Snoops cleared her throat. "Blossom won't spill. She's pretty upset. For the record, I'm not peeved. It's cool you're a doctor. You should do what you want."

"Thanks for the vote of confidence. What exactly am I doing?"

Snoops tore her sandwich into sloppy chunks. "You know what I mean. You're everyone's favorite doctor."

"Not much of a contest. I'm the only doctor in Liberty."

"Finney, at The Second Chance Grill? She tells everyone how you helped her bunions. And Mrs. Percible is getting better, mostly because you bug her about using her inhaler."

In April Ethel Lynn Percible had suffered smoke inhalation and serious burns during her house fire. Just released from the

36

hospital, she *was* healing better than expected.

"We can all agree it's great Mrs. Percible is on the mend. She's still weak, but she's making good progress." Mary paused to run her palm across Blossom's silky curls. When the proffered affection was ignored, she asked Snoops, "What does any of this have to do with promises?"

"Blossom thinks you broke a promise to your family."

"I did? How?" Beneath the table, Sweetcakes nudged between her thighs in search of another snack. Leaning down, she went nose-to-nose. "Have I broken any promises you're aware of? Bark once for 'yes' and twice for 'no.'"

Sweetcakes lathered her cheek with licks. Mary laughed, which was enough to make Blossom toss down her sandwich. "Stop joking around," she snapped. "Snoops is trying to tell you something important."

"Why don't *you* tell me? You're the one who's upset."

"Fine. I will."

She drew her delicate frame upright in the chair, making her even more adorable. Blossom wasn't a big kid. What she lacked in size, she made up for in sass. "No one's saying it's not great how you help everyone in Liberty. The town needs a doctor. You do a good job."

Here it comes. "I'm glad you approve," she replied. Her stepdaughter's accusatory tone knotted her stomach but she kept her expression placid. "I do work hard. If I didn't have a practice here, elderly patients would have trouble finding wellness care. They'd put it off, or endure long drives to Jeffordsville Hospital to see a doctor. It's no different for the working families I serve. They lead busy lives. They'd put off physicals and other services they consider nonessential if there wasn't a doctor in town."

"Sure, but it doesn't change our deal. I should've made you sign a contract or something."

"Sweetie, *what* are you talking about?"

The kitchen phone rang, making Mary jump. She left the girls stewing at the table. She'd barely lifted the receiver when Meade said, "Why aren't you answering your cell?"

"Too busy." Blossom was slouched low in her chair. Mount Vesuvius, with lava churning inside. "Meade, this isn't a good time. Can we talk later?"

37

Soft laughter then, "How much time do you have left? I'm guessing forty-five seconds."

"Actually I'm three minutes off schedule."

"You need a vacation."

Or an interpreter. If Blossom thought Mary had broken a pact of some sort, maybe she also needed a contract attorney. "Meade, can I call you later? In another ten minutes, I'm late for my afternoon appointment."

"Wait. Can you fit in another appointment this afternoon? I wouldn't ask if it weren't important. I can leave work early to bring her in."

Mary snatched her iced tea from the table and glugged it down. Seeking privacy, she looped the phone's cord across the counter, allowing her to slip beside the refrigerator. Hidden from Blossom's icy stare, she asked, "I can fit you in at the end of the day. Say, five-fifteen?"

"Perfect. Thanks."

"Who's the patient?"

"A young woman—she's pregnant. I doubt she's received prenatal care. I can't even tell you how far along. Four or five months, I think."

Worry over Blossom receded beneath Mary's concern for her new patient. "I'd like more details but don't have the time." She wasn't an obstetrician. Thinking quickly, she decided to contact Jeffordsville Hospital between patients this afternoon. An expectant mother would require a referral. "Do me a favor, will you? Come in a few minutes early to fill out paperwork. I'll review it before I see her."

Hanging up, she knew better than to check her watch. Plus she still needed to discuss whatever was bothering Blossom.

The talk would have to wait. Beneath the busy doctor's nose, the girls had vanished.

Feeling like an interloper in her own home, Meade handed over the shiny, jumbo-sized bag. "For you."

She was standing in the hallway of the servants' quarters outside Glade's room. She'd always respected personal space, and wasn't comfortable entering without an invitation. Besides, there wasn't time. Reenie had relayed the message 'about the appointment, and they were due at Mary's office within the hour. Glade blinked at the folds of tissue paper layered in the bag. "What is this?" she asked, giving the bag a shake.

"Clothing. I hope everything fits. If not, we can make exchanges. You might want to pick something out to wear to your appointment."

"You went shopping for me? Wow. Thanks."

"It was no bother. I stopped on my way home from the office," she lied. The impulse shopping trip was squeezed in between afternoon appointments. She'd raced like a madwoman through the department store, barking orders and sending saleswomen skittering to fulfill her demands. Had she left the impression she was a woman unhinged? Throwing off the unpleasant thought, she said, "Why don't I wait upstairs while you decide what to wear? Please try to hurry. You're Dr. Chance's last appointment of the day."

She'd already turned to leave when the excitable girl latched onto her arm. They were both tall women, but Glade weighed considerably more. With a gleeful tug, she nearly hauled Meade off her high heels.

"Don't go! This is like Christmas, only bigger. No one *ever* gets this much stuff at once. Is all of this new? You must've spent tons of money."

Meade allowed the girl to drag her into the bedroom that, if her memories were accurate, had once belonged to a fretful maid with cheeks dotted with freckles and a propensity to squeak when she laughed. Lara or Larita—the name was lost to the mists of time. Now the room was transformed in an outlandish stab at decorating. Grey walls hid behind pages ripped from magazines. The pages were taped above the dresser and beside the bed, on the wall near the closet and one corner of the ceiling. Some of the images of models, cut out like paper dolls, cavorted across the walls in mad disarray. The molested fashion magazines, or what was left of them, sat in a ragged heap on the floor.

"You've decorated," she said, gently freeing her arm from Glade's hold. Was the fashion wallpaper an indication of an extended visit? The dresser also had a lived-in feel. Candy wrappers, a few toiletries and an old-fashioned cookie tin were set out.

Glade lifted a black garbage bag from the bed and hurled it to the floor.

"Is it okay if I put stuff up? I was bored. I didn't want to keep bugging Reenie. She was busy upstairs all day long." She placed the bag in the center of the bed. "Your sister is getting married next weekend?"

"In Liberty Square. We're holding the reception here."

"Your ballroom is bigger than a roller rink. There must've been twenty people in there today, washing windows and scrubbing the floor. Your dog kept barking at everyone. I took him outside to earn my keep."

"Glade, you don't have to earn your keep. You're a guest here."

"I didn't mind taking care of him. We took a long walk." Tearing through the tissue in the shopping bags, she sent a shy glance. "He peed on everything but my shoes. I guess I can't blame him. Boy dogs like to show you who's boss. It's in their nature."

"Melbourne *is* a character. He thinks he's a much larger dog, like an English Mastiff trapped in a miniature poodle's body. I don't have the heart to set him straight."

The quip relaxed the girl. "I'm glad he's small and cuddly," she said, removing the first layer of tissue with care. "Big dogs get mean, and they slobber all over you. Poodles are nice."

"I couldn't agree more." Life didn't afford many opportunities for affection, but her sweet baby always supplied. "Did you walk him through the east woods? It's one of his favorite places."

"We went everywhere. Your property is prettier than any park I've ever seen. I tried to keep Melbourne on the go because, you know . . . he gets frisky."

"Ah, I see."

Glade looked up, as if needing approval to continue. When Meade smiled, she added, "He tried to hump my leg. I mean, all the time. If I stopped to look at the flowers or lean against a tree, he was at it again. I'm glad he likes me but it was gross. You should have his thingies removed."

The remark was the type of comment Blossom would make.

Only Blossom was a child, not a woman in her second trimester of pregnancy.

This morning it was impossible to guess at the progression of the pregnancy. No more. Without a shred of modesty, the girl peeled off her ratty sweatshirt to reveal large breasts encased in a bra two sizes too small, and a belly round with the promise of new life. Several bruises dotted the girl's back. Her hands dipped into the bag.

Embarrassed, Meade pivoted to the wall. She knew not to leave. A rustling of tissue, and Glade chortled.

"Omigosh, this is pretty! How did you know I love purple? The stretchy fabric is great. It's soft but really gives in the right places if you know what I mean."

"It's a summer sweater and should continue to fit. The pants too. They have an elastic panel."

"The pants are great. *Three* pairs? Oh, I love this one!"

A grunt of exertion indicated she'd shrugged off her sweatpants and climbed into the new pants. Still facing the wall, Meade noticed the garbage bag tossed from the bed. The contents had spilled out. Pants, shirts, more magazines and a blue hairbrush spotted with thumbprints of grease. She caught the odor of perspiration and something else, the scent of pine she'd noticed last night when she'd first discovered Reenie comforting their distraught guest.

But a garbage bag—not a suitcase. Did the girl carry her few belonging all the way from West Virginia in *this?*

"Glade, where did all of this come from? I didn't see it last night," she asked, her concern gentling the question.

A long sigh punctuated the air. "When I got here, I thought I should leave my stuff outside. I left it behind the bushes by your front door."

"Why on earth would you leave your belongings in the bushes?"

"In case I needed to leave in a hurry. If I wasn't welcome."

"Oh, Glade."

Another pause as pregnant as the girl broke the uneasy silence. Glade admitted, "It was dumb not to call Reenie before showing up. I haven't talked to her in a long time. There was a pay phone in Columbus I could've used when I switched buses. I

41

felt guilty too—I hardly know Reenie, but she was the only person I could think of. I had to get away."

From what? From whom?

Did the girl think the father of her unborn child was a danger? Was he furious upon learning of the pregnancy? Asking for the details seemed unwise. Better to let Mary uncover the facts during the examination.

Meade caught sight of something else in the bag. Her heart moved into her throat.

With exquisite care, she retrieved the Raggedy Ann doll from the tangle of clothing. The orange yarn hair was unraveled as if by nervous fingers. The apron tied over the blue fabric dress was decorated with hearts and flowers drawn with a variety of colored pens. Taking care not to turn around while Glade dressed, Meade placed the doll on the dresser.

Was this a cherished keepsake, a childhood companion used for comfort or to provide the illusion of safety? There was nothing safe about unwed motherhood, especially for a girl whose maturity was questionable and might take years to appear. How would Glade manage?

Worry accompanied Meade on the drive to Liberty. Her young companion was content to leave her alone with her thoughts.

Glade stared out the window at the rolling landscape unlike the terrain of her youth, the isolated hollows of West Virginia. Soon the farms and fields gave way to Liberty's picturesque streets, the lemony heads of daffodils bobbing in well-tended flowerbeds and the Stars and Stripes waving from many front porches. On Liberty Square Meade pulled in to the lot behind The Second Chance Grill.

The door leading to the second floor boasted new gold lettering on the polished glass: *Dr. Mary Chance M.D. – General Practice.*

Reaching it, Glade asked, "Do I really need a doctor? I feel great."

The comment was outlandish. "Is this the first doctor you've seen since, ah . . . " Meade's voice drifted off in confusion. She didn't have the heart to point out that any sensible woman sought out a doctor if she suspected she was carrying a child. The visit with Mary was merely a first step. A referral would be made to an obstetrician in the area. Explaining the process might frighten the girl. Trying another tack, she said, "You'll like Mary. She's young, and very kind."

"Is she your doctor?"

"We both thought it best if she wasn't." Worry streaked through Glade's green eyes and she added, "You see, Mary and I are good friends. Best friends actually. Because we're close, it's inappropriate for her to act as my primary doctor."

"Seems like a dumb rule."

"A physician never treats her own family for the same reason. She can't perform services well if she's emotionally involved with the patient. Does that make sense?"

"I guess." With thin confidence, Glade pulled open the door. "How did you get so close?"

"Long story. Not worth telling."

"I love stories." Halfway up the stairwell, she cast a sidelong glance hot with curiosity. "Were you best friends in school? I had a best friend until 9th grade. Her dad got a job in a coal mine in Raleigh County and she moved away."

"I'm sorry you lost a friend."

"When did you become best friends with Dr. Mary?"

"Glade, I'd rather not go into it."

The girl paused in the corridor outside Mary's practice. "Is there a guy in this story? There is, right? You're blushing!"

Against her better judgment, she relented. "Before Mary arrived in Liberty, I dated her husband. Briefly. It was nothing serious. After they married, I discovered I had a lot in common with Mary. We've been close ever since."

As if to demonstrate the strength of their bond, Meade swept into the reception area and was immediately flagged by the receptionist. They were escorted past the waiting patients and into Mary's office.

They didn't have long to wait. A black nurse with silvered hair came in to escort a visibly nervous Glade to an examination room.

Anticipating a long wait, Meade settled into one of the two upholstered chairs facing Mary's desk. She practiced yogic breathing to release the day's stresses and regain her center.

Tonight she'd promised to accompany Birdie for the final meeting with the florist. They'd settled on bridal flowers of blush pink peonies nestled with fragrant lily of the valley. The florist, sensing Birdie's adventurous spirit, wanted to create large bouquets for the bride and her maid of honor to carry. Meade was hoping to talk her sister into bouquets of more reasonable size.

Unbidden, a depressing thought wove through her musings. *I'm too old to play the role of maid of honor.* Did she have a choice? Declining her sister's request was never an option since the 'maid' Birdie would have preferred was her elderly cousin Theodora. On the closeness scale, Meade came in a distant second. Of course, choosing Theodora would've been even less appropriate. A young woman of marriageable age, like Glade, should've played the part.

No, Meade wasn't anyone's idea of a great choice for maid of honor. As far as she was concerned, she'd entered the no-man's-land of middle age, a time well past the excitement of wedding vows and the dreams of youth. Her course was set, and she wondered what her forties would bring. The expansion of *Vivid*, certainly. Opening a satellite office in Cincinnati or Pittsburgh made sense—perhaps even one in a southern state or out west. Adding travel to her schedule wasn't a problem. Nothing held her to Liberty except the obligation to care for her father, a duty less onerous since Birdie's return to his life. Over time it seemed likely their relationship would deepen.

Contemplating their bond, Meade seesawed between gratitude and a shameful dose of jealousy. She was no longer the *only* apple of her father's eye. The introduction of a missing daughter into his tragic life was cause to rejoice, and she chastised herself for harboring a small flame of jealousy.

Clinging to more positive thoughts proved difficult. A dreary ennui settled on Meade as she imagined the future. Increasing success and the time to do whatever she liked seemed assured. She'd travel and join a country club. She liked the idea of picking up golf. Children were out of the question—even if she found the right man, dated then married, it would take several years to build a new life with her husband. By then she'd be . . . what? Age forty-four? Forty-five? Too old for a child. Yet she might find a life-mate, a loving husband as committed to her as he was to his career.

She'd find a businessman as lonely as she.

"Meade, what's wrong? You look positively blue."

She hadn't heard Mary enter.

"Nothing. Everything." Swiping a lock of hair from her face, she dismissed the sad musings. There was no sense in sharing her more pessimistic thoughts with a close friend. "Don't worry about it."

"Are you sure? If you need to talk, I'm here."

"And I love you for it." Rimming her voice with false cheer, she asked, "Have you decided on a dress for the wedding?"

"Still up in the air. You?"

"The same. If Birdie hadn't decided to marry with only three weeks' notice, I would've shopped in New York and taken you along. We would've found the perfect gowns *and* had time for alterations."

"And I'd go to escape Blossom. I've messed up in the mothering department." Mary gave a self-deprecating laugh. "Knowing Blossom, it was one of her silly blood oaths. I can't recall pricking my finger much less what the promise was about."

"Did you ask her directly?"

"I tried. She seemed more intent on using Snoops as interpreter."

"Don't ask me for advice. I've never been one of Blossom's favorite people."

"Give her time. She'll have a change of heart."

"Doubtful. She likes down-to-earth people, like you. I'm standoffish, a habit I share with my father. Or I'm a closet introvert. Take your pick. No wonder people think I'm a snob."

The comment was out of character, as if she were begging for reassurance.

"Something *is* bothering you," Mary said. "I wish you'd share. You've been so busy helping with the wedding, we've hardly chatted in weeks. Tell me what's going on."

The simple request gave a moment's respite from the sadness overtaking her. If not for Mary's friendship, she would've tucked away her worries as she'd done for a lifetime, tucked them away to fester in her heart. No wonder she kept people at a distance. She'd spent a lifetime avoiding her emotions instead of processing them in a deep, meaningful way.

"It's the wedding," she admitted, and her ability to pinpoint the problem was a victory. "Watching my younger sister take the next step in her life has me wondering if I've wasted too much time on my career. Oh, I don't mean I'm in a hurry to walk down the aisle—I'm not sure I'd take to marriage. What if I can't? What if I found my independence more important than love?" The more she thought about it, the more certain she was that dreams of marriage were fanciful at best. She *did* enjoy her independence. "All the compromises couples make . . . I like charting my own course. Relationships demand give and take, and an openness to change."

"Meaning you're too old to flex? Don't be ridiculous."

"Spoken with the wisdom of a thirty year old. Just wait. You'll get stuck in your ways. We all do. Oh, why are we discussing this? It's self-serving. It's been ages since I've liked any man enough to consider marriage."

The outburst sent an impish light through Mary's eyes. "I'm not sure I agree." She sat at her desk. "What about Anthony? Not too long ago, you had a crush on him. If he'd felt the same, you might've taken the leap."

"You *would* bring him up," she replied, playing along. It was impossible to feel embarrassment. Her interest in Mary's husband was ancient history, something they both laughed about. "I don't know what I was thinking. He had absolutely no interest, and still I pursued him. A summer of madness."

"You aren't being honest with yourself. You were nearing your forties, an era that strikes many women hard—single women especially. Perhaps you were grasping for that one, last chance to become a mother."

"Perhaps subconsciously. Who knows?" Understanding her deepest motives was immaterial. "It's moot. I *am* forty. A child is out of the question."

"It ain't over 'till it's over."

"I'm aware of the statistics. Even if I hired the best fertility specialists in Ohio, it's unlikely I'd have a child." Meade paused, unsure how to proceed. When she'd organized her thoughts, she added, "A baby isn't what's bothering me, or it's not the only thing. It's the wedding, seeing my younger sister marry. Another example of the life my professional success has precluded me from enjoying. Home, hearth—a man."

"Relationships take work, and you're thinking about expanding *Vivid*. Would you have time to cultivate a relationship? The right man will applaud your success as long as you also make room for his needs. If you don't have time, why would he stick around?"

"Exactly."

"Believe me, I understand the demands. I'm juggling my practice with a new marriage, and I'm blowing it in the parenting department. The way Blossom is acting, I'm sure of it. I don't have a solution, not yet, but I can tell you this. My family comes first. If you're thinking about finding a partner, you know the real question. Are you willing to make room for a man in your life? You're ambitious, Meade. Your career has always been important to you."

The intercom on Mary's desk buzzed. A short conversation with the receptionist ensued. When she finished, Mary said, "I've asked one of the nurses to help Glade complete the patient profile. She refuses to give a current address. She's also confused by a number of questions on the form."

"Is she having trouble understanding?" Meade asked, glad for the change of conversation.

"The nurse is reading each question aloud. It's taking time."

The disclosure was enough for Meade to set her personal troubles aside. "Reading problems?"

"During the examination she mentioned she's a high school dropout. Were you aware?"

"I had my suspicions." On the night of Glade's arrival, Reenie had implied as much. "Did she tell you when she left school? Reenie wasn't sure."

"At the end of tenth grade. I'm under the impression she's moved around a lot since then."

Compassion for the girl tightened Meade's throat. "She has one of those old-fashioned Raggedy Ann dolls in her belongings. For all I know, she sleeps with it at night. How will a girl so immature develop the skills to parent a baby? She needs counseling or another form of professional help—someone to guide her." She looked up suddenly. "Did you get her age? Reenie couldn't recall, and I haven't found an opportunity to ask."

Mary sent a look of consternation. "Isn't Reenie her aunt? It's odd she can't recall the girl's age."

"Glade is the daughter of Reenie's niece in West Virginia. They don't have much contact other than the cards sent on holidays—that sort of thing. With Reenie getting on in years, she rarely visits her extended family. She hardly knows Glade."

Mary glanced at the ceiling, evidently to commit the information to memory. She was an excellent doctor who prided herself on knowing the details of her patient's lives. Her commitment was a rarity in the age of modern medicine.

"Glade turned eighteen in April," she said.

"Just a few weeks ago?"

"I'll admit prying open a clam is easier than getting information from a secretive patient. Again, it makes sense if you factor in how she left her home in a hurry and landed on your doorstep. She's scared." From her desk Mary picked up a pen and rolled it beneath her fingers. "I believe she's in the second trimester. We'll need an ultrasound for a more precise due date. Heavier girls can hide a pregnancy longer. She's been wearing loose clothing to conceal the pregnancy from herself as well as others. Not the best sign, psychologically speaking. By the way, I demanded to see her driver's license. If she were underage, I would've called social services. She's not."

"I'll take that as good news."

"You need to make some decisions."

"I'm sure I'm not ready to hear this."

"Better get ready. I don't advise sending her back to West Virginia. She needs a new start."

Meade shifted in her chair. What would a new start entail?

Today the girl managed to remain out of sight of Meade's temperamental father. If she stayed much longer, Meade had no choice but to talk to Landon. How he'd react to the news of a long-term houseguest was difficult to predict. And what about *after* the baby's arrival? If Glade refused to return to her mother in West Virginia—a mother who wouldn't welcome her with open arms—then what? She'd require assistance finding work, suitable daycare for her child and an apartment.

"Meade." The soft lilt of her friend's voice pulled her back to shore. Gaining her attention, Mary said, "Sometimes it's best to begin somewhere new . . . somewhere safe."

Meade steeled herself. There was more, something worse. Something yet unsaid. It would change the calculus of whether or not she must rise to a woman's obligation to help a kindred soul, an unwed teenager.

Confirming her suspicions, Mary said, "I found bruises on Glade's arm and back."

"I saw the bruises on her back. This afternoon, while she was dressing."

Mary's expression was grave. "If it's a sign of abuse—if the man she was involved with is a danger to her and the baby—then I strongly urge you to keep Glade here."

Chapter 4

The clutter of invoices and receipts was overwhelming. With an eye at tackling a portion of the mess, Hector dug in.

Most of the *Liberty Post's* employees were gone for the day, leaving the newsroom in a state of relative calm. Hugh was out on a story, and Birdie was upstairs in their apartment. Hector planned to spend an hour organizing the accounts before calling it a day. With the wedding only days off, the groom was increasingly frazzled. Hugh's anxiety meant the accounts were badly neglected.

As Hector sorted the paperwork, this morning's conversation with Landon continued to bother him. No matter what the retired banker thought, choosing to stay in Liberty for the summer wasn't ideal. It meant delaying the search for a permanent job in Philadelphia, something long-term that would lead to a career.

Landon's comment by the lake rose again in his mind. *You may lack confidence in your abilities, but you strike me as a man with solid instincts.* Even if Hector was unsure of a career path, did that indicate self-doubt? Sure, he'd bounced through too many jobs. What seemed bad luck or lack of preparation was anything but. Work had taken a back seat to the more immediate concerns that had dominated his life during two ill-fated marriages. A checkered job history didn't mean he doubted his abilities.

Yet Landon's comment stuck in his brain like a taunt

demanding he question every assumption he held about himself.

He'd finished stacking bills on one side of the desk when Theodora marched up the newsroom's center aisle. Given the wedding preparations, she'd become a constant fixture at the *Post.*

Tonight she wore a black skirt and a cowboy-inspired suede jacket with fringe swinging in time with her strides. The leather boots on her small feet were a perfect match. All she was missing was a hitching post for her horse—not that he could imagine her stopping by in anything but her beloved sky blue Cadillac.

She was carrying a basket of peaches.

"Not my first choice for dinner but I'll take one," he said by way of greeting. "I'd head for a drive-through, but I promised Hugh to get the accounts in order. Talk about a mess."

With a grunt, Theodora lowered the basket to his desk. "Go on, take two if you'd like. Birdie can't eat them all. If she does, I'll scare up another basket."

"Since when does Birdie eat peaches by the truckload?" Fruit was always a good idea, but not ten pounds at once.

She studied the female reporter working on the other side of the newsroom. Satisfied the newbie wasn't eavesdropping, she said, "It's the cravings."

"Cravings?"

"You know how pregnant women get a hankering for certain foods?" When he nodded with understanding, she added, "Sabrina, the pharmacist over at the drugstore? Hers were the same—couldn't get enough peaches when she was expecting. Ate them at all hours. Her husband took to sleeping in the guest bedroom. He got tired of rolling into peaches at night."

"Forget about cravings. Find a remedy for Birdie's morning sickness." Last time he'd checked, she was camped out before the toilet bowl in her master bath. There wasn't much he could do other than offer a pat on the back. She'd sent him back to the newsroom with a tepid thumbs up. "I thought morning sickness was a *morning* issue. Birdie's shot the theory to hell."

"Some women experience it at odd hours. You never can tell what'll set it off." Theodora took a peach from the basket and tossed it over. After he'd taken a bite, she added, "My friend in Columbus, Joan Maholtz? She couldn't stand the smell of beef cooking. Made her sicker than a dog."

"No kidding." A discussion of women in pregnancy was unfamiliar terrain. He tried to find his comfort zone, an impossible feat.

"Susan, over at the antique store? She couldn't stand the smell of plastics. Strangest thing. Offer her bottled water and she'd run off, gagging. Jewels, the new girl at the veterinarian's office? She was in hell for months. The sight of eggs in a nice macaroni salad would have her retching for an hour. She was pregnant last spring and stayed clear of every picnic in the county."

The old woman's fascination with all things maternal was touching. Would Birdie's pregnancy soften Theodora's hard edges? Usually she fired off snappish comments or burst into fits of temper. He found this softer side of her personality endearing.

Or not. He suspected she was buttering him up when she said, "Have you talked to Delia? The dress she's wearing to the wedding is a stunner. Real slinky thing. Every young buck in the county will be following her around at the reception."

"They'll score a dance if they carry chewing gum. It's her drug of choice."

"Don't you *care* if she dances with all the eligible men but you?"

Logging into the computer, he fired up the accounting software. "No Theodora, I don't."

"Why not?" She stomped her foot. "Hector Levendakis, I hate to horsewhip your male pride, but you're not young. Aren't you itchin' for a chance at love? Delia is a good woman. She likes you. What more is there to it?"

"A lot."

"Why not give her a chance?"

The reasons were too numerous to share with the diminutive matchmaker. He had more than ten years on Delia. She was too bubbly for his taste. And he wasn't interested in a long distance romance. Despite Landon's urging he stay for the summer, he hadn't warmed to the idea of putting off the return to Philadelphia.

"Theodora, I know you mean well," he said with as much patience as he could muster. "Stop pushing. I'm not interested."

"You fool. I *don't* mean well. I mean to grow Liberty." She shimmied her shoulders with impotent rage. "Didn't I get Mary to stay and wed Anthony? Didn't Hugh fall for Birdie, and start the newspaper at my urging? If mating rituals were left to the young, Liberty would be a ghost town."

Was she feisty *and* diabolical?

He'd assumed her meddling was the harmless pastime of a woman with too much time on her hands. Evidently there was more to it. "If you want to grow the town, convince Hugh to hire more reporters. He might bring in a young buck who's perfect for Delia."

"A bird in the hand is worth two in the bush. You're here, and I mean to make you stay."

Finishing his peach, he tossed the pit in the garbage. "I'm honored, but you're wasting your time. I'm focused on my career."

"You don't have a career. Not yet. I'm working on it. Even if you did, do you want to end up like Meade? All she does is work."

"There are worse fates."

"At the moment, Birdie is the one dealing with a bad fate— the sister kind. Meade is driving her to distraction with suggestions on the proper way to host a wedding."

"Ease off. If she didn't help, Birdie couldn't pull off the wedding. Not with three weeks of lead time."

"Hell and damnation—what are you talking about? Three weeks or three years, it wouldn't matter. Meade's been walking right over her sister, telling her to do this or that for the wedding. She's a tyrant. A regular Attila the Hun. In case you're stupid, let me spell it out. Meade loves nothing more than being top dog."

"Guess what? You're just as irritating. You latch onto ideas like a pit bull."

"Bitch, bitch, bitch."

He nodded pointedly at the clutter on the desk. "Do you mind? I'm working here."

"Then work. All I'm saying is, lack of male companionship has turned Meade into a cranky old maid. You want to end up just as unlikeable?"

"Theodora, no one has referred to women as 'maids' since the Elizabethan era. More importantly, Meade isn't old. There's nothing wrong with focusing on your career. People do it all the time. She's not one of my favorite people, but she's a successful businesswoman. I hope I do half as well."

"She needs to get laid."

Discussing a woman's private life was out of bounds. Rattled, he began punching receipts into the accounting program with gusto. Better to dig in. Theodora would take the hint and push off.

But she'd already dropped the subject. Her weathered face creased with disgust as she looked down the aisle.

"Cain and Jezebel, I've done it now. I've uttered her name and here she is. Hector, pick up the phone. Find an exorcist."

Unsure what she meant, he peered around the basket of peaches. Meade was gliding up the aisle with the calm superiority of a queen at her coronation. As usual she looked stunning, her platinum hair swept back to compliment high cheekbones and large, wide-set eyes. She didn't possess her younger sister's flashy looks. What she *did* have was more dangerous, a refined beauty paired with a mind as scintillating as the diamonds glittering at her ears.

She tossed a dismissive glance his way before regarding Theodora with ill-concealed impatience. From the looks of it, she held them in equal contempt.

"Theodora. Hello." She gave the basket of fruit the once-over. "Are the two of you planning a baking spree? Peach cobbler for twenty? I'm sure it'll give you something useful to do."

Theodora hauled the basket into her arms. "I'm not baking tonight but if you must know, your tone burns my biscuits. Watch it, missy."

Meade retreated from the ire flashing in the tiny titan's eyes. "Let's start over," she replied, and her Adam's apple bobbed in the pillar of her neck. She was haughty but with Theodora nearby, she was also nervous. "Where's my sister? We're running late."

"How the hell should I know? I just got here." To his astonishment, Theodora butted her out of the way and planted the basket in his lap. "Give these to Birdie, will you? I'm late for a fitting. I've got a hankering to wear something glittery to the wedding."

"Cocktail dress or full length?" he asked, following her cue and ignoring Meade. Two could play the hostility game, and he'd had enough of her for one day. If her father was correct and he *did* lack confidence, any none-too-subtle jabs she flung his way wouldn't help.

"I'm wearing a ball gown. A swishy thing in sea green."

"Sounds pretty." He regarded the basket she'd dumped in his lap. "I'll take these up. I'm sure they'll help Birdie feel better."

"I don't know if they'll help, but she'll want them the next time she's hungry. Between bouts of sickness she's eating like a Clydesdale. If the nuptials weren't in a few days we'd have to let out her wedding dress."

"Should you ask the caterer to have peaches on standby at the reception? It's the bride's big night. She ought to have whatever she likes."

"Good idea. I'll call after my fitting."

The light banter lit something in the back of Meade's clear blue eyes. "Birdie isn't feeling well?" she asked no one in particular.

Theodora pretended not to hear. "I'll see you later," she told him. Making a beeline around Meade, she marched out.

Her departure went unnoticed. "What's wrong with my sister?" Meade demanded. "She can't be sick, not tonight. We have an appointment with the florist."

"Reschedule."

"I can't! The wedding is next weekend."

Her distress changed the dynamics of their conversation. She didn't like having her schedule altered, and the panic in her eyes was appealing. He decided to play it for all it was worth.

"Take my word for it. You'll never get Birdie out of her apartment tonight." A woman with Meade's power didn't encounter many speed bumps, and he couldn't resist adding, "You want the facts? She's praying to the porcelain god. She won't finish anytime soon."

"Hector, I have no idea what you're talking about." She came close enough to peer down her nose. "Has Birdie caught a bug? Why didn't she call? Why am I *here* if we aren't keeping the appointment? I've been going since 8 A.M. I'm exhausted."

Revealing her sister's pregnancy was tempting. It wasn't his place. She'd find out soon enough.

Choosing the better gambit, he got to his feet. "Save the temper tantrum," he said, matching her superiority with insouciance. "You're not the only one who's put in a long day. Hugh's got bills from January he forgot to pay. Even better? He stopped inputting receivables in the accounting program last month. Houdini couldn't unravel the mess."

"And you can? Hard to believe."

"I'm trying, which counts for something." He got into her face. "Mark Birdie off your schedule. Call the florist and explain. Or don't. What you do doesn't concern me as long as you stop dumping bad vibes. Find a landfill. I got enough of your negative energy this morning."

Height gave a primal advantage, and he liked the way she unconsciously appraised the sturdy line of his shoulders before lingering on his throat. "Are you baiting me?" she asked. She seemed incapable of meeting his stony gaze.

"It's an idea. Should I? Seeing that you think so highly of me?"

"I *don't* think highly of you."

"And I don't care."

Her lashes were thick and artfully blackened with mascara, her drowsy gaze revealing a heady mix of attraction and unbidden desire. Pressing his advantage, he backed her against the desk. The invasion of her space fisted her long, manicured fingers.

Women were always drawn to him, but Meade seemed unprepared for the sexual awareness heightening between them. Her expression was too open, too expressive. She appeared incapable of hiding a natural reaction most women would conceal behind witty banter or a cool response. Which suggested innocence beneath her demure pose. It was fetching.

As were her eyes, lifting to capture his with a beguiling curiosity. Gone was the rude businesswoman who shielded her emotions behind sharp intellect. For a wondrous moment thought sifted from his brain, his attention narrowing on the scent of jasmine rising off her skin and the flecks of gold strung through the blue of her eyes.

A faint patchwork of lines marred the skin above her upper

lip and between her brows. He reminded himself that she was a woman of forty, a notion difficult to square with her youthful vitality and overall good health. If she were age fifty he wouldn't have cared—the animal magnetism they'd unleashed was potent and pure, as compelling as his desire to run his hand along the pale skin of her throat. He fought the urge.

And understood: if beauty was a trump card, she'd outplayed him.

Needing to break the exchange, he said, "Go upstairs and help your sister. She needs the company. Hugh's out on interviews."

Meade roused from deep waters. "I should."

"I'll take these up." Tamping down his desire, he slung the basket of peaches under his arm. "After you."

The spell he'd cast diminished with each step she took up the stairwell. She seemed no longer aware of him. Inside the apartment, she set her purse down on the kitchen counter without the slightest inclination to draw him back into conversation. The way she withdrew into herself was impressive, the polished calm returning, her gait measured as she moved past.

The lights were dimmed in the living room. From the master suite, the piteous sound of retching sent her to investigate.

With regret, he let her go.

Meade sensed Hector's attention pursuing her down the hallway. His interest was unwelcome. Something electric had passed between them in the newsroom, a jolt of recognition that took her unawares. It left the sensation of expectancy in her belly, and an odd excitement jangling through her nervous system. The encounter was like none she'd ever experienced, nor one she'd gladly repeat.

With discipline, she cooled her thoughts. He'd return to work and leave her in peace. More retching from the bathroom, and she put him out of mind.

Her sister's bedroom was a mess. The cruise wear purchased for the honeymoon sat in heaps in the corner. The bed was unmade. On the dresser a box of saltine crackers shared space with a large bowl. In the bowl was a single peach.

"Birdie?" She heard shuffling in the bathroom.

It was a shock to find her sister kneeling before the toilet.

"Are you wearing perfume?" Birdie asked.

A bizarre question, but she played along. "Of course. Why?"

"Stay where you are. One whiff, and I'll start puking again. It's on my no-no list."

"Since when do you have an allergy to perfume? You love *Flowerbomb.*"

"Not lately, I don't."

"How will you get through the reception if perfume makes you sick? We're entertaining hundreds."

"Menthol cream. I'll dab it under my nose. Hugh says morticians use it when they're examining dead bodies."

"That's disgusting." Would the goo show in the bridal photos? Talk about a disaster.

"It's the best plan I've got. Any and all perfume unsettles my stomach. If the invites hadn't already gone out, I'd ask people to refrain from using it."

Birdie looked dreadful. Her thick blond hair was banded tight at the base of her neck and her skin was splotchy. "How long has this been going on?" Meade asked. Earlier this week her sister had been fine.

"A day or two." Birdie grabbed the edge of the sink and pulled herself up. She resembled a seasick passenger on savage seas.

"Are we canceling the florist?"

"Oh, yeah. Unless you'll take care of it."

"Let's wait until the morning." Dragging her to the appointment was unthinkable. She was too sick. "If you're not better tomorrow, I'll go alone." Meade hesitated. "Do you need anything? A glass of water? Aspirin?"

"No, but thanks." Birdie pressed her hand to her stomach. "Give me a sec. I'll meet you in the living room."

Meade retraced her steps to the living room. She sent a text to the florist to reschedule. Hector was gone, the ripe peaches thoughtfully set out in a glass bowl on the coffee table.

Ears perked, she listened to Birdie shuffling around in the bathroom. A virus was nothing but an inconvenience. Half the town would attend the reception. Meade had also invited a select group of business associates and a few friends from her father's years in the banking industry. How would people react if the bride, smelling of menthol, kept them at arm's length? What if Birdie fell ill during the reception and dashed out? Hosting the affair with the bride absent was a prospect too awful to contemplate.

Her worries vanished beneath a deeper concern as Birdie trudged down the hallway and sank on the couch. She'd donned Hugh's robe and slippers. The slippers were large enough to pass for clown's shoes.

At Meade's appraisal, she said, "No fashion critiques, okay? I need Hugh's gear. His scent keeps my stomach settled."

"You're kidding."

"I'm not." She dragged a fluffy throw blanket across her knees. "I should ditch the wedding gown and wear his pajamas. If I skip laundry day, they'll really smell like him."

"PJs in Daddy's ballroom. That would be a first." And a last. When the photographer snapped the wedding pics, Meade knew she'd hide.

"Does it matter? It'll keep me from turning green while entertaining your cast of thousands."

"I thought you liked the idea of a large wedding."

"Hey, I thought we'd do a small thing in Liberty Square. Family and friends. You're the one who turned this into the event of the season. If it makes you feel any better, Hugh's on your side. He loves the idea."

"I'm glad. By the way, I'd appreciate your assurance you won't change into his pajamas at the reception." Birdie was an iconoclast of the first order. If an idea lodged in her head, there was no telling what she'd do.

Birdie picked at the blanket, her expression clouding. "I'll stay in my bridal gown, but only because it's a big deal to you. The way I've been feeling, I couldn't care less."

"Talk to Mary. She'll give you something to help." Vitamins, a stern reprimand—anything sure to keep the testy bride from bailing out of the wedding would do just fine.

"Believe me, there's nothing she can do." Birdie's eyes held a hint of deviltry. "Meade, it's not what you think. I don't have a bug."

"What then? Cold feet? If you're having second thoughts after all the work I've done—"

"—I'm pregnant."

The announcement hung in the air.

For a split second, Meade thought she'd misheard. Less than an hour ago, she'd driven a very pregnant Glade back to the estate. Now another pregnancy? The coincidence was mindboggling.

Meade's lips were numb. "You're having a baby." She rubbed them together, which didn't help. It dawned on her that her brain was suffering the deep freeze of shock. "Are you sure?"

"The OB thinks I'm in my ninth week. I've never been good at tracking my periods. The due date is a little dicey."

"Wait. Aren't you on the pill?"

"I meant to fill the script. You know how it is. Since we opened the *Post,* I've been running non-stop."

"Birdie, who forgets to fill the script when they're living with a man? You and Hugh have been together since Christmas."

With a huff, her sister threw off the blanket. "Are you trying to impersonate Dad? He asked the same thing."

Meade stared, wide-eyed. "Daddy knows? You told him first? You tipped him off before notifying your maid of honor-cum-wedding planner?"

"Give me a break. I had to beg to get you to agree to the maid of honor gig." Birdie shrugged. "The wedding planner bit I just tolerate."

"Thanks. Thanks a lot. I'd still like to know why you didn't tell me."

Her ire was unbecoming. If Birdie chose to share the news with Daddy first, what difference did it make? It was her right to do whatever she liked.

"I also told Theodora," Birdie admitted. She rolled around a thought then added, "Oh. I almost forgot. Hector also knows."

This was a real stunner. Meade recalled his conversation with Theodora in the newsroom. He *did* know. The taunts he'd thrown out were irritating hints. And he'd brought the peaches upstairs to sate Birdie's cravings. Morning sickness and cravings—he was privy to the most private details of her sister's life. Details she couldn't have guessed.

Burying the shock beneath a cool tone, she asked, "When did you tell Hector?"

The question put her sister on the defensive. She spent an inordinate amount of time returning the blanket to her lap and rearranging it around her legs. The smooth skin between her brows puckered.

When it seemed she'd never answer, Meade said, "It doesn't matter when you told him. I'm curious, nothing more."

"He found out this morning. Not from me."

Hurt centered in her chest, deepening like a festering wound. "Hugh told him?"

"No—Daddy. Hugh isn't sure why he shared the news. It came up when Hector met with him today. Hector was pretty mum when he got back from the estate. Hugh's glad he was told. He likes Hector."

"So do you," she remarked, hating how she shaped the comment into an accusation.

This bothered her sister as well because she tensed. "Yeah, I do. He's not what you think, Meade. Not shallow. He'd walk over glass for Hugh or me. Most people aren't half as loyal, and he's only known us for a month. You should cut him a break."

"What else did he discuss with Daddy?" Also none of her business, but she couldn't resist prying.

"I don't have a clue. Like I said, he wasn't saying much when he got back to the *Post*. Maybe Theodora had something to do with it. You know how she likes to work behind the scenes."

"Well, congratulations. A baby. How wonderful." She tried to escape the feeling of betrayal gripping her. It was mean-spirited, and totally uncalled for. Birdie wasn't in the wrong, and neither was Hector. Meade knew she was overreacting. She ought to be overjoyed. "How is Hugh taking the news?"

"He's thrilled. Boy or girl, he doesn't care. He's loves the idea of becoming a father."

"And you?"

"I'm nervous. Excited too. I was just getting used to the idea of marriage, and now I'll become a mother too." Birdie offered a tentative smile. "What about you? Are you happy for me? I get the feeling you're not."

"Don't be ridiculous. I'm thrilled."
A small untruth. She felt a hundred years old.

Chapter 5

"Blossom you're *not* wearing a micro-miniskirt and heels to the wedding. I didn't even know you owned high heels." Mary wouldn't go near those three-inch stilettos. Her center of gravity was most comfortable in a physician's down-to-earth loafers. "The outfit is too much."

Stalking across the bedroom, Blossom was deaf to the comment. She zipped up the skin-tight dress. The fabric looked glued to her hips. It also revealed most of her thighs.

On the bed, her friend Snoops helpfully put in, "She bought the shoes yesterday at the mall. We looked everywhere before she found the perfect pair."

"You went shopping?"

Blossom opened her jewelry box. "It's not like I could wait for you to take me. All you do is work." She pulled out three beaded bracelets and slid them on her wrists. "Dads chill. He doesn't care what I wear tomorrow. Why should you?"

Good question, and she searched for a suitable reply. "You've shown him your outfit? He thinks it's fine?" She tried adding disapproval to the query, but wasn't sure if she'd succeeded.

"I described it to him."

"So . . . he hasn't seen it?"

"What's your point?"

Anthony sauntered down the hallway. He paused in the doorway behind her.

"What haven't I seen?" he asked Mary. Winding his arms around her waist, he dropped his head on top of hers and took a gander at his daughter's outfit. She listened with relief as his breath wheezed to a startled halt. "Hold on, *muchacha.* You aren't wearing that get-up tomorrow. It's got 'call girl' written all over it."

Channeling a testy runway model, Blossom glided a brush through her curls. "What's a call girl?"

"Never mind."

Mary eased out of his arms and faced him. "Tell her no," she whispered. "I have to decide what I'm wearing. Not many options—can I throw together an old skirt and a blouse? It'll take an hour digging through my closet to come up with something remotely suitable for a wedding. I don't have time to arm wrestle Blossom until she relents."

Anthony dragged his hand through his hair. Splotches of grease from the Gas & Go peppered his shirt. Not that Mary cared. A year of marriage wasn't enough to sate her hunger for him. She never tired of his easygoing nature—or the well-toned muscles shifting beneath his tee shirt. If Blossom slept over at Snoops' house tonight as planned, there was time to seduce him before she left for the hospital.

Guilt ate at her composure. Better to get him naked before mentioning she was driving to the other end of the county and working late at Jeffordsville Hospital.

Catching her lurid glance, he telegraphed the well-rehearsed message: *Time out. Blossom will notice.* Their daughter picked up their more carnal thoughts like radar. Blossom had nearly caught them in the act a humiliating number of times.

Mary's beeper went off. "I should take this," she told her husband. "One of my patients was admitted to the hospital with chest pains." The man had a history of heart trouble. He was scheduled to spend the night under observation.

Blossom climbed into the stiletto heels. "Yeah, take the call." She took a few steps and nearly toppled over. "You've been home for, what? Twenty minutes? Don't kill yourself breaking a record."

Anger rippled off Anthony. He stalked into the bedroom. "Kiddo, apologize right now. Mary's a doctor. She has to care for her patients. You know the drill."

"You don't work stupid hours. Why does she?"

"I own a gas station. It's not like I get emergency calls if someone needs an oil change. A lot of people depend on Mary."

It was time to diffuse the situation before a family squabble ensued, something that happened much too frequently.

"I'm sorry I didn't take you shopping for the wedding," Mary said, wondering if this was the promise Blossom thought she'd broken. "I'll make it up to you. We'll plan something nice, just the two of us."

"Like you'll find the time." Blossom flounced to the mirror and fluffed her mass of curls. "You live for your patients. Shouldn't you also take care of your family? You don't, you know."

The accusation stung. Most nights Anthony made dinner, cleaned up and helped with homework before Mary dragged in from her practice. If the flu struck Liberty, she worked six days a week. On Sundays, more often than not, she dozed on the couch while Anthony entertained Blossom with a game of *Risk* or took her and Snoops on an outing. If they made plans for the roller rink or the movies, Mary usually begged off. After caring for patients all week long, she didn't have the energy.

"I don't mind if you can't goof off with us every Sunday," Blossom said. They'd grown close, and most days she seemed capable of mindreading. "It's okay. I don't always want to hang with Dad on the weekends, or you either. But that doesn't mean I like how you've let me down."

"How have I let you down?"

Blossom stomped across the room in the ridiculous heels. "Mom, for a grown-up you're pretty clueless. It's time, you know? When are you going to give me a baby brother?"

"Or sister," Snoops added. "She isn't picky. She's just sick of being an only child. You're a doctor. Can you make sure you have one of each?"

Anthony, following the conversation with puzzlement, shoved his fists into his jeans. "Just because Mary's a doctor doesn't mean she can choose her baby's sex," he told the girls.

Unable to resist, he winked at her. "Rest assured, I'll do everything possible to help her have one of each."

Mary wiggled her brows. "Thanks, dear. It's a relief I can count on you."

"Whatever I can do, babe."

Blossom, too angry to catch the bawdy interchange, said, "Snoops has brothers and sisters. It's not normal to go through childhood alone. I need someone younger to tell stuff to, and hassle about doing homework. For once I want to be the Big Cheese. And what about Santa Claus and the Easter Bunny?"

"And the Tooth Fairy," Snoops put in solemnly. "Magical stuff is good. It's the best part of being a kid."

"Right! If there's a peewee in the house, we can fake him out about all sorts of stuff. Or her. I'm not choosy. I'll take whatever I get as long as I don't have to change diapers. Honestly, Mom— you don't know what you're missing."

Blossom was mistaken. Mary knew exactly what she was missing. Some nights she cuddled in bed gazing into Anthony's eyes and dreaming so many beautiful dreams. A house brimming with children's laughter. Blossom playing the role of benevolent older sister. Family vacations by the ocean. She wanted children with Anthony's easygoing nature, children as unique as Blossom with her thick, rambunctious curls and wacky sense of humor.

Pulling her thoughts down to earth, Mary checked her watch. "Can we discuss this later? I'll talk about whatever you'd like as long as we also cover what you'll wear to the wedding. I'm no prude, but your present choice of attire doesn't cut it."

The plea dulled the lights in Blossom's eyes. "Whatever."

Her disappointment pricked Mary's heart. "I do need to find something to wear tomorrow."

Together she and Anthony returned to their bedroom. It was still one of her favorite rooms in the large Victorian house they'd never finish renovating. French doors led out to a small, two-story deck trimmed with the same type of frilly woodwork adorning the front of the house. Underfoot the bedroom's grass green carpeting muffled the sound of music if Blossom and Snoops went wild in the living room. Thick drapes in a subdued grey and green stripe were partially open to let in the late afternoon sun.

On the bed, four full-length gowns waited for her inspection. Stunned, she looked to her husband.

He rocked back on his heels. "The timing of my shopping trip could've been better," he remarked dryly. "If I'd run into the girls while they were at the mall, I could've stopped Blossom from buying hooker wear for Birdie and Hugh's big day."

Laughing, she slapped him lightly on the arm. "Keep your voice down."

"Hey, I call 'em like I see 'em. Just so we're on the same page, she's *never* walking out of this house with her butt showing."

"I hope you win the battle." She closed the door, ensuring they weren't overheard. "Face it. This is only the first tug-of-war we'll have over clothing. Wait until she's sixteen. We'll have trouble winning the war."

"I hope you're wrong."

"Why not take her back to the mall tonight? If she prefers a shorter dress, it's fine. Help her find something that isn't *too* short. Look for decent shoes. High heels aren't appropriate for a girl her age."

"I'll take her after dinner." His eyes were unbearably hopeful as he asked, "Can you go with us?"

"We've been on the outs for weeks. She'd rather spend the time with you." An evasion, but he let it pass. She walked to the bed and surveyed the gowns. Each was stunning. Her devoted husband had even purchased matching shoes for each selection—and none with intimidatingly high heels. Four shoeboxes sat open beneath the gowns.

Removing her blouse and pants, she stepped into a sapphire blue sheath. Anthony helped tug the sensuous fabric past her hips. He took his time, clearly enjoying the task. It was impossible to get enough of the feel of his hands on her body, the sure possession combined with a reverence that spoke volumes about the depth of his love.

She pivoted to the mirror. "I can't thank you enough for taking care of this." She regretted not mentioning she'd leave soon for the hospital. Stalling, she added, "I like this one, but let me try the others. They're all beautiful."

"Try the shoes too."

"After the dresses."

The second gown boasted a crinoline skirt beneath folds of eggplant-colored taffeta. More elegant than the first, she liked how the band of satin cinched tight at her waist. The bodice lifted her breasts, creating an enticing peak of her cleavage.

"Game over." Anthony's voice was gruff with desire. "Check the shoes. If they're comfortable, that's the one."

"You're certain?" Standing before the mirror, she wanted to recall the question. This *was* the gown.

Nearing, Anthony wound his hands through her chestnut locks. He lifted her hair to reveal the line of her neck, his languid movements sending quivers of sensation down her spine. In the mirror, their gazes mingled.

"Do your hair like this," he murmured. Pressing the locks to the base of her skull, he kissed her neck. "Wear your silver earrings."

"Your first gift?" The delicate threads of silver with tiny gems were as cherished as her wedding band.

"They'll look great. Skip a necklace—you don't need it."

He straightened, and she leaned back against him. "Do you agree with Blossom?" she asked. A tentative question, and she feared his answer. A baby *and* a growing medical practice—the possibility was overwhelming. Of course, women juggled careers and childbearing all the time. No one said it was easy, but the rewards outweighed the added responsibilities.

"Mary, we've been over this a hundred times. It's your decision. If you're asking if I think you put your patients before your family, I do. What's the alternative? You're Liberty's only doctor. Do I mind? Sure, at times. You're my wife. I don't like sharing. That doesn't mean I'm not proud of you. I am."

"I'm beginning to feel guilty." She tried again. "Nothing would make me happier than to have a baby with you. I want to have several children. Most of the time I feel guilty because I put off making a decision as to *when* to begin."

"You're under no pressure."

She faced him. She draped her arms across his shoulders, needing his understanding—needing his acceptance of her choices even though his own preference was painfully clear.

"I'd like more time," she admitted. "I never imagined my medical practice would double in less than a year. I've hired a third nurse, but it doesn't seem to help. I never catch up. How can I think about starting a family?"

"Blossom sees it differently."

This was a new tack, one he'd never used before. "You think what our daughter wants should factor in?" she asked, treading new ground.

"Next year she enters high school. We'll lose her to the activities teenagers love. She doesn't view this as an issue with your medical practice. She's self-centered like any kid, and wants a baby brother or sister while she's still around to enjoy the experience."

"Not all teens fly the coop."

"Ours will. She lost the best years of childhood to leukemia. Now she dreams of independence. She's making up for lost time."

There was no denying the assessment. Blossom was a new member of the junior high theatre troupe and the debate club. She was thinking about trying out for next year's cheerleading squad. The mutual crush she shared with Tyler Reevak was ongoing, and he loved to take her out for putt-putt golf or to baseball games at the junior high. The demands of Mary's practice kept her busy, and though she'd witnessed Blossom's increasing maturity, she hadn't processed what the changes meant.

"Our bundle of joy won't curb her schedule," Mary said. "The baby will only be three years old when Blossom takes her SATs for college."

"All the more reason not to delay. In another four years, she's off to college."

Mary laughed. "Are you arguing the case for Blossom? Or yourself?"

"Both." He tugged her close. "If you want to wait, we'll wait. I'm only asking you to consider this from the cheap seats. Blossom does want a sib—desperately. Why not give her a few memories before we pack her off to college? A few precious years to enjoy a younger sibling?"

The questions hung between them, as tantalizing as they were troublesome. She *did* want Blossom to have an opportunity to enjoy a sibling before reaching adulthood. Was it possible to grant her wish? And Anthony's?

The familiar hunger swept through her. Waiting until her mid-thirties to begin a family was risky. Any competent doctor knew the odds of becoming pregnant diminished significantly with each passing year. If they waited too long, would they only have one child together? Only one, when they yearned for a larger family?

She went up on tiptoes and kissed her husband full on the mouth. Drawing back, she whispered, "There's a lot to consider. Give me time to sort it out."

In Liberty Square Birdie and Hugh married on a flawless May afternoon.

Half an hour before the ceremony, traffic was blocked off around the Square. In the close-knit town, no one complained. Shopkeepers streamed into the park-like setting along with the other guests to celebrate the wedding of the season.

At Meade's instruction, the florist had decorated an arch with blushing pink peonies, lily of the valley and sprays of baby's breath. The whimsical arch stood in the middle of the green surrounded by flowerbeds bright with yellow daffodils. Folding chairs formed concentric circles all the way to the sugar shack at the end of the green, where guests and curious passersby, unable to find a seat, stood and watched. At the opposite end of The Square, people with business in the county courthouse paused to watch the proceedings.

Throughout the ceremony, Meade traded worried glances with Hector. The town wasn't yet privy to the news of Birdie's pregnancy, but the maid of honor and the best man *did* understand why the nervous groom broke tradition and kept a steady arm wrapped around his bride. Pressed close to Hugh's side, Birdie was fetching in her strapless gown. Her hair was swept into a loose chignon beneath the veil, her violet eyes transfixed on her groom. When Minister Givens turned to Hugh and intoned, '*You may now kiss the bride*', Meade said a silent prayer of gratitude.

As if on cue, everyone broke into applause. The thunderous joy seemed to shake the storefronts surrounding The Square.

Landon and Theodora were the first guests to rush forward.

They offered the newlyweds hearty congratulations. Meade and Hector, largely forgotten, stepped out of the crush of people. The buzz of conversation was deafening.

Leaning close to Meade's ear, Hector said, "We need to get Birdie out of here. Much more of this, and she'll faint."

Shielding Meade from the crowd swarming around them, he led her to the relative calm of the courthouse steps. If he was at all perturbed about their snappish words earlier in the week in the newsroom, he gave no indication.

She craned her neck. A failed effort. The throng swallowed Birdie and Hugh. "Let's give it five minutes," she decided. "Then we'll go in and drag them out. Birdie can rest before the reception."

"I have the limo on standby."

"Behind the courthouse?"

"I took two parking spaces to ensure we aren't blocked in. I also have a jar of menthol cream I'll keep handy until late tonight." From the pocket of his tux he retrieved the jar, and she laughed. He really did think of everything. "This morning Hugh was so rattled, I didn't trust him to remember. If Birdie gets nauseous, we'll dab it under her nose. Sad she's under the weather on her wedding day. I wish I had the cure."

He said the last of it with warmth, reminding her of how much he cared about her sister and Hugh.

She was still hurt he'd learned of Birdie's pregnancy first. The reason was easy to surmise. His affable nature made him the perfect confidante, and his eyes were as inviting as a Yule log burning bright at Christmas. If perfect strangers revealed all to him, who could blame them?

"You never miss a beat, do you?" she heard herself say. "The limo, the salve for Birdie's nausea—you'll probably recite the perfect toast at the reception. You try not to let people down."

He glanced at her warily. "I do my best."

"Is that why my father met with you before the wedding? Because you're caring? I tried getting the details."

"But didn't succeed?"

"He brushed off my questions. Was it one of those man-to-man conversations not meant for women?"

"That's one way to characterize it." He loosened the silk tie

73

knotted at his throat. "Are you in the habit of grilling your father about his affairs? I can't imagine he welcomes your curiosity."

"If you must know, I grill him constantly. There's not much choice." She tried to pick out his silvered head in the crowd. He was probably with Theodora. Their friendship was well established. "I'm sure you understand."

"About his depression? Birdie mentioned it. Something about mood swings and medication."

"He hasn't been the same since my mother's death."

"Birdie gave me the basics. You were just out of college when your mother died." Compassion glossed his features, making him even more likeable. "I'm sorry for your loss."

"Me too." She couldn't refrain from adding, "So you see, I have a good reason for asking about your meeting. My father worries. When he's anxious, he becomes erratic."

"Relax. From what I could tell, he's fine. Even if he were upset, I wouldn't share our conversation. I don't break confidences."

Like her father, he refused to give ground. Despite instincts to the contrary, her estimation of him grew.

On impulse, she said, "May I ask a personal question?"

This time he held her in his sights, his face unreadable. "I'd go with 'no thanks' but it wouldn't stop you."

"You see? We are getting to know each other." At the newsroom he'd caught her off-guard. Not this time. "Why do you care about my sister and Hugh? Everyone knows you're leaving for Philadelphia. Your hometown, isn't it? Why waste time helping a couple who'll drift out of your life?"

"What makes you think *I'll* drift out?"

"Won't you?"

The mask slipped, and his eyes flashed with a charming blend of annoyance and glee. "You don't pull any punches, do you?"

"Not usually." She didn't see the point.

"Then I'll give it to you straight. I don't have to live next door to Birdie and Hugh to keep them in my life. They're family—the kind of family we all need, friends who never let you down or try to make you into something you're not. I don't like rehashing my past, but Hugh knows my darkest secrets. The memories I don't like to think about, much less share. I appreciate how he never judges. He listens, period." He chewed something around in his head before adding, "Your sister is the same, true blue to the bone. You ought to try letting her into your life instead of ordering her around."

"Birdie doesn't follow anyone's dictates, Hugh's included. Why presume I order her around?" The idea was ludicrous. Herding cats would be easier.

"The wedding, for starters. She didn't care about a party costing more than a down payment on a house. She would've happily married Hugh barefoot by a stream in the woods."

"Oh, please. Who marries barefoot?"

He leaned in, as if to ensure she'd comprehend a complicated theory. "People who don't care about pomp and ceremony, that's who." Satisfied when she couldn't muster a comeback, he lowered his voice, adding. "Here's an idea. Stop mothering your sister and your father. They're adults. They'll make their own way down life's rocky road. Or they won't. Either way, it's not your problem."

"I love them. If I didn't, I wouldn't work hard to make them happy."

"Who makes *you* happy?"

She stared at him.

"Don't tell me. You have a deep-seated fear you deserve less than everything? Listen up. You deserve all the happiness you can find. Stop doing the right thing, or what you *think* is the right thing. You don't need to earn your family's love—it's yours for the asking." He didn't give her an opportunity to respond. Enjoying himself, he added, "Now it's my turn to ask something personal. Fair warning. You won't like it."

The challenging tone of his voice sent a heady exhilaration sweeping through her. She tried to subdue the tempo of her pulse. When a man narrowed in on her as Hector was doing now, it meant only one thing. A bold move. She'd started this, but he'd cornered her. Having negotiated countless business deals, she knew not to quibble.

"Hector, let me save you the trouble of asking. I am attracted to you." She paused a beat, to let the admission sink in. "Sexual attraction rarely makes sense."

Triumph shone in his eyes. "I know you are, Meade. You're determined to dislike me because, well . . ." He paused, grinning, his eyes carrying heat that tingled across her skin. "Because you'd prefer *not* to like me."

"I have no idea why I feel this way. It's crazy. It's equally crazy that you're attracted to me, which I should take as a compliment. I don't. We aren't well-suited."

"No common ground, nothing to build on. Is that what you mean?"

"Precisely."

"Does it matter? As you said, I'm leaving."

Was he seeking an invitation to stay? She wouldn't dream of asking, for reasons as logical as they were disheartening. They didn't have anything in common. They operated in different spheres. She wasn't a thrill seeker, like Birdie, or confident, like Hugh. She *was* like her father—careful, consistent, and certainly not in the habit of investing in dicey commodities.

Or people.

Reading the emotions scuttling across her features, he chuckled. "This *is* a conundrum," he murmured. "I've never been attracted to a woman who'd throw me under a bus before she'd agree to a date. What's your usual preference—a suit earning six-figures? The type with 'stability' stamped on his first coronary?"

"Stability is a virtue."

"You need a vice. A man with blood in his veins is a good start."

His mocking tone galled nearly as much as his dark gaze enthralled. "Meaning you?" she demanded.

"What have you got to lose? I'm game for a challenge, and you sure as hell aren't easy. We should explore this, see where it leads."

About as direct a proposal as a man could offer, and she gave him points for sheer nerve. She was still trying to get her neurons to fire when he nudged her, breaking the exchange.

"Head's up." He motioned to the crowd. "Looks like Mary needs you."

From behind, she heard her name called out. With a wave, Mary worked her way free of the people jostling to congratulate the newlyweds. Meade sent another prayer of gratitude heavenward, her second this afternoon. If the conversation with Hector went much further, she'd foolishly consider his request to go on a date. At the least, his bravado would ensure stimulating dinner conversation.

Throwing off the thought, she did a double take. Gone was Mary's dull physician's white coat and scruffy loafers. She was a vision of elegance in an eggplant-colored gown of shimmering taffeta.

The astute doctor sensed the supercharged air buzzing around them. "Am I interrupting something?" Mary asked.

"Don't be silly." The interruption was a relief. Or an inadvertent if well-timed rescue. The last time Meade fell for a man's seductions, she was a blushing college sophomore. Avoiding a repeat performance was wise.

Mary drew them further from the crowd. "Meade, your father left with Theodora. She's driving him home. He needs to lie down."

Meade gave Hector a meaningful glance. He'd questioned why she kept tabs on her father. Perhaps now he'd understand.

"What happened?" she asked Mary.

"I only caught snippets of the argument."

"He was arguing with Theodora?" Usually they got on well. If there was anyone he trusted completely, it was Theodora.

"She tried to calm him down. They had words about Glade. He's angry she's staying at your house. Complaining up a storm right after the ceremony. Theodora asked him to pipe down. She practically dragged him to her car."

"Glade wasn't within earshot, was she? She's been through enough." Meade wasn't sure where she and Reenie had chosen to sit during the nuptials.

"She didn't hear a thing. Reenie took her to the back row, near the sugar shack."

"Next he'll think Glade is staying at the house to spy on him," she said, more for Hector's edification than Mary's. "I'll never hear the end of it."

The comment hit the mark, and Hector looked nearly apologetic. "Your father is paranoid?"

"That's one way to characterize it. Last year he was convinced the gardeners were peeking in the windows. I spent weeks convincing him otherwise. Poor Reenie. She began scheduling the men to arrive at dawn. Paid them twice the going rate for their trouble. They finished before my father woke each morning."

Mary asked, "What set him off this time? I can't believe having Glade at the house is the true source of his rancor."

"Blame the wedding. All the last-minute preparations were too much for his nerves. Now we have a pregnant teen bunking in the servants' quarters. It's not the girl's fault. Under normal circumstances, my father wouldn't mind if Reenie had a relative visiting. She's worked for us for decades, and my father loves her. This is just bad timing."

"No wonder Theodora tried to host the reception." Mary rubbed her chin. "There's a limit to the amount of activity Landon can tolerate before his depression resurfaces."

"We should've let her host. I blame myself for nixing the idea."

"Nonsense. Landon insisted on hosting in the ballroom. Remember? We were joking about finding a cleaning service capable of performing miracles on short notice."

"So much for miracles. Now my father will be impossible all night."

"I'll help you keep an eye out during the reception. If he looks stressed, we'll encourage him to leave the reception early."

Hector asked, "Is there anything I can do?"

The apology in his eyes was now distinct, and she wondered if he regretted the impromptu sexual banter. All things considered, she suspected he did.

"Thanks for asking." It was a relief he'd dropped the flirtation. "Would you escort my sister to the limo? We don't need her suffering a bout of morning sickness in front of her guests."

Chapter 6

Amidst the lavish floral arrangements gracing the ballroom and the band's dreamy music, Mary yearned for nothing more than a waltz with her husband. The demands of her profession put the wish on hold.

On the dais at the far end of the ballroom, the band struck up another slow number. The dance floor was already crammed with couples moving slowly to the ballad. Weaving past tables clogged with guests, she reached the bridal party.

She stopped behind Birdie's chair. "How are you holding up?" she whispered.

Birdie smiled gamely. "I'm done dancing for the night."

"Still nauseous?"

"Comes and goes. Thanks for sending up the ginger ale. It's helping."

Hugh slung his arm over the back of her chair. "Baby, we can leave whenever you're ready. The party is in full swing. No one will notice."

"My father will. He went to all this trouble. Let's stay until midnight."

Mary looked around. "Where is your father?" At the far end of the table, only Theodora remained. She was chatting with several women.

Birdie regarded the sea of couples swaying to the music. "Somewhere out in the crush. Meade got him to dance. Naturally he tried to get out of it."

"Meade won?"

"She insisted. Talk about a battle of wills."

"Is he still complaining about Glade?"

"All through dinner. I asked him to stop. What if Glade overhears? She's just a kid."

"Don't worry. Meade will keep him away from her. She'll never hear a word."

"It's silly. I've never seen him act this way. Why does he care if his housekeeper has a relative visiting?"

"He doesn't, not really." Mary reminded herself that less than a year ago, Birdie hadn't known Landon was her father. They hadn't met until last autumn. To this day, his depression was something of a mystery to her. "Getting Landon up and moving will help. Meade knows what she's doing. Now, try to enjoy yourself. Let your sister worry about your father. She's adept at handling his moods."

Mary excused herself and merged into the crowd. The noise level in the ballroom had increased, the adult guests pairing off to the music or chatting in loud, boisterous voices. Younger guests, including Snoops and Blossom, were milling around in the ballroom's much smaller antechamber. Drawing up the rustling folds of her gown, Mary impulsively changed direction. Why not check on her stepdaughter? It might provide an opportunity to mend their relationship.

In the antechamber the lighting was brighter, the music muffled. Decks of cards were quaintly set out on the tables as if the teens, texting on cell phones and taking photographs of the opulent surroundings, might notice. Two waiters served ice cream from an old-fashioned brass cart. Several dozen junior high and high school students, lucky to have received an invitation, clustered in small groups.

"Hey, kiddo," Mary said, hooking her arm through Blossom's. She steered her away from the others. "Having fun?"

"I've always wanted to see the mansion. Can I look around? Check out the upstairs? I won't touch anything."

"Not on your life. This isn't a museum. There's no tour."

"Meade's your best friend. If you beg, she'll crumble."

"Blossom, *no.*"

"Take a chill pill. I was just asking." Blossom clasped the

hem of her dress and wagged it around. "I guess I should thank you for this."

"No thanks are necessary. I'm glad we struck a truce. You look beautiful."

The eggshell blue prom dress was too mature, but a compromise had been in order. The gold sandals boasted respectable one-inch heels, and she'd allowed Blossom to wear eye shadow and clear pink lipstick. The final result was startling, and more than a little unnerving. Throughout the night's festivities, Blossom drew glances from a number of young men far older than she. The only consolation? At age thirteen, she was too young to comprehend their interest.

Needing to heal the rift with her stepdaughter, Mary said, "I want to tell you something. I do understand how badly you want a sibling. Being an only child is lonely. I can't promise I'll have a baby soon, but I am thinking it through."

Blossom's eyes rounded. "You are?"

"Sweetie, I can't drop everything to get pregnant. Reducing my work hours will take a serious game plan, and I'd prefer not to use daycare. There's a lot to map out."

"You'll figure it out, right?"

"Yes, but keep in mind this will affect you too. Once there's a baby in the house, you'll have to deal with inconveniences like quiet hours during naptime. You and Snoops can't blast the house with music whenever the mood strikes."

The warning couldn't dent the glee warming Blossom's face. "No *problemo.* We'll be as quiet as mice. Can you deliver by Christmas? We'll hang a fourth stocking on the mantle, fill it with stuff for my little buddy."

Her excitement made Mary laugh. "Slow down. Babies should take nine months to bake, not seven," she joked. "And I said I was *thinking* about it. Let me work out a plan."

Blossom bounced on the balls of her feet. "How long do you need? A week? Two?"

"Kiddo—"

"Hey. Names. Who gets to pick? Do we vote? I'll get started on a list. Like immediately."

The issue of naming the baby should've been anticipated.

In the Perini household, democracy ruled. Votes were cast

on a silly number of issues, everything from what to eat for dinner to who'd take out the garbage on Tuesday nights. What to watch on TV brought on a squabble only a quick show of hands subdued. If Mary had deluded herself into thinking she'd handle the lovely task of selecting the baby's name with Anthony alone, she should've known better.

Yet she couldn't entertain disappointment. Blossom loved a mission. She loved stratagems, devising plans, and anything requiring a hundred lists and a dose of cunning. At least this particular mission wouldn't land her in detention at the junior high.

"Go on. Research a few names. I'll give your input some consideration." Mary gave her a peck on the cheek. "Now, if you don't mind, I'd like to find your father. It's time I asked him to dance."

For the fifth time tonight, Hector mused, Delia had tracked him down.

At the bar, on the ballroom's balcony, when he tried to sneak back to the bridal table with another peach the caterer had kindly sliced for Birdie—regardless of where Hector went, Delia materialized before him like a dreaded mirage.

In her next life, she'd make a great PI. She had the stalking thing down pat.

"Ready to dance?" he asked. Encouraging her flirtations wasn't smart, but they'd run out of small talk.

"I thought you'd never ask." She wagged her wrist in his face.

If this was an invitation to kiss her hand, she was in for a long wait. "Let's go." Taking care not to make bodily contact, he dived into the crowd certain she'd follow.

The band switched to a faster beat. It seemed an act of mercy. Hector gyrated along with everyone else, knocking shoulders and trying not to land a foot on the hem of any of the gowns spinning past. He nursed the sinking suspicion he didn't have long before Delia found a way into his arms.

The irony was hard to miss. There *was* a woman he'd like to lead across the dance floor. Not the gum-popping waitress from

The Second Chance Grill.

Meade.

Throughout the night's festivities, he'd been in a funk. After the wedding he'd come on too strong with Meade in Liberty Square, returning her blunt questions with the bald suggestion they begin dating. Putting the moves on her wasn't inspired. In truth he hadn't meant to ask her out. At least not consciously. He sure as hell didn't mean to plunge in without a game plan.

Yet the facts were hard to miss. In an elemental way, they were drawn to each other. And, he was embarrassed to realize, he'd ask her out again if the right moment arrived. Would she agree to a date? Whether her calculating mind would cede to her more passionate nature was impossible to assess.

The only certainty? She'd revved his emotions without trying. What to do about it, if anything, was up for grabs.

Yanking him from his musings, Delia asked, "Do you like my dress?" She twirled, releasing a cloud of cloying sweet perfume. Hoop earrings smacked against her flushed cheeks.

"Nice choice." He avoided staring at her breasts, half bared in the low-cut number.

"Think so?"

"Yeah. Sure."

"Red isn't too much for a wedding? I almost changed my mind, but I love how the dress fits."

In traditional circles, red at a wedding *was* taboo. Pointing out the fact was cruel and so he said, "It's perfect. A real stand-out." Between her rousing dance moves and the fire engine-colored dress, would she burst into flame? A pyrotechnic display, and half the young men in the ballroom were already staring at her. Which is why he added, "Mind if I give you some advice? Friend to friend?"

Her hips throttled to a stop. "Okay." She resumed dancing with less enthusiasm.

He chose his words with care. "Take the flirting down a notch." He stamped compassion on his face, hoping to soften the blow. "The world is full of hungry men."

"I don't understand."

Lord, she looked like she didn't. He reminded himself that she was a kid in small-town America, barely out of her teens.

"Don't dress like you're a free meal. Bide your time until the right man comes along. Women are smart. You'll know when you've found the right guy."

Her lower lip trembled, but he gave her credit. She kept dancing, her feet kicking out jerky steps and her arms swinging in tight arcs. At length, she said, "Does this mean you won't ask me out?"

"It means I'm not the right guy."

"What if I think you are?"

"Delia, I'm pushing thirty-six. I've been married and divorced twice. You're young. Find someone with a clean slate."

"Oh, I don't care about your divorces."

"You should."

"At The Second Chance, Theodora and Hugh talk about you all the time," she said, and he wondered at her eavesdropping capabilities while waiting tables. "You married your wives because you felt bad for them. Like a good humanitarian thing. They were both hurt in car accidents, right?" The music slowed. To his horror she flung herself into his arms. "I'd hate being stuck in a wheelchair. You're a hero for helping them walk again."

She jostled against his chest, and he tried to pull back. "They did the hard work, not me. Physical therapy takes grit and perseverance."

"You're still friends with them."

A statement, not a question.

"Great friends. I married for the wrong reasons. They were smart to divorce me." He got back on track. "Enough about me. The point I'm trying to make? Let a man approach you. Don't make it easy on him. Hold out. Make him prove he's worthy." The way, he realized, he'd prove his worth if Meade agreed to a date.

"So you don't like me?"

"You're great. But, no, I'm not attracted." Spinning her in a circle, he sensed something different. He struck on it. "Where's the gum? This is the first time I've seen you without a wad stuffed in your cheek."

"I ran out."

"Run out permanently. It's a child's habit. You're a beautiful woman. Act like one."

She offered a watery smile. "I'll try."

Over her head, he spotted Glade.

All night long she'd been on his radar. The pregnant teen was gussied up in a cotton dress, the ballooning evidence of her pregnancy impossible to miss. Long hair, parted in the middle, was combed straight to her shoulders. Her eyes were in constant motion, taking in the dimly lit chandeliers sparkling overhead, the people clustered in raucous groups and the wait staff moving seamlessly through the ballroom serving drinks. She reminded Hector of a kid on a roller coaster that proved a terrifying ride.

In the rough Philly neighborhood where he'd grown up, there were countless girls like her. What they lacked in looks they made up for in other ways. Most were as faithful as a lap dog. They cracked their knuckles and their hearts when fast boys, on the lookout for an easy score, charmed them into bed.

Inspiration struck, and he glided Delia from the dance floor. "Would you do me a kindness?" he asked her. "There's a girl over there who's not much younger than you. She doesn't know anyone here."

Following his gaze, Delia gasped. "Wow. How far along is she?"

"You'd have to ask Mary."

"She's Mary's patient?"

"New patient, from West Virginia. I think Mary is lining her up with an obstetrician at the hospital. The kid sure needs one."

"What's she doing in Liberty?"

He explained her tie to Meade's housekeeper. Summing up, he added, "Why don't you talk to her? She could use a friend."

The request extinguished Delia's vamp routine. Wrapping her arms around his neck, she pulled his face close. "Hector, it's true what everyone says. You *are* a nice man." She dropped a chaste kiss on his cheek. "Introduce us. I'll take it from there."

Having never met Glade, he muddled through the introductions. Relief passed through the girl's eyes—she appeared thrilled they'd noticed her. Her hands, as plump as a toddler's, fluttered from her belly to a neck splotched with hives. If she didn't put a lid on her anxiety, she'd soon go as red as Delia's flaming dress.

"Can we sit down?" Glade whispered. She put one foot forward, revealing a swollen ankle. "I've been on my feet too long."

Freed of her role as seductress, Delia put her arm around the girl with motherly affection. "Of course! We'll chat and get to know each other. Where's your table? Or would you rather sit at mine? I came with friends. They'd love to meet you."

"Can we go to your table? I don't have one."

Hector asked, "Where did you eat dinner?" Not while standing, he hoped.

"Oh, I didn't eat. Reenie's busy in the kitchen, ordering maids around. I went out to the front steps."

"You were outside?" He couldn't imagine why.

"I didn't want to get in the way. It's not like I'm supposed to be here."

"I'm sure the Williamses are glad you're here."

With dismay, he reflected on Mary's comments after the ceremony. She'd mentioned Landon was angry about his houseguest. What if Glade learned of his complaints? They'd find her camped out in the forest rimming the estate. She'd do her best to avoid detection.

Anger at Landon competed with his pity for the girl. Snapping his fingers, he flagged down a waiter tall enough to brush the ceiling. "Bring out another plate. You have a guest who missed dinner. Skip the wine." The waiter started off, and Hector grabbed him by the sleeve. "Can you scare up a glass of milk?"

Glade licked her lips. "Is it okay if I have two?"

Hector winked at her before telling the waiter, "Make it a pitcher of milk. Ice cold." To Delia, he asked, "Where's your table?"

She explained. The man left to fetch the meal.

On the dance floor, shouting erupted. Startled guests scurried out of the way, creating a circle around their wild-eyed host. The bow tie at Landon's throat hung awry and he was breathing fast. The band stopped playing for a heart-stopping moment, hurling the room into silence and halting the venom spewing from his mouth.

He pushed a waiter out of the way. The tray in the man's arms teetered. China crashed to the floor. A heavyset matron screeched with fright. The bandleader, scrambling back into position, struck up a lively pop song.

Landon stalked out of the ballroom. The crowd merged forward, blocking Hector's line of sight.

He didn't see Meade follow her father out.

Music floated across the moon-washed acres.

Tall hedges threw shadows the cold light couldn't penetrate. Tripping on the stone path, Meade cried out. She counseled herself to slow down. Up ahead her father, muttering oaths, disappeared around a wall of boxwood. At least the path he took was easy to follow. Whenever gripped by depression, his sanctuary of choice was the boathouse.

Gathering the folds of her gown, she sprinted after him with her heartbeat drumming in her ears. She hated these confrontations, the sad, circular weaving of her father's words whenever his grip on sanity loosened. A memory, a photograph, the arrival of an unexpected guest—there was no predicting what would set him off. That this latest bout of rage erupted in the midst of Birdie and Hugh's wedding reception was humiliating. It seemed small solace that any further harsh words would be uttered far from the people gathered to celebrate their union.

The walkway leading to the boathouse shimmered with evening dew. Further off, the lake undulated like waves of black satin. The dock was partially obscured by mist. Not wishing to risk another stumble, she removed her pumps. The night was balmy, licking her skin with soothing warmth. She took a steadying breath before venturing further.

"Daddy?"

In the eerie gloom, the roses clinging to the boathouse shuddered. The door opened with a creak and she went inside.

"Daddy, where are you?"

By the window fishing rods and tackle jumbled together on a table. The scent of marine life was strong here, the taste of decay clinging to her lips. With clumsy movements, she found her way in the dark and grappled for the window. She yanked open the curtain. Moonlight spilled across the floor.

In the center of the room her father stood with head bowed.

For ballast she gripped the table. "Don't shut me out. I'm

here." These confrontations made her fearful, the unpredictability of the outcome an affront to her ordered mind. No matter how often they took place, she was forced to beat down the dread. "I want to help."

"Meade, go away."

"Don't be angry. As soon as I'm able, I'll find somewhere safe for Glade to live. She isn't spying on you, and she won't stay with us forever. She's a girl in trouble. Daddy, she's Reenie's great-niece. Where's your sense of charity?"

"Don't talk to me about charity," he growled. She planted her feet. If he threw something, she'd have to duck. "Where was your mother's sense of charity? She whored around while you spent your days in the nursery and I worked myself to the bone. Why should I feel charitable? Why?"

"Slow down. Are you upset about Glade or my mother?" Both, probably. Or neither. Logic was a useless commodity when grief overran his thoughts.

"Leave me!"

"Not until you start making sense. I'm sorry Mother hurt you. Try to remember the good times. Remember the picnics? All those afternoons relaxing in the sunshine and playing games? You loved those days. Mother adored croquet and you taught me how to play. We didn't have a care in the world."

"Your mother was a whore."

"Daddy, stop." She pinched the skin between her brows. Tomorrow he'd forget every attack on her mother's memory. He'd forget, and she'd carry another scar from his forgotten rage. "You loved Mother. She loved you too. We were happy, at least some of the time."

The comment stoked his rage. "You have no idea what's bothering me," he shouted, weaving onto a new tangent. "You're too self-centered to understand how upsetting this is. Why wasn't I consulted about the song list?"

She tried to keep up. "The songs chosen for the reception?"

"Have you no compassion? I never would've agreed to *Dancing in the Dark*. Why was it selected?"

Suddenly she understood.

The Big Band classic had been a song adored by her mother. In an unfortunate coincidence, it was also one of Hugh's favorites.

Naturally Birdie had added it. In the rush to organize the wedding, Meade forgot to check the final song list. A tragic error.

The instinct to protect her younger sister sent the words rushing from her lips. "Oh, Daddy—I shouldn't have added *Dancing in the Dark*. I should've remembered how much it upsets you."

"You're careless, Meade. An embarrassment."

"I wasn't thinking."

"How do you think you made our guests feel? We wouldn't have had words in the ballroom if your sensitivity were intact. Good breeding matters, girl. Without proper etiquette, the world devolves into chaos. Haven't I taught you anything?"

Another blow she took with thinning grace. "Let's go back to the house. If you're tired of the party, I'll help you to bed."

"Dammit, I don't need your assistance to find my way to bed. Stop treating me like a child."

The outburst snapped her head up. What had Hector said in The Square when he'd revealed his attraction to her? *Stop doing the right thing, or what you think is the right thing. You don't need to earn your family's love.* Good advice, all of it, and she was weary of playing nursemaid during her father's indiscriminate rages. Regardless of how she tried, she couldn't prepare or lessen the impact. She was tired of trying.

The knowledge stole the compliancy from her voice. "I won't stand here arguing. You're hurtful, and I don't have to listen to your complaints. You're only upsetting yourself more, and me along with you. Enough. We're going back."

During his tantrums, she usually she kept her distance. Not tonight. She strode forward with newfound courage. It *was* time to put her needs first. She was done coddling him every time he became abusive.

Her approach caught him off-guard. "Get away." He batted the air.

"No, Daddy. You're coming with me. I'll take you to bed. If you're upset in the morning, we'll talk then."

"Get back!"

"I'm not leaving you out here stewing."

Recklessly, she reached for him. His arm ratcheted skyward. With surprising force, his fist struck her cheek. Pain shot through the delicate bones underneath. Pinpricks of fire radiated down her neck and stars whirled past her eyes, blackening her vision for a dreadful moment. The sensation was mild compared to the despair swamping her.

Crying out, she stumbled back.

She was still trying to regain her senses when the brutality of his actions slackened her father's jaw. Never before had he struck her. Not once, in all these years of sad and groundless bickering.

Horror leapt into his eyes. "What have I done?"

On a moan, he crumpled to the floor.

"My darling child. Meade, I would never hurt you—" Tears choked off the apology.

Her cheek burning, she fell to her knees and bundled him into her arms.

Chapter 7

The last guests departed the mansion at 1:00 A.M. Hector was not among them.

Unable to bring himself to leave, he circled back to the ballroom. Twenty members of the wait staff were removing wine-stained tablecloths, and stacking chairs. Hugh and Birdie had said good night to their guests right before midnight, and made the drive to their apartment above the *Post.* The band, claiming the place of honor where the bride and groom had spent the evening, was stacking sound equipment and tucking musical instruments into black cases.

Landon had never returned to the reception. By Hector's count, he'd been missing for two hours and ten minutes.

Was Meade with him?

Hector strode into the two-story foyer where a butler was stationed during the festivities to welcome guests or bid them farewell. The man was gone, the foyer's chandelier dimmed. Frowning, Hector peered up the grand, L-shaped staircase. People as polished as the Williamses would never retire for the night before seeing their guests off.

At the opposite end of the mansion, he detected the murmur of voices. Following the sound, he walked through a dimly lit corridor. At the end was a kitchen large enough to do double duty in a restaurant. Maids clustered at the center island sorting dishes into stacks, and drying crystal. Beyond them, the Williams' housekeeper sat at the table jotting notes on a checklist.

He went to her. "Reenie, have you seen Meade and Mr. Williams?"

"Hector. Hello." She set the pen down. "I thought you left with everyone else."

"Mr. Williams—where is he?"

"Why, he's in bed."

"You're certain?"

"I checked on him an hour ago. He's fast asleep."

"Where's Meade?"

"In bed, I assumed." Reading the worry in his eyes, she added, "Should I check?"

"Please."

When she returned, the gravity of her expression matched his. "It's not like Meade to leave for her apartment without telling me," she explained. "She rarely stays there and besides, she's planning to spend Sunday with her father. I called and left a message. She's not picking up her cell either."

Meade wasn't at her apartment. He was sure of it. The housekeeper was correct—she wouldn't leave without alerting someone, and certainly not on the night of her sister's wedding. She was somewhere on the grounds.

"I'll find her," he assured Reenie.

Intuition sent him in the direction of the boathouse, a destination he hoped to reach by memory. The humidity was rising and he shrugged out of his suit jacket. Tossing it over his shoulder, he started across the lawn that formed a green necklace around the mansion. In less than a minute he was out of the glaring floodlights, his pace slowing as his vision adjusted to the night.

Clouds scuttled across the moon, leaving patches of black and grey on the estate's rolling hills. Using the meager light on his smartphone, he rounded the cutting garden alert for the murmur of the lake's waters. If the moon didn't come back out, he wasn't sure he'd find the way.

He did, despite the near darkness. The door to the boathouse was ajar. There was no one inside.

Worried now, he walked down to the beach. The lull of the waters provided a haunting music. To the left, he made out a thin band of sand merging with the night. Ears pricked, he prayed. In the distance, the faint and harrowing sound of weeping lifted on the air.

"Meade?"

Anxiety increased the perspiration slicking down his chest. Pulling off his tie, he left it with his jacket on the bench where he'd chatted with Landon. The breeze kicked up, balmy with summer's promise. Walk the beach with only his cell phone to guide him? He muttered a curse. If Meade chose to evade discovery, finding her would take time.

Borrowing a flashlight from Reenie would've been smart.

"Meade, are you here?"

The snuffling broke off. "Hector?"

The startled response got his feet going. Like a homing pigeon, he went toward her voice.

"Mind giving me a hint? Where are you?"

"Right here."

He found her twenty yards off, huddled on the sand with the gauzy folds of her gown pooling around her. What he could see of the dress didn't look good. A ragged tear ran through the fabric, as if she'd torn it while walking in the dark. Her hair was unbound, flailing like streamers of indiscriminate color.

Gingerly he lowered himself to the sand.

"You okay?" Obviously not. Tears glistened on her cheeks.

"Why are you here?"

"Looking for you." He declined to add he'd been frightened he wouldn't find her.

"Go on back. I'll be in later. I need to sort myself out."

"Meade, it's late. The reception ended thirty minutes ago. Everyone's gone."

"Did Birdie make it to midnight?"

"Barely. She left with a bag of peaches. Gift from the caterer."

"Where's Daddy?"

"Sleeping. Your housekeeper says he went to bed a while ago."

She drew her knees up, her back curved by grief. "I tried to get him to the house. He wouldn't let me help him."

"He didn't go back to the party. Hugh noticed."

"Did Birdie?"

93

"She was more focused on the peaches."

The news brought a sigh of relief. "Thank God he stayed away from the ballroom. He was too muddled to entertain guests."

Hector studied the clouds scuttling across the heavens. "Did you have an argument?"

"We always argue."

She began to cry. The tears stripped away the art and artifice cultivated by a woman of high standing. The transformation was difficult to witness. He was thankful for the darkness concealing her misery from too close an inspection.

Meade prided herself on her deliberate speech and intimidating poise. The tears felled these attributes like a scythe to wheat. Yet with Hector's pity came unbidden gratitude. A rare gift was this, to glimpse the vulnerable heart of such a unique woman.

"Meade, it's all right," he said, needing to end her suffering.

"Believe me, it's not. Have you ever known anyone with serious depression?"

Chewing it over, he said, "Not that I'm aware. I have an uncle in remission for cancer. He gets pretty low. Most of the time he manages fine. My aunt keeps his spirits up. They're both troopers."

"This is different. My father can go a long time, months on end, and seem fine. Then a song dredges up a bad memory or something changes in his routine. He goes off the deep end. Rages, or days of moping—he gets mean. I've always found it ironic how someone so thin-skinned has no consideration for other people's feelings. Oh, he's not like that every day. But when his depression takes hold, it's like living with a hostile inmate."

"Break him out of prison."

"I've tried." She dug her fingers into her hair, pulling needlessly on the flowing locks. "He refuses to leave his bedroom or he stews in the greenhouse. Like he's stuck in a cage of rage."

"His cage of rage," Hector repeated, shaking his head. "A sad poetry, but I like it."

"You would."

"Meade, get him out more often. No one should live like a hermit."

"Do I look like a miracle worker? If not for his friendship with Theodora, he'd never leave the house. She has a gift, a way of reaching through his darkest thoughts and giving him peace, if not happiness."

"Ask her for pointers."

"As if it'll work. They've been close longer than I've been alive. He trusts her."

"But not you?"

"I'm his daughter, not his friend. He doesn't view me the same way."

"Sure he does," Hector protested, and the softness of his tone convulsed her back with a new wave of sorrow.

She fought to find her voice through the tears. "Caring for him year in and year out is hard, frustrating—like dragging granite. He goes as cold as stone, and there's no reaching him. No way to end his grief. I'm tired of trying to make him happy when all he does is make me sad. I'm tired of *him*. Does that make me an awful daughter?"

"Not at all. You're a great person. The best."

"Oh, sure." More tears, and she buried her face in her hands.

Which was all he could take. "Come here," he murmured. "You're on the verge of an all-out crying jag."

Scooting closer, he took her into his arms and she let him, her head drifting to his shoulder, her chest heaving with the brunt of her heartache.

Held close, she was smaller than he'd imagined, more delicate, her fingers endearingly fragile as he curled them beneath his much larger hands. Her perfume became a lure, the light floral scent stirring his senses, the feel of her skin moist beneath his fingertips. His caresses were clumsy as he stroked her arms and murmured words of comfort that proved incapable of staunching the outpouring of grief.

She'd begun to settle down when the moon escaped from behind thick clouds. In the bluish light the beach came alive. The water brightened and the ribbon of sand grew visible. Yet the moon's glow seemed a warning to Meade. She raised her head from its perch. Regretting the loss, he tightened his hold on her hands.

Then he saw the welt. It was an angry red on her cheek.

95

"How did this happen?" Careful not to hurt her, he tested the bruised flesh. Her skin was hot to the touch. Then the truth jolted him. "Your father hit you? Meade, did he?"

She flinched. "It was an accident. I tried to make him leave the boathouse." She scooted back an inch, and he felt the loss like an amputation. "I shouldn't have come at him. It was stupid. When he realized what he'd done, he was devastated."

A chilling anger filled Hector. "Has this happened before?"

"No, never. Daddy isn't violent."

"Like hell."

"Hector, I swear to you—he didn't mean to strike me," she insisted, and her voice broke on a sob.

"It's all right. Please don't start crying again." He folded her back into his arms and began rocking. It was a relief when she leaned into him, her gestures tentative as she reached across his stomach to find purchase. Without stopping to consider his actions, he pressed kisses to her forehead, adding, "We should get some ice to stop the swelling. I'll run back to the house."

"Don't go." She relaxed fully against him.

"Let's go together," he suggested, but he didn't move. He didn't want the moment to end.

"I'm not ready to leave. Let Reenie get to bed. I couldn't bear her questions. She's so protective. If she sees me like this, she'll be up all night worrying."

"Whatever you want."

She rubbed her cheek against his shoulder as if testing his strength. "Do you ever wonder why life works out the way it does?"

He grinned into the dark. "All the time. Everything makes sense when you're young. You get older, make a few decisions with outcomes you sure as hell don't expect, and you end up wondering how to keep score. The game changes."

"It shouldn't."

"Learn to flex. If you don't, you'll break."

She nuzzled closer. "I've always believed if you follow the rules you'll come out ahead. Get an education, work hard, and everything falls into place. The successes outweigh the failures. No guarantees but, for the most part, everything works out."

"It does, for some people."

"Not me."

"Luck changes. You stay in the game."

"I'm tired of the game."

Her fingers dug into his ribs, telegraphing fear or despair. Whatever the emotion burdening her, it brought his protective nature to the fore. He didn't like seeing women hurt. This instance was particularly difficult. Meade was capable, accomplished, a woman firmly in charge of her destiny. She wasn't the type easily knocked down by a bad run of luck. The injury to her cheek would heal. But the altercation with her father—what if it broke her?

At risk to his heart, he urged her into his lap, settling her in the cradle of his thighs as he would a lover. She came readily, her eyes moist and her expression open. Her compliance filled him with awe and the notion he'd unexpectedly found himself in the center of one of the most precious moments of his life.

Often the most pivotal events of life passed by unnoticed, the importance hidden until much later.

Tonight was different; he understood the portent of her willing affection, the ease with which she settled against him as if she would trust him forever. As if she might, should he prove deserving, allow him to lay claim to her heart. The possibility left him yearning to taste the forbidden fruit of her lips. In his chest, his heart thundered.

Oblivious to his dilemma, she said, "It's pathetic, the way I try to keep everything going. What's the point? Control is an illusion. You were right in what you said after the wedding. I can't please everyone."

"You mean your father."

"And my mother before him. She had my entire life scripted. The right friends, the best schools, even my career. I never would've founded *Vivid* without her prodding. She loved France, discovering small perfumeries. She loved the pretty shops with the soaps and bath products made from recipes handed down for generations. On one of our mother-daughter shopping sprees in Paris, she hatched the idea for *Vivid*. Daddy thought she'd found the perfect career for me."

"If you hadn't gone along with the plan, what would you have done instead?"

"Who knows? I never gave my own interests time to surface."

"You have no idea?"

"I don't. I thought if I was the perfect daughter, accepting my parents' choices instead of forging my own path, my achievements would bring happiness. I knew they were miserable. Oh, I wasn't aware of my mother's liaisons or my father's affair with Wish Kaminsky until Birdie showed up in Liberty. But I always knew something was wrong between my parents. So I compensated for their misery by giving them perfection. Perfect Meade. My work, comportment, everything."

"A heavy load to carry." Too heavy in his estimation.

"Do you think I'm a fool?"

She gazed at him solemnly, as if his opinion were more priceless than the stars coasting out from behind the clouds. That she cared what he thought elevated him to the heady position of her equal.

The change, though subtle, unhitched the control he'd valiantly kept in place.

"Meade, you're not a fool. You're an exceptional woman."

"I am?"

"Absolutely." Torn between propriety and desire, he added, "I hope you'll forgive my honesty. I'm crazy about you."

Impulsively, he pressed his mouth to her throat. She bent gracefully, giving him room to explore. The invitation was intoxicating. The beach spun beneath him.

Breathlessly she said, "You are kind, Hector. I was wrong about you."

She couldn't think. The intellect she'd inherited from her father, the ceaseless weighing and judging of a trained mind—all thought vanished beneath the questing heat of his mouth.

Needing to give as well as take, she stopped his lovemaking by holding his head between her palms. She memorized the hard planes of his face, lingering on the tiny scars running at the edge of his thick brows. He drew still, ceding control, and she brushed her lips across the coarse stubble on his jaw. His hair was lustrous, wrapping around her fingers in thick bands. When his eyes locked on hers, dark with passion and need, an accompanying longing plunged to her belly.

98

"We should stop," she whispered. "We're opening ourselves up to a thousand regrets."

"We're not."

"Are you sure?"

In one, fluid movement, he turned her onto the sand and covered her body with his. Muscle and bone, they became acquainted with each other. His caresses roamed freely, lighting fires on her waist, her shoulders, her neck. The wonderment on his face stole her breath away.

"Meade, you're beautiful." Dipping his head, he left lingering kisses on the tender skin beneath her ear. "Tell me what you want. Not what you think is proper—what you *want*."

"I'm frightened."

"Of falling in love? We won't walk away from this." He went up on elbows, forcing her to assess the sincerity in his eyes. "If I make love to you, it won't end here. I'll pursue you."

"You shouldn't."

"I will, and I mean to keep you."

Moonlight surrounded him like a halo, and there *was* something angelic about the purity of his motives. Beneath the desire thrumming in her rib cage, she felt contentment wholly unfamiliar, an emotion rich with promise. It stilled the reservations lodged in her brain, the countless reasons why she should get up and say goodnight. Was this a stolen season? It had been far too long since she'd lain beneath a man who professed an affection untested yet that might prove durable.

On a wish, she steered his mouth to hers.

Whether or not their relationship would develop into something lasting was a question better left for time to reveal. On Sunday all Meade cared about was how uncommonly *good* she felt.

After the altercation with her father in the boathouse, Hector's appearance on the beach was nothing less than a rescue. He'd arrived an interloper of whom she was suspicious, but he'd effortlessly displayed his true worth through a dozen kindnesses—including a bout of temper over the injury on her cheek. His impulse to protect her and the generous manner in which he soothed her tattered emotions had revealed a man of more depth than she'd anticipated. The discovery had transmuted her suspicions into admiration and a fast-growing attraction.

They'd remained on the beach until the first notes of birdsong broke the night's grip, and dawn painted the treetops in rosy shades of pink. After they'd made love, they talked until their voices were hoarse and sleep threatened to overtake them. No one saw the car leave the estate at dawn.

Stepping from the shower, Meade toweled herself dry. She shrugged into the sinfully thick Turkish robe she kept at her father's house, her miniature poodle Melbourne yipping at her feet. Even with less sleep than normal, she brimmed with energy.

The cozy sitting room was awash with noon light. The suite she kept at the estate wasn't overlarge, but it was comfortable. Located at the end of the hallway from her father's private rooms, with three bedrooms in between rarely graced by visitors, the suite offered ample privacy. Unlike the sparsely furnished apartment ten minutes from her office at *Vivid,* the country suite was charmingly old-fashioned with floral wallpaper and overstuffed chairs in a matching rosebud pattern. The king size bed's coverlet was spun of lace, a lucky find on a recent buying trip to France.

After she'd donned slacks and a silky tee shirt, she retraced her steps to the bathroom to apply makeup. The bruise on her cheek wasn't large, but it was turning a dull shade of purple. She dabbed concealer on top then finished with a liquid foundation. From a distance, the mark wasn't visible. Satisfied with her handiwork, she did her eyes then rimmed her mouth with lipstick.

She'd just finished drying her hair when a knock on the door brought her back to the sitting room. Melbourne, alerted by the rapping and eager to escape the confines of the suite, ran tight circles around her ankles.

Laughing, she tried to shoo him back. To no avail—the moment the door was opened, the poodle darted out to freedom.

"Traitor," she muttered.

Glade held up a silver tray laden with breakfast treats and a pot of coffee. She looked frightfully young today, her hair plaited in a hasty braid and her face devoid of make-up.

"Reenie thought you were too tired to come down," she said shyly.

"I didn't expect to sleep this late." Sensing an opportunity, she took the tray and smiled. "Won't you come in? I hate to dine alone."

The invitation elicited a bashful nod. "Okay."

She led the girl to the small balcony attached to the suite. In Meade's opinion it offered the best view of the grounds from a perch on the southern corner of the mansion. The view showed off Reenie's cutting garden behind the house, and the forest further off. To the southwest, the lake rippled in silvery bands.

"Did you enjoy yourself last night?" Meade set the tray on the glass table. She pulled out the wrought iron chair, and waited for Glade to get comfortable. "The dress Reenie bought for you was lovely. I hope you had a good time."

"I met a girl named Delia."

"Delia Molek? She's a waitress at The Second Chance Grill."

"She's nice." Glade's eyes lit with interest as Meade removed lids from the various plates. "Hector introduced us."

"I'm glad you hit it off with Delia. She's only a few years older than you."

"We're going to the movies this week. She said she'd call to set it up."

"A great idea. You're too young to be stuck in this house every minute."

Meade surveyed the ridiculous amount of food Reenie had sent up. Memories of her night with Hector flitted through her mind, stealing her appetite. She felt giddy. Her young houseguest, on the other hand, looked ravenous.

"Have you eaten?" She poured a steaming cup of coffee.

Glade fidgeted with her hands. "Oh, yeah. Twice."

"Twice?"

"Reenie made a big breakfast. Later I had a snack. Doesn't matter what I do, I'm hungry all the time."

"You're pregnant. You're eating for two." Lifting the plate of eggs and crisp slices of bacon, Meade placed it before the girl. Next she presented the bowl of pretty melon balls and the plate heaped with croissants. "Go on. Enjoy. I'm not yet awake. Coffee

101

will suffice."

"You don't mind?"

"Not at all." She took a grateful sip of coffee as the girl dived into the food. Recalling the distressing conversation with Mary at her office, she asked, "Have you called your mother? You should let her know you're safe."

The girl set down her fork. "I meant to call." She appeared loath to explain. "I wasn't sure what to say. Reenie finally called. It was a short conversation."

"You haven't spoken to your mother directly?"

"What's the point? All we do is fight. She told me never to darken her door again. I'm not kidding. Her exact words."

"People say terrible things when they're angry." A depressing truth she understood all too well from years of handling her father. "Don't give up. Try to talk to her. If you don't raise your voice, she might cool down."

"Doesn't matter what I do. She'll start yelling. I can't deal with it right now."

"That does sound difficult. Well. You've tried to speak with her. There's nothing more you can do."

Letting it go, Meade searched for a silver lining. At least the woman knew her pregnant daughter wasn't wandering the streets. Glade was safe with Reenie, a distant but caring relative. Far better than the alternative—being forced to file a missing person claim with the police.

Meade tried to imagine how she'd feel if she had a daughter with whom she'd experienced a similar falling out—how she'd react upon learning there was a grandchild on the way, a child she might never meet. The notion was impossible to entertain. Regardless of the sadness that had poisoned her parents' marriage, she'd known they loved her. They'd cherished her. Was Glade's mother different? There was no denying the girl's choices were reckless. Still it was inexcusable for her mother to shut her out.

With less enthusiasm, Glade resumed eating.

Meade asked, "How do you feel about becoming a mother?"

"It doesn't seem real."

"It doesn't?"

"I keep thinking I'll wake up and be my old self. Like my

body will go back to normal. I'm so *big.*" The skin between her brows puckered. "I don't want to have a baby. I don't know how."

"Stay positive. Your moods affect the baby. Anxious mommy, anxious child."

"How can I feel positive?" She drew in a breath that didn't appear to boost her confidence. Expelling it, she asked, "How much will it hurt? The delivery, I mean."

Sugarcoating the facts was irresponsible. Childbearing was arduous. Many women endured a long labor. "There may be quite a bit of pain during delivery, especially if you give birth naturally. If you'd rather not, your obstetrician will discuss alternatives to make you comfortable."

"What would you do?"

"Glade, you must decide for yourself."

"I'm asking is all."

"I'd choose natural childbirth. Pain medication is risky for the baby. That doesn't mean you shouldn't explore other options. Every woman must make her own choice."

"I'm not sure."

"Think it through. You have time."

The girl mulled this over. Then she asked, "Are you sad you didn't have kids? I mean, when you were young enough to have them?"

She chuckled. "Believe it or not, a woman can have a baby in her forties." Even a woman who'd enjoyed a beautiful and unexpected night of making love without using protection—her first night of intimacy in years. Thankfully she needn't worry. Even though her cycle was erratic, she wasn't near the time of ovulation. "I'm not saying it's common, but a woman can have a child in middle age."

None of her friends, certainly. Most conceived naturally or did the rounds of in-vitro by their mid-thirties. Or they relinquished thoughts of motherhood and focused on their careers.

"A crazy woman, maybe," Glade decided. "Forty is too old. Who'd want to deal with a bratty teenager in her fifties? I'd rather have my teeth pulled."

Meade laughed outright. "Are you describing yourself? Were you a bratty teenager?"

"Maybe." Mirth tugged at the girl's lips. "Okay—yes. I knew how to get on my Mom's nerves."

"I bet you did."

"Were you tempted to have a kid? Like, when you were my age?"

"I was engaged once. Ages ago. We met in college. If we'd married, I would've had several children."

"Why didn't you get hitched?"

"My mother died, and I had to care for my father. It didn't seem fair to string along an impatient fiancé. I broke off the engagement. Then my company became profitable. The more *Vivid* expanded, the less inclined I was to look in the rearview mirror." She took a last sip of her coffee. Setting down the cup, she added encouragement to her voice. "Glade, I want you to trust me. If there's anything you need to discuss about the man you were involved with, I'm here. I won't judge."

"I don't want to think about him."

"Did he hurt you?"

"He was okay."

A dodge, but she didn't press. After the baby was born, she'd hire a therapist to work with Glade. Abuse was a serious matter. Far better to find a psychologist to help the girl heal.

"Do you know what you'd like to do after the birth? For example, you might complete high school. Earn your GED online, or in night classes."

"I'm not good with books." Folding her napkin, Glade returned it to the serving tray. "Reading gives me a headache."

"When was your last eye exam?"

Glade fixed her attention on stacking the plates. On her neck and fleshy cheeks, spots of color appeared.

Her refusal to speak *was* a reply. Evidently medical care was out of reach for a girl raised in West Virginia's coal country.

Silently Meade devised a to-do list. This week's visit to the obstetrician was just the start. The girl needed an eye exam. A visit to the dentist too. She'd instruct Reenie to schedule the appointments.

A visit to the library was also in order. On her way home from work tomorrow, Meade decided she'd pick up several books on pregnancy to read to the nervous girl. If the stages of

104

pregnancy were understood, they'd seem less frightening. The librarian would also have information on the GED exam's requirements. A pamphlet, or something similar. Finishing high school was important. Knowledge gave a wealth of advantages.

It was time to set Glade's world straight.

She followed the girl downstairs then they parted ways. Dealing with another task was also important, if more problematic. Given the argument with her father at last night's reception, the conversation couldn't be put off.

The sunroom's French doors were shut tight. Bracing herself, Meade pulled them open.

Clumps of chocolate brown soil speckled the floor. A trailing pothos was out of its pot, scattering broken leaves on the workbench. On the shelves directly behind, her father reached for a terra cotta pot.

"Daddy."

The greeting stilled his movements. Eyes averted, he finally took down the pot and trudged to the workbench.

She handed over the trowel. "We have to talk about last night," she said. "I know it was an accident, but you can't ever hit me again."

He reached for the plant, his hands unsteady. "My behavior was inexcusable."

"It was."

"I don't know what I was thinking."

"That's the point. When you're overwrought, you're *not* thinking. Practice better self-control. You're perfectly capable."

He looked at her, his eyes red-rimmed. "I swear, I'll make it up to you."

"There's no need for grand gestures." Temper tantrums were often followed by lavish gifts—the emerald studs she wore on special occasions, theatre tickets to a sold-out Broadway play. Small tributes that didn't assuage the hurt.

"My behavior was beyond the pale. Let me make amends."

"Daddy, stop it. If you want to make it up to me, start back with Dr. Simon. He's been a great help in the past."

"I refuse to spend the rest of my days on a psychiatrist's couch."

"What about your paranoia? It's not normal to go over the

edge whenever something new happens in your life. Do you understand how hard this is? I never know what will make you sad or angry, or so frustratingly stubborn I can't reason with you."

Never before had she taken a direct approach. Had last night's lovemaking with Hector made her feel invincible?

Oh, the second thoughts would come, and with them a million reasons why a relationship would never work. For now, she let the bright emotion guide her. If her honesty was too much, let her father sulk all afternoon. What was the harm? None of his petty remarks or hurtful comments held the power to affect her today.

In a small voice, he asked, "Am I paranoid?"

"Sometimes." She laughed with relief. At least he was hearing her out. "All right—most of the time. You'll be less convinced everyone is spying on you if you make new friends. The only person you trust is Theodora. She must tire of propping you up every time you're blue. Branch out."

"I like my life the way it is."

"If you won't help yourself, I should call Dr. Simon." When he opened his mouth then closed it again, evidently startled by her take-charge attitude, she added, "All right, I won't—on one condition. Stop moping about Glade. For heaven's sake, she's young. She'll become a mother at the age most girls are picking out prom dresses. I'd like to help her get on her feet, and I won't have you scaring her with your mood swings and temper tantrums. You should be ashamed. Have you introduced yourself properly? Or is she ducking into corners every time you stalk by?"

Fingers of rage climbed her father's neck. He went red clear to the sagging pockets of skin beneath his eyes, but his eyes—they were filled with confusion.

"What's gotten into you?" he asked, gripping the workbench as if the sheer power of her desires carried gale winds. "You're filled with piss and vinegar today. I don't approve."

"Daddy, I'm about ten minutes from middle age. I don't care if you like it or not."

Reenie tapped on the French doors. She tiptoed in.

"Hector's calling," she said, assessing the situation with a nervous smile.

Grasping for the threads of his tattered composure, her father reached for the phone. "Ah. It's about time. I've been expecting his call."

Reenie cleared her throat. "He's calling for Meade."

The news sent a wave of excitement through her. She'd known Hector would call. But this quickly? She wasn't sure if she should laugh or succumb to a bad case of nerves.

Anxiety won out. Which must have been contagious because her father tossed down the trowel.

"How odd," he muttered. He peered down his nose like a ship's captain spotting land where there should be nothing but ocean. "What business does Hector have with you?"

CHAPTER 7

Chapter 8

Behind the mountain of books, Blossom typed madly. If this was a last-minute school assignment before summer break, she was valiantly scaling the peaks of the Himalayas.

"What kid works on a Sunday?" Hector asked.

She paused long enough to smirk. "I'm not working on a post," she said of the blog she wrote for the newspaper's online edition. "It's something else. I can't do this at home. It's classified."

He scanned the spines of one book after another, the copy of *Bullfinch's Mythology* warming the cockles of his heart.

"Buttering up your English teacher with a paper you forgot to hand in? If you need help with the Ancient Greeks, I'm your man."

"Thanks. I've got it covered."

He picked up a copy of the Bible. There was also a book on Native American culture and another about the Celts. "Must be some paper. What's the subject? If you're letting mythology duke it out with theology, religion usually wins."

"This isn't for school. Go away."

Hugh sauntered up. "She won't divulge intel," he told Hector. "If an investigative journalist can't pry the information from her, nobody can."

Blossom wheeled her chair around to glare at Hugh. "Hey, at least I have a good reason for being here. Aren't you supposed to be on your honeymoon? Earth to Hugh. You got hitched last night."

"Yeah, well . . . we cancelled the island get-away."

"Did you break the news to Birdie? Geez, at least my dad took Mary on a trip when they tied the knot. You should talk to him since you're pretty clueless. He'll give you pointers on how a man is supposed to romance his wife." She channeled one of the adult expressions she kept on standby. "I'm disappointed in you."

"Save it." Hugh offered a loopy grin. "Birdie isn't mad about skipping sand and surf."

"She's not? What gives?"

"All will become clear in the near future."

"Tell me now." The adult disapproval morphed into childish curiosity. "If it's really good, I'm all ears."

"You first. Share your secret."

"Pass. But mine is better than yours." Blossom swung the office chair from side to side. "Best news to hit Liberty *ever*. You'll be begging to run my scoop on the front page. It's monumental."

"Nice word choice," Hector put in. The kid took her job at the *Post* seriously, and was keen on expanding her vocabulary. To Hugh, he said, "Got a moment? I need advice."

They went out to Hector's RV, which had become a permanent fixture beside the renovated barn where the *Liberty Post* was located. The RV's rectangular living room was surprisingly airy with a man-sized couch of buttery leather, built-in TV and golden oak storage cabinets. On the opposite wall, the kitchen boasted all the gadgets a chef needed—mixer, food processor, coffee grinder, even a crock pot for those busy days when Hector didn't have time to cook an inspired meal.

He grabbed two beers from the fridge and handed one over. Seeking courage, he took a swig. "It's about Meade," he said.

Hugh left his beer on the counter and flopped on the couch. "Stop fighting with her. News flash—some people don't mesh." Changing topics, he craned his neck to peer at the fridge. "Got anything to eat? Birdie's pregnancy has put the kibosh on my culinary skills. I'm afraid to shop. Half the groceries I bring into the apartment make her sick."

"How about three-day old lasagna?"

"Sold."

Hector took down a plate and pulled the lasagna from the

110

fridge. "How is the new bride?"

"Lounging in bed with her laptop. Nesting, you know?"

"She's not upset about canceling the honeymoon?"

"I doubt it. She's roaming websites, getting ideas on how to turn our guest bedroom into a nursery. I left the AmexCard on the nightstand. She's as happy as a pig in mud." Hugh chuckled. "Hell, I am too. I'd start painting the baby's room, but the smell will make her gag."

"Have her stay with Meade when you're ready to paint. I'll pitch in. We'll air out the place before she comes home."

Hugh sat up. "Hold on. Are you staying in Liberty? Another week, a month? No pressure, man. Of course, I can use the help at the newspaper."

There was no question he was staying. For how long depended on Meade.

Pulling open the microwave, he said, "Count on me at least through May. I'll stay longer if I'm still dating Meade." Carrying the food to the table, he scowled. "Close your mouth. You look like you're catching flies."

Hugh's jaw snapped shut. When he'd composed himself, he asked, "How long have you been seeing Meade?"

Last night's torrid lovemaking on the beach was private. "Not long," he said, blocking the memory before his heartbeat jumped like a jackrabbit. "Tonight I'm taking her to dinner."

"Pal, you don't need advice. Get a check of your mental health. Call Mary. Not exactly her field of expertise, but she'll see you."

The quip sent him back to the cupboard. Ditching the beer, he poured a shot of whiskey. Downing it, he carried the bottle to the table and refilled. Hugh was already seated, plowing through the lasagna.

He came up for air long enough to shake his head with bewilderment. "Let me get this straight. You're bailing me out of a tight spot at the *Post* for an indeterminate amount of time because you're on the prowl for Birdie's sister?"

"Essentially."

"The sister who thinks you're a flake because she's sitting on millionaire's row and you never stick with a job for more than ten minutes? Not that I think you're a flake. You're still finding yourself."

"Thanks, Hugh. You're making me feel about two feet tall."

"You're welcome." Hugh finished the food, the mirth in his eyes both irritating and bright. "Does she know you've been married twice? Unless Birdie spilled the beans, she's in the dark."

Hell, he hadn't thought of that.

During his twenties he'd married Sil then Bunny in a misguided attempt to make amends for the traffic accident that took his mother's life. She'd asked him to run an errand, but he'd been nursing a hangover from a college party and had refused. He'd lost his mother, and though his younger sister Calista was doing great in her career as an accountant, she'd never walk again.

He poured another shot and stared at the glass. Thinking about the mistakes of his youth made him blue, but he tried to brush it off. If he'd run the errand on that fateful day, could he have swerved out of the way? Could he have avoided the years of heartbreak that followed? Would his mother be alive, content in her golden years?

As his sister liked to point out, wallowing in regret wasn't necessary. She'd never blamed him for the head-on collision with the drunk driver.

After a moment he said to Hugh, "If Meade doesn't know about my divorces, I'll find a way to bring it up."

"Leave a chat about your divorces for later," Hugh replied. "First weeks of dating? Stick to easy topics."

"I can't wait too long. It's not right." Considering, he downed the shot. "For the record, Meade isn't what you think. Get her alone, and she's nothing like her public persona. She's caring. Really sweet."

"Meade, sweet? She ran the wedding like a military operation. Trust me, Birdie didn't play the role of General Patton."

"You don't know her well. Birdie doesn't either. Meade is big on doing the right thing, or what she thinks is right. She's also vulnerable, more than she's aware."

"You're in love with her."

Hector pushed the glass away. "No one falls in love that fast." Or, more precisely, after one spectacular night on a moonlit beach. Still, he was troubled by Hugh's observation. Needing to lighten the conversation, he added, "The jury's still out. What if she doesn't like camping? I didn't buy the RV for show. I like taking my baby out on the road."

The quip didn't fool Hugh. "Man, you've got it bad. I can see it in your eyes. You need advice? Here goes. If you want her, don't think twice. Win her. Pull out all the stops. Don't think about the reasons it can't work—make it work. Look at me and Birdie. When we met she was a thief living by her wits. From the start I knew she was the one—the *only* woman for me. I wasted too much time pushing her away. I didn't think I could reform her."

"But you did."

"Not even close. Birdie turned her own life around. If I'd had the guts to believe in her, I would've seen how hard she was trying. I thought it was my job to put her on the straight and narrow."

"Loving a woman doesn't give you the power to change her."

"You got it. If you love a woman, you help her lead her chosen life." Settling back, he crossed his arms. "It's premature, but I've got to ask. If the relationship goes long-term, are you all right with *Vivid?*"

He didn't see how Meade's company came into play. "Why wouldn't I be?"

"She's thinking about expanding, meaning travel. Lots of it. If you decide to set down roots in Liberty, she won't always be around to warm your bed."

"I'm more concerned about Meade thinking she's the bread winner. If we go the distance, I need her to know I'll pull my own weight." He backpedaled. "Not that I'm thinking that far into the future."

"Pal, wake up. I've known Birdie for less than a year and we're married with a baby on the way. Some relationships take time to build. Others are lightning-quick. If you're at step one, who knows?" In a more serious voice, Hugh asked, "You're fine skipping the parenting gig? I mean, you probably haven't thought about it."

No, he hadn't considered children. It seemed ridiculously premature. "If we go the distance, what makes you sure we won't have children?"

113

"*Vivid* is Meade's passion. You can't expect a woman running a multimillion-dollar corporation to switch to part-time hours to make you a Daddy. Besides, she's forty years old. If she'd wanted kids, she would've settled down by now."

No, he wasn't fine missing out on fatherhood. He didn't see the point of living without the joy of children. Some people weren't cut out for the toil and the sacrifices, but he was. He'd never met a kid without some redeeming traits, even the smart-mouthed boys in his old neighborhood in Philly with their jeans pulled low and their cocky mannerisms. Hector had done more than one stint with Big Brothers, something he'd pick back up if he remained in Ohio.

"My cousin Lexie and her husband traveled to China," he said. "Cutest baby girl you've ever seen."

"Adoption. Good thinking. It might be the solution." Hugh shook his head, grinning. "Man, we're something, aren't we? Baby-talk like a couple of old women. We ought to turn on the ballgame. Home game for the *Indians.*"

"No time. Meade said she'd meet me here at seven." The prospect sent nervous tension through his muscles. "I wanted to pick her up, but she thought this was easier."

"I'll bet Landon doesn't know she's got a date. It'll throw him for a loop. From what I hear, Meade hasn't been in a relationship since the Neolithic Era." An evil grin toyed with Hugh's lips. "Does she know you live in a house on wheels and drive a rental car? She probably thinks you're staying in our guest bedroom."

Hector groaned. No, he hadn't mentioned the RV. He'd call her back, in case she thought they were meeting inside the *Post.*

Hugh slapped him on the back. "This is a side of the tracks she's never seen."

From her pose in downward dog, Mary caught a glimpse of Blossom racing through the front door and up the stairwell.

"Where has she been?" She tossed the query to Anthony, watching the baseball game on TV.

The *Indians* stole second base, and he punched the air. "I think she was out at the *Post.*" His eyes remained glued to the

114

tube. "She's working on something."

"She seems excited." Heavy thumping upstairs, and Mary went into child's pose to stare at the ceiling. "What's she doing?"

"No idea."

"Aren't you curious?"

"Nope." He dug into the bowl of popcorn beside him on the couch. Kernels bounced across the carpet, and into Sweetcakes' waiting chompers. Kettle corn was the dog's favorite. "Thanks to your announcement, she's dropped the demon act and gone back to her old self. As long as she stays out of trouble, I'm cool."

He meant the conversation she'd had with Blossom at last night's reception. "I'm glad she's on board. Actually I am too. What about you? Think we can pull this off?"

"A baby? No *problemo*. We'll work swing shifts like we discussed. You'll take mornings. When you leave for the office, I'll come home from the Gas & Go. You'll skip your 1 P.M. appointment, and Blossom will take over when she gets home from school."

The plan, though workable, didn't assuage her doubts. "We need more coverage." She rolled up the yoga mat and joined him on the couch. "What if Blossom has an event after school, or tires of helping with the baby? Or she starts dating? We can't assume we'll hold her to a strict schedule, certainly not after she begins high school. We aren't being realistic."

Shivering, Anthony feigned terror. "No dating. She's now thirteen, but that's it. No more birthdays. I'm not thrilled about the detentions for cutting lunch period, but at least she's not riding around in some kid's souped-up Chevy."

"Gutless wonder." She moved in to cuddle, spilling popcorn on his thighs. Sweetcakes lapped up the mess. Mary placed the bowl on the coffee table out of the dog's reach. "We'll need to hire someone at least part-time. An older woman, preferably someone with experience in infant care."

"You think we can't manage with the three of us?"

"Not long-term. You and I will have days when we can't leave work on time, and Blossom's schedule is never fixed in stone."

Like their daughter, Anthony was delighted about the prospect of increasing their family—and woefully unprepared

115

for the real-world logistics.

"I wish we could afford a nanny," he said.

"We'll manage with another set of hands. I'll stop taking patients on Saturday afternoons, which will help. The office will close at noon."

"When are you telling your staff? Fewer patients means fewer hours for your employees."

"Soon, I guess. I can't hold off."

"They won't like it."

No, they wouldn't. The three nurses and two receptionists in her employ were all raising families. All five of the women were married, and their paychecks mattered. Losing several hours of pay wasn't news they'd welcome.

Blossom rumbled down the steps cradling a stack of books. She was out the door in a flash. Mary's newly acquired mothering instincts warned her that her stepdaughter was up to something. What, exactly? Given the impending discussion with her staff, she was too nervous to find out.

She rose. "I'll soak in a bath before dinner. It might cheer me up."

"Want company afterward?" Anthony's smile was rife with meaning. "I've got a roast in the oven, and time to kill."

"What about the ballgame?"

He pulled her back down onto the couch and into his arms. "Forget the *Indians.* We need to make a baby, right?" He nibbled on her ear, sending sparks of desire through her blood. "I'll let you be on top. Well. For starters. After that, I'm taking over."

She chortled. "Thank goodness I can always count on you."

Hector was knotting his best tie when the rap on the door sounded at five minutes to seven.

Sweating profusely, he tugged off the tie and bolted for the bedroom. The RV was long but not particularly wide. He swiped the kitchen counter, stumbled then made a mad dash to the bedroom.

"Be right there!" He swabbed his armpits with a towel before selecting a new shirt. White like the last one, it looked great with the striped silk tie.

Buttoning his suit jacket, he went to the door.

At the bottom of the RV's steps, Meade was smoothing down a blouse that showed off her long waistline and the curve of her breasts. One look and a new film of perspiration made his chest as damp as the rainforest.

"Come in." He stepped back, and she climbed the steps. Inside the RV, she paused. Her khaki slacks were as simple as her blouse, an outfit for the weekend. On her feet were Top-Siders.

She took in his suit. "I thought we were dining casually."

"I'm taking you to *Brick*. I hear they have great lobster." Absurdly, he felt guilty. "Wasn't I clear when we spoke on the phone?"

"My apologies," she said, matching his formal tone. "I wasn't alone when you called. I missed the part about *Brick*. Should I go home and change?"

"No, no—I'll change. It'll only take a sec."

In record time, he returned in jeans and an oxford shirt. He rolled up the sleeves, hesitating as she turned in a circle to take in the kitchen, the living room and the small dining area beyond. What she thought of his current residence, however humble, mattered more than it should. He hoped she wasn't disappointed.

"This is where you live?" she asked, the question void of judgment. She seemed genuinely curious. "I thought you were staying with my sister and Hugh."

"The RV's home, for now."

She noticed the food processor and the crockpot. "You enjoy cooking?"

"It's a passion. I've been hooked since childhood. Hugh thinks he knows his way around a kitchen, but I have him beat."

"No one cooks better than Hugh." She smiled shyly, a relief. She was just as nervous about their first date as Hector. "In my opinion, Hugh's a marvel in the kitchen. Birdie's lucky."

"I don't know about Birdie's luck, but he's not in my league."

"Is that confidence or arrogance I detect?"

"Both. I've mastered Greek, Italian and the basics of French cuisine. Next up? Mexican." He struck on an idea. "It's a gorgeous evening. Why don't we forget about *Brick* and have a picnic in The Square? There won't be anyone around on a Sunday night."

She plucked at her blouse. "If you don't mind. I'm not

dressed for a five-star restaurant."

He offered a glass of wine, which she declined as he bustled around the kitchen cutting thick slices of French bread and heaping prosciutto and sun-dried tomatoes on top. From the table he snatched pears from the fruit bowl then rummaged in the pantry for other supplies. When he'd finished preparing the meal, he found a red and black-checkered blanket and a wicker basket.

As predicted, The Square was theirs to enjoy. Gone were the crowds that had swarmed the center green for the wedding. The arch created by the florist had been carried off. The Gas & Go at The Square's south end stood dark, and all of the shops were closed. Only The Second Chance Grill, with a few late diners inside, was abuzz with activity. Meade was grateful for the privacy.

"Let's spread out over there," she suggested, leading him toward the sugar shack. They chose a spot.

He placed the picnic basket between them like a demarcation line. Evidently he planned to keep his distance tonight, an oddly disappointing prospect. She chastised herself. Because he thought highly of her, he was playing the role of a perfect gentleman. Last night they'd rushed headlong into intimacy—a first, for her and, she suspected, Hector as well.

Searching for an icebreaker, she asked, "Did my father convince you to stay?" Hector looked up, nearly dropping the sandwiches. Reading the curiosity in his eyes, she added, "Yes, I got him to tell me what you'd talked about. After you called to ask me out."

"You're intrepid." He made her plate and set it on the blanket. "I don't mind helping Hugh for a while. The pay's good, and I can't complain. Whether or not I'll stay the summer is up in the air. The *Post* is great, but not my idea of a permanent career."

Not the answer she'd hoped for, but she took it with grace. "However long you stay, it's a kindness. Hugh's proud. He won't tap Birdie's inheritance for the money to hire a full-time office manager. You've given him a face-saving solution."

"Can't say I blame him about the inheritance. No man worth his salt wants to rely on his wife's money. Besides, it's immaterial. The *Post* gains new subscribers every day. Soon he'll have the cash flow to hire an office manager, at least part-time." He produced wine glasses from the basket and uncorked the Chenin blanc. "He'll get the newspaper into the black. He's determined. What he really needs are professional writers. He wastes half his day revising copy produced by his staff of newbies."

"Experienced journalists don't come cheap."

"I suppose they don't." He handed her the glass of wine. When she took it, his fingers hovered in the air. Coming to a decision, he lowered his hand to her cheek and traced the precise location of the welt she'd artfully hidden beneath foundation. In a voice soft with concern, he asked, "What's it like beneath the war paint? Painful?"

"No, it's fine. Just a bruise." Still his hand lingered, and she couldn't resist leaning into his caress. He took the invitation greedily, allowing his fingers to trace a path to her lips.

"Did you talk to your father?"

He meant last night's argument in the boathouse. "I told him he can't ever lose control again."

"Will he listen? Because if he won't—"

"He'll listen."

If he didn't, what would Hector do? The answer came immediately. He'd confront her father, reason with him—he'd do everything in his power to protect her. The knowledge made her heart heavy with an emotion hard to identify. When had she last needed a man's protection?

Never.

She guided her life with an expert hand, choosing well and relying on experience to make smart choices. Her father wasn't a danger. Yet Hector's desire to protect, his very masculine response to a perceived threat to her wellbeing, made her lightheaded. No, she didn't need a man to guide her. She unfailingly chose well through the tools of cool thought and hard intellect.

Except now. Now she was choosing wildly, and she was in free-fall.

She hung on Hector's gaze. "We had a good conversation," she said. "Mostly I talked, and Daddy listened. He was terribly sorry. He promised it wouldn't happen again. I have no reason to doubt his conviction."

"Daddy." Hector repeated the word with relish. "It's darling. I've never heard you refer to your father that way."

She hadn't caught the gaffe. "It's childish." She only used the endearment in private conversation with Birdie or Reenie.

"More like adorable. Daddy's little girl. I bet you were." Sobering, he added, "You have the prettiest eyes. Blue with a starburst of gold. Like sunlight on the ocean."

"You're a romantic."

"Guilty. Do you mind?" He glided his hand over her hair, taking pleasure in the task. "A cliché surely, but men do fall for blondes."

"Including you?"

"There's one blonde in particular I'm falling for." His expression fluid, he looked off over the green. He seemed to wrestle with a decision. At length, he added, "About last night . . . I should've held off. You were upset, and I took advantage. For the record, I've never had a one-night stand. I lost my father a long time ago, and most of my role models have been women. I value every one. I don't take women for granted."

His sincerity was touching. "I didn't think you did."

"You aren't upset?"

"Hector, I wanted to make love with you." She wasn't a prude, and she refused to allow him to blame himself for a faultless night. "It's been a long time since I've slept with a man. I'm glad it was you. Last night was perfect. I've been waiting for the regret to take hold, but it hasn't. It won't."

"Thank you."

An edgy laugh escaped her. "For what?"

"Giving me a chance. I want to do this right. Take you out, get to know you properly. There's so much I want to know." He smiled, relieving the tension between them. "For example, what's your ten-year plan?"

"I suppose you've guessed I have it all mapped out."

"No surprise there."

Giving in to temptation, she caressed the hard line of his jaw. "Let's see," she murmured, thrilled when her touch dilated his pupils. "*Vivid* will have a national presence by then. I'll double my staff. Open a southern distributorship and another out west."

"Travel?"

"Lots. I love to travel. Whenever I'm in France on a buying trip, I take several days to vacation. Tuscany, London, Amsterdam—next year I'm seeing Istanbul." She rested her hand on his neck. "Have you been? To Europe, I mean."

He gave her a look that needed no interpretation. "You're kidding, right? Outside of a stint in Afghanistan, I've been exactly nowhere."

"Hard to believe."

"Okay, I've camped in Pennsylvania, New York, and a few spots on the east coast. I'd like to take the RV on a longer trip, say across the country to California or all the way south to Texas. Not sure when I'll mark those dreams off my bucket list."

"I've never been on a road trip in an RV."

"We'll plan a trip together." He pushed her plate forward. "Now, eat."

For the remainder of May, Hector kept Meade's social calendar filled. He rescheduled dinner at *Brick* and took her to an art show. He began inviting her to dinner in the RV, often with her sister and Hugh joining them.

Meade's culinary skills were nonexistent, but she enjoyed learning how to sauté veal for exactly three minutes per side for scaloppini, and fold delicate sheets of filo dough for baklava. In a nod to Birdie, whose morning sickness made every meal a dicey proposition, Hector whipped up a pork dish with peach glaze, peach salsa, and enough peach pies throughout the month to put Meade's waistline at risk.

He also became a real asset to the *Post*. With long distance guidance from his sister, the accountant in Philadelphia, he put the newspaper's books in reasonable order. His natural people skills provided other benefits. He kept the newspaper's inexperienced staff on deadline with stories and interviews, and helped coordinate work schedules. In early June, Meade was ecstatic to learn he'd told Hugh to count on him for another month.

The only disappointment, if it could reasonably be characterized as such, was his determination not to initiate sex.

Each night he said his farewells with increasingly passionate kisses then climbed into his car, face flushed and eyes glittering, for the ride home. Or he sent her off from the RV with a smoldering look, but without the slightest indication he'd ever take their deepening relationship to its logical conclusion. She was beginning to think they'd never again enjoy the pleasures of intimacy unless she took matters into her own hands.

So she'd decided on a course of action, beginning with a frank conversation with her dearest friend.

Despite the late hour, several patients were in Mary's reception area. Twin boys in soccer uniforms waited with their mother, and an elderly man discreetly coughed into his handkerchief. Meade strode past.

She counseled herself to keep the visit short. As it was, Mary skipped too many dinners with her family.

The receptionist, a phone cradled in her ear, waved Meade inside. "Go on back," she whispered. "I'll tell Mary you're here."

In the corridor, the door to each examination room was shut. Mary's voice was audible in the second room, her tone measured as she explained something to the patient. From the end of the corridor, Blossom dashed from the good doctor's office.

"Hello, Blossom," she said. "Are you waiting for your mother?"

"She doesn't know I'm here. Don't tell, okay? I want to surprise her."

"With what?" The kid was notoriously mischievous. If the surprise came wrapped in a detention slip for skipping lunch period, her mother would *not* be amused.

"Trust me, you'll get it." Blossom's eyes twinkled. "My mom will too."

Without further explanation, she sprinted off.

True to her word, the surprise was clear the moment Meade stepped into the office.

A two-foot tall Christmas tree, the one Anthony stuck in the window of the Gas & Go during the holidays, took center stage on the desk. Only the fake evergreen wasn't trimmed with its usual holiday ornaments. With a decidedly springtime flair, it was rigged up with silk flowers, everything from daisies and roses to large peonies reminiscent of the fresh blooms used for Birdie's wedding. At the base of each flower hung a string of pink or blue. At the bottom of each string was an index card with a name written in a rainbow of colors.

"Meade! What a nice surprise." Mary closed the door, her brows rising. "Did you bring a gift? Something to spruce up my office? It's a little over the top, but thanks."

"Don't look at me. It's from Blossom. She's come and gone." Meade fingered a silk pansy of dark purple. On the card she read *Ceridwen*. "What's with the names?"

"They're baby names."

"I don't think so." Meade checked another card. "*Hypatia*. Wasn't she an ancient philosopher?"

"You tell me. I'm no historian. Biology and chemistry were my preferred subjects in college." Mary checked one name after another. "*Zenobia, Cleopatra, Titus*—oh, look. This side's from Disney movies. There's another group of Native American names. Hmm. I'm not sure *Squanto* works for me."

"Why is your eccentric kid picking out names? Are you getting another dog to keep Sweetcakes company?"

"This is Blossom's idea of pitching in. Or hurrying me up."

"Hurrying you up for . . . what?"

Mary leaned against the desk, her smile rife with meaning. "Meade, they *are* baby names. At least Blossom's idea of suitable names. Anthony and I have been talking about adding to our family. Blossom's excited. In fact, she's pressuring us for a younger sib."

The news brought a startled gasp from Meade. "Are you thinking about it? I thought you were planning to wait until you'd paid off more of your college loans."

"I was."

"Change of plans?"

"I'm pregnant. We haven't told Blossom."

"Pregnant!" She hugged Mary. "I'm so happy for you and Anthony. This is marvelous!" She held her at arm's length. "Why aren't *you* happy? This is wonderful news."

"Oh, I am."

"Then what's bothering you?"

"Logistics, I guess. Once I'm well into the second trimester,

I'll refer new patients to a few doctors at the hospital. I'm worried about telling my staff about the baby. Once I stop taking new patients, I'll have to reduce their hours. Not much, but they won't like it."

The concern was understandable. *Vivid* had a growing crew, from office workers to personnel in the warehouse, and Meade was conscious of her own responsibilities as an employer. There was never a time when employees welcomed a reduction in hours. "You won't have to lay anyone off, will you?" she asked.

"Reduced hours will suffice."

"When will you tell Blossom?" Meade eyed the wildly decorated tree. "Better make it soon. If you don't, she'll paper your office walls with names. Believe me, artwork is an anything-goes activity for teenagers. You should see Glade's bedroom at my father's house. She's covered the walls with photos cut from fashion mags."

"Fashion wallpaper?"

"Basically." Meade crossed her arms. "Well? How long do you plan to keep your kid in the dark?"

Mary feathered her hand across her brow. "After I've safely reached the second trimester. Anthony's so thrilled he's having trouble keeping the news to himself. I made him promise."

"I'm glad you trust me enough to share. Whenever you're ready for the baby shower, I'll get to work. Don't try to talk me out of hosting. You know how I love to plan a party."

"And weddings." Mary added in a more chipper voice. She tipped her head to the side. "Did you stop by for a reason? I'm surprised to see you. From what I gather, Hector keeps you busy most nights."

"He does, which is why I need to talk." She was more embarrassed than she'd anticipated. In a shameful dodge, she wandered to the window. A boy ran through The Square's center green with a kite that refused to stay aloft. Finally she composed herself. "We aren't sleeping together, not yet, but I want to discuss options. Not the pill. I tried it during my twenties. I never felt right on it. During my next relationship, there was no reason to worry."

"Vasectomy?"

"A relief, to tell you the truth. We didn't date long, and I'm not sure why I consented. He was the most high-strung man I'd ever met. Caffeinated every minute. Trying to get a word in edgewise was a chore."

Mary glanced at her knowingly. "Is Hector your type?" she asked.

"I think so." Meade caught herself, and sighed. "Yes, he is. I'm positive. Don't look so shocked—I'm stunned enough for both of us. He has a zest for living, a real ability to live in the here-and-now. Whenever we're together, I forget my worries and do nothing but enjoy myself. I've never had this much fun."

"There's more to a relationship than having fun."

"Yes, and we're moving rapidly. He's caring and gentle—classy in a way I didn't expect."

Mary gave a withering look, and Meade regretted the comment. "Good breeding has nothing to do with a man's net worth," Mary said. "Hector comes from a tight-knit Greek family. Only one sister but, from what I gather, he has enough aunts, uncles and cousins to populate northeast Ohio. Given the traditional background, he'll pull out the stops to court you properly."

"Like Anthony did with you?" The Perinis were just as traditional.

"He tried to do everything right. Flowers, gifts, proper handshakes combined with glances that made me weak at the knees. Those looks still turn me to pudding." Her mossy green eyes grew inquisitive. "Has Hector indicated he'd like to become intimate?"

"On the contrary. Oh, he's attracted—we've had necking sessions hot enough to peel paint off the walls. Nothing more. He won't take it further." She returned to Mary's side on a wave of frustration. "I'm crawling out of my skin. I'm honored he's working so hard to do everything right, but this is more waiting than I can handle. In the middle of business meetings, I start daydreaming about the ways I'll seduce him once I find the nerve. My employees are beginning to think I've lost my edge. If I start on birth control, it'll give me the confidence to initiate."

"Perhaps you shouldn't."

"Why not?"

"From what you're describing, he *is* courting you. He won't go further until he's sure you're both in love. Given his track record, can you blame him?"

She had no idea what her friend meant. "What track record?"

"Meade, he's twice divorced."

"Twice?"

"Don't jump to conclusions. It's not as bad as you think."

Cold comfort, in her opinion. "How do I avoid jumping to conclusions?" she demanded. "Why hasn't he told me? We've been dating nonstop for a month."

"I can't speculate. I can tell you that both of his ex-wives were in traffic accidents similar to the one that killed his mother and cost his sister the use of her legs. Birdie has the details. She's chatted with them both."

"Birdie talked to Hector's ex-wives?"

"She got to know them, long-distance as it were, after Hector came to Liberty to help hunt down Wish Kaminisky. They'd call occasionally to check up on him, see if he was all right."

"Birdie never mentioned them." Not that she'd given her sister the chance. Organizing the wedding had dominated their conversations.

"Hector's ex-wives are nice women. Very protective of him. Sil and Bunny each divorced him after coming to the conclusion he hadn't married for love. He was desperate to help them heal, as if doing so would make up for his mother's death and Calista's injuries. They set him free because they felt it was the right thing to do."

The wheels in her mind turned swiftly. Hector had mentioned his sister Calista was wheelchair bound—he'd also mentioned his mother had died in the accident. Had he then married to make amends for his mother's death? A tragedy for which he was blameless?

"You're saying these women—Sil and Bunny—were also injured in a collision with a drunk driver?"

"Exactly."

"Two women, two separate accidents . . . who did he marry first?"

"I'm not sure."

"How did he meet them?"

"His sister Calista talked him into joining a community group for grieving families, I think. I can't recall exactly what Birdie mentioned. I do know that during each marriage, he helped his wife through years of rehabilitation."

Her heart softened. "Good Lord. I can't imagine." Hector was devoted in ways hard to comprehend. Her affection for him grew.

Mary was saying, "Now you know how he spent the better part of his twenties. He took Sil and Bunny to physical therapy, worked hard to get them walking again—all the odd jobs he held? If I had to guess, he skipped around a lot to dovetail his work hours to each wife's therapy schedule. If a job didn't fit, he quit and found another. Meade, I've seen this in my own practice, people who drop everything to ensure they're available to care for a seriously ill loved one."

The revelation sent pity and gratitude through Meade. Hector hadn't drifted from job to job because he was irresponsible. He'd put his own ambitions aside to help two women heal.

She asked, "How are Sil and Bunny today?"

The question pleased Mary. "They both enjoy full mobility. I believe Sil is a psychologist. Bunny is a librarian. It goes without saying they both love Hector in a sisterly way." She walked around the side of her desk and opened a drawer. She took out a handful of brochures. "It's not my place to advise whether or not you should become sexually active. You're a mature adult. Given your long-term abstinence, you may be unaware of the newer contraception options on the market. Read these, and let me know if you have questions. I'm here to help in any way I can."

Taking the brochures, Meade asked, "And as my friend? What do you advise?"

"Don't push the relationship further," Mary said. "Be patient. For once in your life, let someone else lead. Trust Hector to initiate full intimacy when the moment is right."

CHAPTER 8

Chapter 9

For a woman used to getting what she wanted, waiting for intimacy was difficult. Most of the time Meade felt like a lovesick girl in the throes of her first crush, a shocking and amusing status for a woman of forty.

Today was no exception.

As they strolled down the beach hand in hand, she tried to suppress the enticing memory of their night together. The effort went unrewarded. The memory of their physical intimacy was now ever-present, clouding her thoughts at work and stealing upon her each morning as she awoke. Though he didn't know it, Hector was expanding her emotional terrain by leaps and bounds, and making her remember all the excitement of young love.

He led her past the spot where they'd made love on the night of the reception, his dark eyes lifting to appreciate the horizon's soft bands of purple and burnt orange. Did similar thoughts taunt him? Ever so slightly he loosened his hold on her fingers; with his thumb, he teased the pulse point at her wrist. His touch sent shivers of need through her body. He followed up with a darting glance filled with fire. She didn't dare reciprocate, keeping her attention firmly on the waves crashing onto the beach.

Today he'd brought a sack of stale bread undoubtedly pinched from The Second Chance Grill. Releasing her hand, he tossed out the treat for the sharp-eyed seagulls gliding overhead.

Gulls swooped to the sand with a mad cawing.

The flock of birds fought for the last crumb. Steering her past the skirmish, Hector asked, "How about dinner at my place tonight? I have chicken marinating in teriyaki sauce."

They'd established a habit of meeting at the estate when she got home from *Vivid.* Dinner usually followed.

"I can't go," she replied. "I'm working up the fall orders from my suppliers. A mountain of paperwork. I tried to finish at the office, but spent most of the day fielding calls."

"Did you pick up the company in Columbus?"

She was pleased he'd remembered. "They called this morning. I'm in. *Vivid* will begin deliveries in late August. It's a promising account."

"What's the name?"

"*Beautiful You.* They have three locations. Each facility is a combination beauty salon and day spa. Next year they'll open a fourth location in Cincinnati."

Studiously he kept his eyes on the rolling waves. "When is your next trip to France?"

She'd planned a scouting trip this summer to add more specialty soap makers to *Vivid's* lineup. Small factories were forever popping up in Marseille, where luxurious blends had been created for centuries.

"I'm not sure," she hedged. The trip could wait. Leaving Hector during these first months of their romance didn't appeal. The easy routine they'd forged was still new, and she looked forward to seeing him. "I can wait another month or two before traveling. Actually I can wait as long as October before placing orders for next spring."

At the surf's edge he came to a standstill. "I'm not putting a monkey wrench in your schedule, am I?" He threaded his arms around her waist. "Meade, if you have obligations, it's not a problem. I'll be here when you get back."

It was the first time he'd given an indication of extending his stay in Liberty. "I'm glad," she said, trying not to read too much into his words. He wasn't promising to stay permanently. "When I do set my travel schedule, you'll be the first to know."

"Thanks." His hands moved in a tantalizing journey up her back to her shoulder blades. "Don't get me wrong. If you boarded a plane in the morning, I'd miss you."

"Would you?" A childish question she instantly regretted.

In response, he took her lips in a kiss as ripe with longing as it was controlled. The heady moment didn't last. A seagull alighted at their feet, drawing them apart.

With amusement Hector appraised the bird. "Sorry, pal. The feast is over." The bird flew off, and he regarded her. "I should walk you back to the house. You can get something to eat before digging into work."

"Can the teriyaki wait until tomorrow? I'd like to spend the evening with you."

He squeezed her fingers in reassurance. "Sure thing," he said.

Like many of the rooms in the Perini's rambling house, the dining room was a work in progress. The walnut table with claw feet was a recent antique store find. The nicks in the glossy surface were barely visible after a diligent buffing with lemon oil. The eight chairs were comfortable even though they boasted a mishmash of designs.

From the table Mary removed the vase of pink tulips and deposited it on the sideboard. Then she gave Blossom's flower bedecked Christmas tree a position of prominence. The cards dangling from every branch flapped soundlessly as she stood back to appraise her work.

Appearing in the doorway, Anthony arched a quizzical brow. "What is this? Christmas in June?"

Mary reattached a silk rose to one of the tree's drooping branches. "It's a present from Blossom. I'll give you three guesses what this is about, but you'll only need one."

He grunted when she held up a card for his inspection. "You're kidding, right?" he said. "Are these baby names? Some are from Ancient Greece."

"And Rome. I'm partial to Claudius, but don't feel restricted to ancient history." Mischief flirted with her lips as she held up another card. "If it's a girl, what's your take on Pocahontas?"

"I was thinking Lily for a girl."

"Lily? I like that."

"It goes with Blossom." He grinned like a pirate. "And if you're asking, I've got nothing against Anthony junior. We'll call him Tony."

"I'll take it under advisement."

He switched tracks. "Did you talk to the women in your office?"

They both knew the answer—she was dodging the issue. Broaching the subject meant disappointing her dedicated staff.

"I'll get around to it. There's no hurry."

"You're the one who thought they should hear about the reduction in hours well in advance. Remember?"

"Change of heart." Or, more precisely, loss of nerve. She adored her staff. Why reward their diligence with upsetting news when the changes were months off? "I won't cut hours until I'm well into the pregnancy, but what if someone quits? I don't want to go back through the drill of resumes and interviews. Building the perfect staff took time."

"Give options and you won't lose anyone. Let the women make the new schedule. You're not asking anyone to drop down to twenty hours a week. They'll find an equitable solution."

His confidence propped up her flagging spirits. "If each woman works one day less a month, we'll manage." They'd certainly prefer to choose which day to take off. "Thanks. I'll talk to them soon."

"Good deal." He drew her close and rested his palm on her abdomen. "How are you and the munchkin doing?"

"Don't tell Birdie, but I feel great. Not a hint of morning sickness." She loved the munchkin endearment. Once she started to show, Anthony would surely dream up a host of amusing nicknames for their baby. The thought lifted her spirits even more. "I'm waiting for something to turn my stomach. A scent, a taste—so far, it's smooth sailing."

"Some women don't experience morning sickness, right? I vote we keep you in the 'feeling great' category." Deftly, he switched topics. "About Blossom. Why don't we tell her? I know you think we should wait, but I can't stand the suspense. We'll get party hats and ice cream. After she pigs out on dairy, we'll drop the bomb that *we're* naming the baby without her interference. We'll stick her with diaper duty."

"You're awful."

"Just excited. I didn't think we'd get pregnant our first week trying." He sent the heated glance that never failed to make her dizzy. He squelched the romance by adding, "Want to head upstairs for a quickie? We have ten minutes."

She batted him on the arm. "Quiet! Blossom will hear." Stepping from his embrace, she looked around. "Where's Sweetcakes?"

"Out back. Before you ask, I fed her as soon as I got home. By the way, Blossom isn't here. We're meeting her at The Second Chance."

Mary peeled off her physician's coat with more than a little frustration. "Why don't we stay home tonight? I have patients at 8 A.M. tomorrow."

He held up his hands in surrender. "Don't blame me. This afternoon Delia stopped by the Gas & Go. Something about Finney needing to see you. While we're there we might as well grab dinner."

Finney Smith was the cook at The Second Chance Grill. Two years ago Mary had inherited Liberty's only restaurant, and Finney, with her bossy personality and locally celebrated cuisine, ran the establishment. Privately Mary was batting around the idea of making the cook part owner of a restaurant now prospering under her guidance. Given the demands of a medical practice, Mary was well aware she couldn't operate the restaurant without her most dedicated employee.

"Why didn't Finney talk to me today?" The restaurant was one convenient floor below her practice. Then she remembered. "This morning she *did* mention something about hiring a new employee. I put her off. I was running late."

Anthony gave her a peck on the forehead. "Go change. You can talk to her now."

They reached Liberty Square as the dinner rush was winding down. Several waitresses were clearing tables and seventyish Ethel Lynn Percible was at the cash register. For decades she'd worked part-time at the restaurant, but she wasn't supposed to be working now. Mary had given her strict orders to rest.

In April she'd been in a house fire. The fire department had doused the flames before the first floor was engulfed, but Ethel Lynn had suffered smoke inhalation and several second-degree burns on her arms. The bandages were gone, but the ordeal had taken a few pounds from her slender frame and slowed her usually frenetic gait. Now her arms, with a starburst of scarring from elbows to wrists, were hidden beneath a long-sleeved vintage dress. The spring frock boasted a pretty daisy pattern. She'd finished off the ensemble with orange pumps and a yellow pancake hat that was the height of fashion in 1957.

Mary stepped behind the cash register. "How many times must I tell you?" she whispered to Ethel Lynn. "It's too soon to work. Let one of the new waitresses handle the cash register."

Her stubborn patient shrugged off the light reprimand. "Heavens, child. I'm only helping for half an hour." Ethel Lynn slammed the cash register shut. "What's the harm?"

"It's half an hour too long. You're still weak."

"I've had all the bed rest I can stand." Ethel Lynn fluttered her fingertips in the direction of the long counter and the bar stools packed with customers. "Stop fussing over me and deal with Blossom. In the last hour she's eaten two sundaes. There isn't a child from here to the Pennsylvania border with a bigger dairy obsession."

"She's had *two* sundaes?"

"Jumbo-sized. Finney told us to cut her off. If we hadn't, she would've asked for a third sundae."

The disclosure was less than welcome. Sure enough, Blossom was camped out on a barstool with one of Finney's mixing spoons in her fist. She was hunched over the last of a chocolate sundae large enough to share with her best friend Snoops. With gusto, she polished off the treat.

Anthony, following Mary's line of sight, started toward his daughter. "I'll drag her to a table and order dinner," he assured her. "Don't keep Finney waiting. See what she needs to talk to you about."

Grateful for his intervention, she darted behind the bar and went into the kitchen.

Finney was stalking before the six-burner stove. Her meaty arms were in constant motion as she flipped steaks and then threw a handful of mixed vegetables into a skillet. Her brassy blond hair was cinched tight in a rubber band. To her left, one of her assistants was pulling a tray of pies from the oven. Mary couldn't recall the young man's name. Unlike Finney, he rarely spoke unless prodded.

At the table in back, the very pregnant Glade was peeling a bowl of Grannie Smiths for more pies. Papery shreds of bright green were scattered across her protruding belly. They reminded Mary of the festive nonpareils one might use to decorate a cake. Glade was humming as she worked.

The image of the expectant mother happily immersed in a task captured Mary's imagination. Would she find time for similar pursuits during the final months of her own pregnancy? Nesting at home, baking a luscious treat from scratch or papering the baby's room—a physician's routine left little time for life's simpler joys. Could she find a balance between her professional duties and private life?

Finney placed one of the steaks on a plate. "It's about time," she said, whipping her spatula in Mary's general direction.

Mary set her thoughts aside. "Finney, I just got off work."

"Excuses, excuses. The way you've been acting, I'm beginning to think you're avoiding me."

The idea was ludicrous. "You know I love you as much as I love pancakes," she joked. "Especially if it's a batch you've whipped up. Not that I'd like breakfast at the moment." She sighed. "Well, I'm here. What do you need?"

"Can you make the dinner rush end? I've fed the nation and run ten miles. My feet aren't happy about it."

The complaint didn't mask the cook's pride.

"We're busy because no one in Liberty can resist your banana pudding and tonight's pork loin special," Mary replied with a smile. "It's a good thing."

The praise puffed up the cook's well-endowed chest. She nodded for her assistant to take over at the stove.

When he had, she led Mary to the corner in back.

"Whatever happened to our morning coffee breaks to discuss local gossip and business at The Second Chance?" Finney asked. "I fix you a nice cup of my special blend, and you listen to whatever needs discussing. Don't go changing my routine, Mary. I like things the way they are."

135

"This morning I was too busy to stop in." Now that she was pregnant, she'd also given up coffee. Caffeine wasn't good for the baby. Not that Finney knew. Like everyone else, she wasn't yet privy to the news about the pregnancy.

"Why didn't you stop in yesterday? Forgetting two days in a row isn't like you."

Had she forgotten? Since learning she was pregnant, she'd been in a fog of excitement peppered with nerves. Motherhood promised many joys but she harbored niggling doubts, the typical worries about her breast milk coming in properly or rising cheery-eyed for a 3 A.M. feeding. Medical training gave no guarantee a woman would glide gracefully into motherhood.

A more worrisome thought intruded. What if she slept through her newborn's howls, and Anthony did too? They were both heavy sleepers.

At the cook's impatient look, she set aside her private concerns. "My schedule has been hectic," she explained. "I didn't mean to throw your routine out of whack. Honestly, this week has been long."

"We're women. Every week is too long." Finney lifted her foot, encased in a size-11 shoe. "My bunions are killing me. They're playing bongo drums against my toes."

"Don't stand every minute. We've added employees. Let one of your assistants take over whenever you need to rest. They're perfectly capable."

The suggestion sent the cook back to her stove to prowl like an enraged lion. Her young assistant scurried out of the way.

"To hell with that. No one goes near my stove. It's mine. My helpers work the ovens and handle prep, but The Second Chance Grill has *only* one cook."

Mary rolled her eyes. Everyone at the restaurant manned the stove at one time or another. Who couldn't fry an egg?

"What do you need to discuss?" She regarded Glade, filling the table with neat piles of apple peels. "And why is Glade helping with tomorrow's special?"

The cook had concocted an event to honor John Chapman, better known as Johnny Appleseed, with everything from apple fritters to the mouthwatering pies spiking the air with the sharp scent of cloves.

"You've already guessed it. I need to talk to you about Glade. Now, I know she'll be a Momma soon. That doesn't make her less a teenager. Stewing out at Landon's house with nothing to do but walk Meade's dog and stare at the countryside—the child's bored. It's not like Reenie has time to keep her young relative entertained."

"I suppose the routine *is* dull."

"Delia suggested we have her work at The Second Chance. Part-time, mind you. I like the idea."

Another pair of hands in the kitchen was welcome, and work during a healthy pregnancy wasn't an issue. To Glade, she asked, "Would you like a part-time job?"

The girl stopped peeling apples long enough to bob her head. "Oh, yes! If Reenie is too busy to drop me off, Delia will pick me up for my shift. We've already worked it out. I told Finney I'd do a good job."

"I'm sure you will—but stick to light prep. No carrying dishes or heavy items from the freezer. We don't want your baby arriving ahead of schedule. Deal?"

"Deal." Beaming, she returned to her task.

To Finney, Mary whispered, "Please keep her to four-hour shifts. If she plans to hang around longer, ask Blossom and Snoops to get her outside for fresh air. Don't let her sit for hours doing nothing but reading fashion magazines. You might suggest they walk her over to the library. Meade thinks she's interested in taking the GED after the baby's arrival. The librarian can scare up material on what's needed to pass the high school equivalency exam."

Finney muttered choice words. "For a doctor, you're slow on the uptake. Meade's already bought her a manual to study for the GED. Also got the poor thing contacts. Don't suppose she could see worth a damn without them."

"Meade took her to an ophthalmologist?"

"Bought her eyeglasses too, but she prefers the contacts. Teenagers. They care about surface appearances, don't they? Look real close, and you'll see she's wearing mascara too. Another gift from Miss High-and-Mighty."

There was more. A leather purse in the prettiest shade of tangerine was slung across the back of the chair, and her linen maternity dress was perfect summer wear.

Finney released a heavy sigh. "I may have to revise my low opinion of Meade. The way she's been treating Glade has got me thinking. Maybe she's not the devil after all."

"Oh, please. Why does everyone have it out for Meade? She's nice when you get to know her."

"She won't get more fans like you if she keeps sticking her nose in other people's business."

"You've been miffed for over a year. Can't you let it go? So she pointed out that low-fat dressing shouldn't include mayonnaise. Big deal."

"When did a little mayo hurt anyone? And have you forgotten how she treated *you* when you first took over The Second Chance? If there'd been a way, she would've plowed over you to get her mitts on your husband."

"At the time, he wasn't my husband. Now I love her dearly." She eyed Glade, to ensure she wasn't listening. She wasn't. She was bent over her task with single-minded devotion. Changing the subject, Mary asked, "When did Meade get the material for the GED?"

"Last week, right after she took Glade to the dentist. How does a girl walk around with three cavities and never tell a soul?" The cook shivered as if a dentist's drill were aiming for her mouth. But she perked up when she said, "What's even better? Meade is paying for the obstetrician."

The news took Mary aback. "The bill will run into the thousands." There was no such thing as an inexpensive pregnancy or a discount hospital stay.

"They were talking about it when they stopped in after the visit to the eye doctor. They were chatting up a storm at the counter. Thought I'd pass right out. Of course, Meade is rich. She can afford to be generous. And don't forget Reenie. This is Meade's way of thanking her for years of service. She's worked in the Williams household since Meade was a bitty thing."

"There's more to it. Meade cares about Glade."

"I suppose she does." Finney placed a clean skillet on the stove and poured oil in a slow stream. "Some of life's greatest blessings come disguised as hardships. Meade never expected one of Reenie's kin to land on her doorstep, certainly not a pregnant teenager. *Vivid* is her passion. She's made her choices—good choices, some might say—but when will she get another chance to use her mothering gifts? Not that I would've guessed she had any. I hate to give her a compliment, but she's doing a lot of good for a girl who needs a helping hand."

It was true. Meade was enjoying a taste of parenting. Even though Glade was an adult, she had much to learn. How to live independently, care for a baby while working a job—and it was imperative she earn a high school diploma. Later on she might learn a trade or enroll in college part-time. Whatever her choices, it was clear Meade would continue to help in ways large and small.

Glade wasn't the only positive addition in a life structured around the assiduous growth of *Vivid* and caring for an aging parent. Who could've predicted Meade's romance with Hector? They came from different worlds yet their affection deepened by the day. Mary was sure they were in love. Whether or not they were conscious of the fact—whether someone as precise as Meade could give herself over completely—remained to be seen. For her part, Mary was confident the relationship would continue.

Feeling pleased for her friend, she retraced her steps to the dining room. It was a relief to note Ethel Lynn had abandoned her post by the cash register. She'd joined a table of women from her knitting circle. They were sipping tea and daintily sampling each other's desserts.

Directly ahead, Anthony had chosen a table near the picture window.

She took the seat opposite. "Has Blossom wandered off? This far into summer vacation, she's liable to roam."

The quip brought a chuckle from Anthony. "Give her a sec. She's outside with Snoops. She'll come back."

"One can hope." Mary opened her menu. "If she's not here in five minutes, please get her. I'd like her to eat something nutritious. I'm not willing to wait. I'm famished."

"Let's order. When we do get her planted in a chair, I'll make sure she orders something with veggies on the side."

Delia walked up, order pad at the ready.

"I'll have a steak," Mary said.

Anthony flopped his menu to the table. "Seriously? What happened to chicken girl? Chicken on salads, grilled chicken, chicken parmesan—since when are you into steaks?"

"What's wrong with variety?" Since learning she was pregnant, she harbored a lion's craving for red meat. It was amazing he hadn't noticed. Yesterday she'd wiped out the roast beef reserved for his sack lunches, and she'd snitched half a burger Blossom had foolishly left in the fridge. Until the cravings were under control, no cow was safe.

His eyes twinkled, and she got the distinct impression he'd finally caught on. "Whatever you need, babe." To Delia, he said, "Bring us two steaks with all the trimmings, and salads on the side."

Delia scribbled on her order pad. "Should I come back for Blossom?"

"Might as well. After half a gallon of ice cream, it's up for grabs what she'll order for dinner."

"Anything else? Something to drink?"

Anthony squeezed Mary's fingers. He asked, "How about a glass of milk for the baby?"

The blood drained from her head. Revealing their secret to Delia meant the news would cross town at the speed of light.

Gauging her reaction, he shoved his fist into his mouth. He looked ready for a full court tongue lashing, which wasn't on Mary's mind even if she *was* furious. Alarm sent her stomach into free-fall.

Delia squealed with delight.

She hopped in a circle like a crazed bunny. "You're pregnant?" Stumbling to a halt, she shouted, "Finney! Why didn't you tell me the news?"

Mary leapt to her feet.

Finney barreled from the kitchen. "What are you jibber-jabbering about?" She pointed her spatula at Delia like a sword. "Screaming at the top of your lungs—this is a fine dining establishment. Where's your sense of decorum?"

Her displeasure merely started the waitress giggling. Every eye in the dining room was fixed on the unfolding scene. Mary snatched at Delia's apron, to stop her from catapulting to the cook and blowing the lid off the secret. She wasn't fast enough.

Delia sprinted forward. "Mary's pregnant!"

The announcement brought gasps from diners throughout The Second Chance.

Blinking wildly, Finney landed her attention on Mary. "You are? Good heavens, why didn't you say? What are we, chopped liver? This is wonderful!"

Grabbing them both, Mary hissed, "Keep it down! If my staff finds out through the grapevine, they'll wonder why I haven't mentioned it."

"Your staff. Right." Finney nodded sagely. "You deserve to tell them when you're good and ready. When's your due date?"

"Late winter. Months and months from now."

"Sure seems like it's raining babies in Liberty. Birdie, Glade, and now you."

Delia hopped up and down. "Let it rain!"

The exuberant waitress looked over the cook's shoulder, to the door. Blossom came in from the street. Mary experienced one of those free-fall moments of horror, the warning locked in her throat through some mischievous device of fate.

And Delia shouted: "Blossom, let's do the happy dance. Mary's pregnant!"

Cutting the engine of his car, Hector frowned with confusion. Theodora was joining them for dinner? In the circular driveway before the Williams' mansion, she got out of her sky blue Cadillac.

She dropped her keys into her buckskin satchel. "How's Birdie? I meant to stop by the *Post* to check on her. The day got away from me."

"Same old, same old. Nesting, puking, eating too many peaches. Plan a day trip for her. Hugh won't be happy until we get the nursery painted."

"Hugh *is* happy. With all your pitching in at the newspaper, you're helping to keep him that way." She tipped her head to the side. "Think I can interest Birdie in a day trip? Might be good to get her out and about before she's bigger than a barn."

"I wouldn't characterize her pregnancy that way but, yes, she could use an adventure." He changed topics. "Are you here for dinner?" He'd expected to dine alone with Meade and her father.

"Meade called with an invitation. We're making it a foursome." Theodora cast an appraising glance. "Son, I figured you'd take a liking to a girl like Delia. Didn't know you were shooting for the stars."

"Am I overreaching?"

"Hell, no." She took the hand he offered. Together they climbed the mansion's steps. Without bothering to ring the doorbell to alert Reenie, Theodora went inside. "Planning on making it permanent?"

"Meade, or my stay in Liberty?"

She made a beeline for the library. "Both."

Arriving at a decision had plagued him for weeks. Soon Hugh would hire an office manager, leaving him free to pursue a career better suited for his abilities. None of the options looked great. An entry-level job in sales or marketing wouldn't match the income Meade took home from *Vivid*. Which was the real issue. In a primitive way, he was driven to prove his worth by garnering the highest income possible.

But how, exactly? A checkered work history didn't make his resume a standout. In fact, it left the impression he was incapable of settling into a respectable career.

Theodora snorted, drawing him from the reverie. "What are you fretting about?" she demanded. "It's a simple question. Are you staying in Ohio or not?"

"Nothing's simple, Theodora."

She went behind the wet bar and retrieved a beer from the fridge tucked in beneath. "Since we've opened this can of worms, let me pry. Are you serious about Meade?"

She withdrew a second beer, which he declined. "Before getting involved with Meade, I planned to go back to Philly. Start at the bottom somewhere—anywhere. No big deal, and I didn't mind making up for lost time. I can't regret the decisions I made in my twenties."

"No sense ruminating over the past. What's done is done."

"My ex-wives? They're both fantastic women. I'm lucky they had the sense to let me go. But I couldn't have helped them literally get back on their feet if I'd been climbing the corporate ladder. So I assumed I'd start over. Low pay, long hours. Eventually I'd move into a great job."

"You can do that in Ohio."

"No, I can't," he blurted, the frustration welling. "What if Meade thinks . . ." His voice plummeted into silence.

"You're not good enough?" Theodora supplied.

A pebble of doubt scraped against his pride. Meade was nothing like his ex-wives, two good women he'd married for reasons other than love. Sil and Bunny had grown up in the same working class neighborhood he'd called home, a place where most parents worked odd shifts and grew old fast, and getting your kids educated was cause for celebration. Each summer the families held block parties in the street; the yearly vacation was a camping trip in The Poconos or something equally inexpensive. No one traveled to Paris or made a habit of dining in 5-star restaurants. Not unless they were celebrating a major event like a twenty-year anniversary.

"Hector, you're a fool," Theodora snapped. "There's no shame in an honest day's work."

"Easy for you to say. You aren't dating a millionaire. Meade deserves more than I can give her."

"I *am* a millionaire. If I took a mind to it, I'd date anyone I damn well please." She took a swig of beer, considering. "What's inside a man's heart is more important than the cash in his wallet. Some of the noblest jobs in the world don't earn much. It's work of the spirit, more valuable than chasing money. By the way, I'm pleased as punch you caught Meade's interest. It's about time someone did." Her black eyes glittered. "You got a mind to keep her?"

"If I can." He'd never wanted anything more.

"What's the matter with you, son? Woo her. Simplest thing in the world. I don't see what's stopping you."

"You want the laundry list?" He took the beer from her grasp and guzzled it down. When he'd finished, he said, "Gainful employment is just the start. Assuming I lock down a good job to demonstrate I'm worth her time, what about kids?"

"Meade's forty, past the age of making babies. Even if you could talk her into it."

"Which is why I'm wondering—is it too soon to broach the

subject of adoption? Even if she agrees, am I willing to be the primary caregiver? Meade travels, and someone has to go to teacher conferences and take the tot to little league."

"I suppose so."

"What if I want more than one kid? Will she consider it? If she will, am I ready to play the role of Suzy Homemaker?"

"Hold on," Theodora said. "Let me drum up a visual of you in a frilly apron."

He ignored the jest, saying, "She can't run *Vivid* and deal with all the tasks related to parenting. If we have a family, I'll have to do the heavy lifting."

Theodora looked like she'd won the prize pig in the state fair. "Seems this romance is putting your testosterone to the test."

He sank onto a barstool. She was right.

"This isn't like Birdie and Hugh falling in love and starting a newspaper." He dragged his hand across his scalp. "They live above the *Post* and can wing it with the baby. Meade has an established career, and I'll need to find my own path. I refuse to stand in her way, but I don't want to give up every aspect of a traditional marriage. I can't think about giving her up either." Pausing, he thought of something else. "Come to think of it, where is she?"

Theodora filled a glass with Jack Daniels and shoved it under his nose. "Drink." After he took a healthy sip, she added, "She's probably down at the boathouse. Last week Landon asked me to help pick out her gift. The powerboat was delivered this afternoon." Sliding onto a barstool, she added, "I can't say why Landon got it into his head to buy her a fancy speedboat, but she does love the water."

Clearly Theodora was in the dark regarding the gift. But Hector quickly deduced the reason. Landon was making amends for his altercation with Meade on the night of the reception.

"I wasn't aware she loves the water." Two months in and there was much to discover about the woman he loved.

Emotion seized his heart. He *was* in love. Completely, no-holds-barred—he couldn't imagine life without her. He loved watching the light dance in her eyes when she laughed at his jokes, and the careful wending of her thoughts as she discussed the day's triumphs or challenges. If they strolled in Liberty Square or at one of the summer craft fairs they enjoyed discovering together, she touched him constantly, as if she couldn't get enough physical affection. Which made sense. She was used to leading people, standing apart. Yet in the special, private moments he'd come to cherish, she allowed him to breach every barrier. She never held back, never hesitated. Even if he didn't always like the reply, he'd learned to trust in her honesty.

True to Theodora's word, Meade came in with her hair windblown. Landon was right behind her.

"Let's go out on the boat after dinner," she said, landing a kiss on his cheek. Dressed in shorts and a tee shirt, she looked much younger than her years, loose-limbed and relaxed. His heart seized again. "Daddy just bought it. Almost a perfect replica of the powerboat we once owned. Talk about memories. When I was in high school, you couldn't get me off the boat."

They went into the dining room, and Landon seated himself at the head of the table. Reenie carried in a platter of chicken. The tangy scent of rosemary spiked the air.

"My daughter is quite the mariner," Landon said to Hector. "Captain of her own skiff before most children learned to ride a bike. A natural mariner."

"I wasn't aware," he said.

"Gets the aptitude from her late mother. Cat loved the water. Regattas, pleasure trips, an afternoon racing from our dock with Meade at her side." He regarded Meade. "Dearest heart, do you like your gift?"

"You know I love it." A dozen times he'd asked since unveiling the surprise moored at the end of their dock. Standing there in a suit with her briefcase swinging in her grip, she'd been utterly taken off-guard. It hadn't taken much urging to get her to dash to the house and change into shorts. Finally she added, "Excuse the pun, but you went overboard. I can't imagine what you spent."

"Ah, it's a small gift. I have something larger in store."

Reenie brought in salad and rolls. Meade took the dishes to pass them around.

"Something larger?"

"Don't try to pry it out of me. A surprise isn't a surprise if I tell."

"Daddy, please don't buy anything else." The gifts were meant to reassure there would be no repeat of his abhorrent behavior. Since the reception, he'd treated her with nothing but respect. No raised voice, no tantrums. A relief. "The boat is enough. I don't need anything else."

"I don't care what you *need,* sweet girl. I'm more interested in seeing your dreams take flight."

"My dreams? Whatever do you mean?"

Tightlipped, he brimmed with cheer as he poured wine for all. He held up his glass. "To *Vivid.* May your company expand beyond your wildest imaginings."

They clinked glasses, and he moved the conversation to new topics. She was still trying to work out the meaning of his comments when dinner ended. He suggested they enjoy dessert on the patio out back. Summoning them from the dining room, he was like the grand master at a parade. At his side, Theodora kept him busy with light banter.

Meade stopped Hector before he stepped outside.

"What's going on?" She drew him behind the long curtains fluttering on the French doors. "You seem far away tonight."

"I'm fine."

"You're not. What's worrying you?"

"Nothing."

"Hector—"

"You're too perceptive. You know that, right?" He stole a kiss, and she leaned into him eagerly. When they'd finished, he asked, "What was your father talking about? Making your dreams take flight—he's planning something for your company."

"It would seem." She shrugged. "I can't begin to guess. He adores grand gestures. It could be anything."

"Grand gestures. I know exactly what you mean. Did you know your father wanted to buy a house for Birdie and Hugh? Talk about a grand gesture. Hugh turned him down."

"Daddy *would* think a house is the perfect wedding gift. He doesn't understand Birdie's independent streak, or Hugh's. They prefer living above the *Post.*"

"Now, maybe. It won't last. All those stairs from the

146

newsroom to their apartment? Wait until the baby is a toddler. Grabbing stuff off tables, dashing past their knees. Little kids are slippery. Birdie and Hugh will start looking for a real home."

The description of a child's slippery nature was comical. "You have a lot of experience with toddlers?" she asked.

"I'm Greek. We breed."

Was their relationship keeping him from a better destiny? A strange ache centered beneath her breast. A man like Hector would make a fine father, something he wouldn't become if their relationship endured.

He kissed her again, but sadness darted through his expression. He snuffed it out, saying, "I'll take you to Philly sometime. I'd like you to meet my family. Be warned. I have enough cousins to populate a small country."

"I'd love to meet your extended family, especially your sister."

"Consider it done. Whenever you like, we'll schedule a weekend trip."

Her heart sinking, she murmured in agreement. When would she find a free weekend? *Vivid* demanded her constant attention. She'd try to carve out the time, she promised herself.

He peered over her head, his smile widening. She turned to see what had caught his attention.

At the other end of the foyer, Glade gave an energetic wave. Her hair was knotted at the base of her skull. Stray tendrils spun out in all directions. In her hands she carried a quilted satchel made of colorful squares of fabric. A snowy substance dusted her light blue shirt. Flour?

Meade cocked her head to the side. "Are you just getting in?"

If Glade was embarking on a social life in her new hometown, it was all for the good.

"I was at The Second Chance." A fizzy expectancy swirled around her. "I got a job."

"Oh, how wonderful! Congratulations."

"Part-time only, but I really like it. I'm helping Finney in the kitchen."

Hector sniffed the air. "You smell like cinnamon. Were you baking pies for tomorrow's special? I'm looking forward to Finney's culinary tribute to Johnny Appleseed."

147

She nodded in the affirmative.

Meade asked, "Are you sure you have the energy to work?" Glade's pregnancy was more pronounced each day, a teenager's bouncing gait long gone. These days, she lumbered at a slower pace.

"Oh, I want to work. I get to see Delia all the time now. She's my best friend."

"Good choice," Hector said. "Delia has lots of friends. She'll expand your social life in no time."

"I hope so." Her brows knit together, Glade paused. After a moment, she revealed, "Finney yells a lot, but never at me. Mostly she yells at Ethel Lynn. Really loses her temper. I like Ethel Lynn even if she is flaky. Today she filled all the salt shakers with sugar. Boy did that set Finney off. She was furious. Delia had to fix the mess. I helped."

Meade grinned. "Ethel Lynn is a bit absentminded, and Finney runs a tight ship."

Hector pointed to the satchel slung over Glade's arm. "What's that?

She patted the bright fabric. "A gift from Ethel Lynn. She's making a quilt and had some extra squares. Isn't it pretty?" She unbuttoned the top, revealing two books and a clutter of paper. "I got some stuff at the library to help me with the GED. Blossom and Snoops took me over."

"Do you have the workbooks I bought? They'll guide you," Meade suggested. "If you need anything else, let me know. I can pick it up on my way home from work. Come to think of it, we can find a tutor. Would you like that?"

"You've done enough already. I don't want to be a bother."

The girl darted a glance across the foyer, and Meade understood why. She was still avoiding Landon. But she wasn't a lowly serf even if she *was* avoiding the inhospitable king of the castle. It was a state of affairs in desperate need of resolution.

Meade was still trying to work out a solution when Hector boldly reached into the satchel. He extracted a grammar book with a frayed binding and a worn green cover.

"Do you need help with this?" He flipped through the pages. "Most students have trouble with grammar."

The familiar rash blossomed on her neck. "Oh, I'll figure it out."

Concerned, Meade pursed her lips. "Are you sure? Perhaps I should find someone to work with you."

"Tutor's cost money. You've spent too much already. The workbooks must've cost a fortune."

An afternoon relaxing at the spa would've cost twice as much. Of course, everything in life was relative. To a girl of Glade's limited means, the workbooks were prohibitively expensive.

"Nonsense. A tutor will keep you on track. Once you have your GED, you can enter a trade school or a four-year college. One of our state colleges has a satellite campus nearby." She smiled encouragingly. "We'll discuss the options whenever you're ready."

"There's no need for a tutor," Hector put in. "I'll help."

The ready offer pleased Meade. "Are you sure?"

"In Philly, I tutored through the Big Brother program. Two of the young men I worked with? On Saturday nights you'd find us knee-deep in books at the local youth center. It was a struggle, but they both passed the equivalency exam." He sent Glade a reassuring look. "I'm betting you're less stubborn, and more apt to study than they were. Are you?"

"I guess." Glade sounded doubtful. "How much homework will I have to do?"

"As much as you're willing to handle. There's no deadline. I'm sure the school district offers the test several times each year. Take it once you're good and ready."

"That sounds great."

"Call me at the *Post* tomorrow. We'll set up a tutoring schedule. Trust me, this isn't the first time I've bailed a kid out. I worked with a dozen kids in Philly through Big Brothers. Some needed help just getting through junior high coursework." He winked at her. "Not that you're a kid."

"Thanks." The offer sent her rash in fast retreat. "I'll call you tomorrow."

CHAPTER 9

Chapter 10

In a town the size of Liberty, gossip traveled faster than Internet chatter.

Arms filled with an energy drink, purse, and her medical bag, Mary climbed the final steps to her medical practice. Producing the key to unlock the office, she nearly stumbled over the assortment of gifts tucked before the door. The festive grouping looked like offerings at a shrine.

Sweetly wrapped packages sat alongside an assemblage of envelopes bright enough to do a rainbow proud. A handful of chocolates was stuffed inside a pink coffee cup. Lest Mary think the locals were only rooting for a girl, there was also a blue Teddy bear with a tiny baseball cap on its fluffy head. Someone had even tied a balloon to the doorknob. The purple dirigible was emblazoned with the words: *We're having a baby!*

By the time her staff appeared, she'd consigned the baby booties, nappies and festive salutations from patients and friends to a corner of the receptionist's desk. Tonight she'd need a box to drag it all home. Or a wheelbarrow.

The oldest of her nurses, Alma Lindgren, batted the lively balloon away from the phone that would soon start ringing, and wouldn't stop until they'd seen the last patient of the day.

Alma was the natural leader of Mary's staff. A six-foot tall commando with blunt cut golden hair, she possessed the build of a weightlifter. Although she didn't in truth lift weights, she was quite adept at restraining feisty retirees and truculent children on those rare occasions when drawing blood or administering a shot proved trying. Despite her stern demeanor, patients were reassured her listening skills and easy humor. Even when the office was crammed with people, she never rushed a patient along.

Now her face betrayed no injury as she waited for an explanation as to why the town was apprised of news kept from Mary's devoted employees. The other women on staff, ears perked and eyes lowered, hung sweaters and deposited purses in preparation for the morning's first arrivals.

How to form an apology to soothe the proud nurse and the others?

"I wasn't trying to keep you out of the loop," Mary told Alma. She regarded the others. "Any of you. I just found out I'm pregnant. Just a few days ago. Last night Delia shouldn't have blasted the news across The Second Chance. In fairness, she didn't know my pregnancy was a secret."

"She's the least of your problems." Alma's composure was so complete, it was impossible to gauge a reaction on her square, bulb-nosed face. "Ethyl Lynn must've burned the midnight oil. It couldn't have been Finney. If she knew you were keeping the news private, she wouldn't tell anyone."

"What are you talking about?"

"A dozen women are waiting for the craft store to open. They want to get started knitting whatnots for your bundle of joy."

"You think Ethel Lynn called them last night?" A distinct possibility—Ethel Lynn did enjoy gossip.

"That's not all. If I had to guess, half your patients are building a phone tree. Last night I got four calls in row. Probably more tried to call. I took my land line off the hook and shut off my cell."

Mary, steering her arm into her lab coat, stopped short. "My patients put together a phone tree? Tell me they didn't."

"Oh, I believe they did. Father John over at St. Mary's? At this morning's Mass, he made an announcement right from the pulpit. Said how happy he is about the addition to your family. Not many people in the crowd on a weekday, but they'll spread the news."

She groaned. Father John's sentiment was laudable, but whatever happened to privacy? By nightfall, she wouldn't be able to walk the streets without people rushing her to offer congratulations.

Alma sighed. "What do you expect? People love you. They're excited."

"It's too much, too soon." Father John actually mentioned her during Mass? She'd have to remember to thank him when he came in next week for his annual physical. "I'm only a few weeks pregnant. The due date is months off."

"Will you keep a full schedule?"

"Barring complications, yes."

"What about after the birth? Mary, you aren't the first woman doctor for whom I've had the pleasure of working. Handling a full caseload will tax your energies. And what about on-call duties if someone in your care is hospitalized?" Alma's golden brows lowered the barest degree. "Long-term, what are your plans?"

A hum of voices, the morning's patients, grew in volume as Mary explained to her staff that, as Alma had implied, she'd need to reduce her workload after the baby came—and perhaps sooner, depending on how she was faring toward the end of the pregnancy. She reassured the women that no one's job was in jeopardy. If they worked together, they'd devise a schedule suitable to all.

No one was particularly happy about the prospect of reduced hours. In the end, each woman gave Mary a hug and offered the warmest wishes.

Although they took the news with grace, her worries increased with the day's hectic schedule. Was she prepared for the combined demands of motherhood and a growing practice? A shortened workday didn't guarantee ease of entry to motherhood. She'd seen enough in her own practice to understand some babies glided into childhood with even temperaments and few illnesses. Others caught every virus that swept Liberty or suffered allergies that made them fidgety and unable to settle into a schedule.

What if the baby cried every time Mary readied for work? Or arrived in the world with gluten allergies or threw volcanic temper tantrums? Little Timmy Greene, now age five, was the mysterious offspring of two bashful and sweet-tempered parents. What if Mary gave birth to a child with a similar propensity to bash people on the head and scream siren-like through doctor's offices?

At six o'clock, she trudged across the green to the Gas & Go. Anthony was at the vacant pumps with Blossom. One look at Mary's mussed hair and mascara-smudged eyes, and her husband knew something was up.

"Bad day?" Delicately he rubbed beneath her eyes, banishing the offending mascara.

Before she might reply, Blossom asked, "You weren't crying, were you?"

"Timmy Greene was my last patient. He poked me in the eye." Pulling out of her malaise, she blinked rapidly at Blossom. "Tell me. Do they still work?"

"You aren't blind if that's what you mean. Why did Timmy go after you?"

"Why does Timmy go after anyone?" She tousled Blossom's curls. "A zest for living?"

"He's a terror. As bad as Meade's dog." Blossom reconsidered. "Strike that. Melbourne is worse. He pees on everything. Why doesn't Meade have his thingies removed?"

"She's not a fan of unnecessary surgery. Plus she loves Melbourne, and he likes his thingies where they are." To Anthony, she said, "How do you feel about hauling gifts home? I have dozens in my office."

"Well-wishers? Yeah, I've had my share too. I gassed up Theodora's car and she gave me a twenty-dollar tip. I tried to give it back but she insisted. Said she's glad I put my loins to good use."

Mary laughed.

Blossom tried to follow along. "What are loins?"

Anthony slung his arm around her shoulders, pulling her near and drawing giggles. "Why don't you show Mary the *other* surprise? She needs cheering up."

The last of it was said with thick sarcasm, alerting her to more trouble.

"Oh, no. What now? I've had enough surprises for one day.

As it is, I'm afraid to go home. We've probably lost the front door to a deluge of baby gifts and balloons."

Blossom offered a winning smile. "I'll keep the balloons. It's not like you need them."

"As long as you write the thank you notes, why not?"

"Forget it. Keep your balloons."

"Let me know if you change your mind." As if.

Blossom nudged her toward the Gas & Go's office. "C'mon. You'll love the surprise."

She didn't. The window behind the cash register was covered top to bottom with baby names written on blue or pink cardstock. They were dishearteningly similar to the cards Blossom had used to decorate the Christmas tree that was now the gaudy centerpiece of their dining room.

A banner ran along the top of the gas station's window: *Vote for Your Favorite!*

Mary fended off the impulse to weep for real. Beneath each name, people had left checkmarks. It was distressing to note that Pocahontas had three checkmarks; the dreaded Claudius had gained five.

"I like Romans, your father especially, but I'm not naming a baby Claudius." She couldn't think of anything more dreadful. Or maybe she could.

Titus had a checkmark. So did Hypatia.

The meaning of her father's grand gesture became clear to Meade the following Thursday.

The call, arriving early in the morning, threw her usually composed assistant into a state of panicked excitement. Siki nearly toppled out of her stiletto heels relaying the message.

Shooing her from the office, Meade dropped into the leather chair behind her imposing granite desk.

Nels Norling owned the Norling department store chain, a flagship operation across the southern United States. The average customer was affluent, worldly—the perfect consumer for *Vivid's* boutique perfumes and bath products. The fastest way to expand beyond the northern states? Gain a foothold in the south by securing the Norling account.

Meade couldn't imagine why Nels was calling. She wasn't planning to expand *Vivid* any time soon. Pitching Norling's was a year off—or two.

Calming herself, she picked up the receiver. "Mr. Norling, hello."

"Call me Nels," he said in a booming voice. "I don't stand on ceremony."

"Nels. Of course." With practiced calm, she got down to business. "Thank you for calling. How may I help you?"

"Start by booking a flight."

"Excuse me?"

"I expect to see you in Atlanta tomorrow. Don't tell me there's anything more pressing on your calendar than securing the business of the fourth largest retailer in the United States. There isn't."

"You're considering my product line?"

The confusion in her voice brought a chuckle across the line. "Weren't you apprised of the real estate deal?" When the query was met with silence, he added, "Meade, I've been trying to unload the building on the east side for years. I can't tell you how pleased I am to get it off the books."

The east side—he meant Atlanta. His company was headquartered in Atlanta. Then she remembered. "You mean the original Norling department store founded by your grandfather. You moved to midtown to build the new, larger flagship. The old store is sitting vacant."

"Like a gaping hole in one of the nicest malls in the area."

"You found a buyer?"

"Your father."

If a ballerina whirled into her office, naked and unannounced, she couldn't be more surprised. "My father bought the property?"

"To open *Vivid's* southern distributorship. He not only paid the asking price, he convinced me that Norling's customer base needs your specialty products. Hell, he's a persuasive bastard."

"Yes, he is." Or was—before retirement, he'd lorded over Ohio's banking industry with panache and savvy.

Now he'd conducted a multi-million dollar deal to jumpstart *Vivid's* expansion. It was crazy, shocking—wonderful. With the

Norling account, she'd easily win the smaller southern chains. Afterward, expansion to the western states seemed assured.

"I guess I should congratulate you," Nels said. "So congratulations. You're coming, yes? I'll pencil you in for ten o'clock."

"Count on me." With dizzying elation, she stood. "Thank you, Nels."

Without alerting her staff to the potential windfall for *Vivid*, Meade arranged the flight and hotel reservations. Landon agreed to drive into town, and they spent a leisurely lunch discussing the opportunity.

Would her company become a national presence within the next five years? The amount of work this would entail, the refurbishing of the building in Atlanta and the need to hire competent employees for the southern office, the travel required on top of a schedule that already demanded she visit Europe several times each year—all her doubts melted away. During lunch she felt as if she dined with the benevolent father of her earliest childhood memories, a man not yet plagued by the loss of his wife to a miserable drowning accident, a man not yet mired in depression.

At the Blue Lake Restaurant they ate lobster salads and sipped champagne as Landon escaped the demons of his current life, resurrecting his younger self through witty rejoinders and astute observations on how *Vivid* must proceed.

Meade traveled through the remainder of the business day in a fizz of expectation.

At dusk, she pulled into the lot in front of *The Liberty Post*.

Hector's rental car and RV were parked beside the barn housing the newspaper. The RV was ablaze with light. Was he still tutoring Glade? Since making the offer to help with her studies, they met often. Deciding to give them more time, Meade went into the *Post* instead.

Hugh's newbies were clacking away on keyboards and talking into smartphones. On the front desk—Hugh still hadn't hired a receptionist—the landline rang shrilly. Meade tiptoed past before anyone flagged her down to answer the call.

She went up the stairwell to the apartment on the second floor. In the bedroom, Birdie was rooting through shopping bags.

"Check this out," she said as Meade stepped inside. From the bag she produced a loose, draping shirt. "What do you think?"

"Looks comfy." The knit top was blindingly neon green like a Popsicle. It went frighteningly well with the neon pink shorts next produced from the bag. The shorts boasted a thickly elasticized waist.

"My baby bump is getting serious. Look." Birdie lifted her tee shirt, revealing her sweetly protruding abdomen.

"It's darling." Meade smiled. "Pregnancy becomes you. Well. Pregnancy with garishly bright colors tossed in for shock value."

"I didn't know I was into them. As big an addiction as peaches. Do you think it's my hormones?"

"I hope so. If you're planning on neon colors for the baby's room, I'll plan an intervention. Think soft, soothing colors. You don't want your child over-stimulated. Unless you're planning to raise an insomniac."

Birdie flicked a glossy length of ash blonde hair over her shoulder. "Thanks for the tip." She followed the grudging respect with a double take. "What's going on? You look great."

"Meaning I don't usually?"

"You don't have a sex life. Sometimes you look . . . peevish."

Technically it was true, and Birdie didn't know about Meade's one night of intimacy. Of course, landing a major client like the Norling chain would make anyone look perkier than usual.

She arched a brow. "I never look peevish. Busy, maybe."

"Too busy, if you ask me. You work too hard." Birdie threw herself on the bed like a starry-eyed teen. She went up on elbows and dropped her chin on her knuckles. "If you're curious, Hugh thinks Hector is in love with you. Head-over-heels. He won't lay a finger on you until he's sure he can keep you."

"Hugh should talk to Mary. She thinks the same thing."

"And . . ?"

Lowering herself to the edge of the bed, Meade regarded her inquisitive sister. "Birdie, I don't have your adventurous streak. I can't date a man for a few months and think wedding bells. Do I love him? Yes. Do I want a deeper intimacy? Absolutely. But relationships take time to grow. They *should* take time to develop." Impulsively she began folding the clothing strewn across the bed. After she'd made a neat stack, she added, "Daddy bought a building for me."

Her sister gasped with surprise. "A *building?* First he tries to give Hugh and me a house for a wedding gift. Now he buys you a building. This is like Monopoly for grownups."

Chuckling in agreement, Meade shared the details about tomorrow's meeting with Nels Norling. Summing up, she added, "Daddy has an architect lined up to renovate. Before the year's out, *Vivid* will have a presence in the southern states."

"Incredible. You're becoming a titan of industry."

The impish remark sent Meade's fingers to her brow. The headache was back, along with the sour stomach. For days now, she hadn't felt well. If she was coming down with a summer cold, she'd better hold off until after the meeting in Atlanta. Negotiations rarely went well if one of the principals was sneezing all over the contracts.

On her belly, Birdie scooted closer. "How does Hector fit in to your plans to take over the world?"

"He'll applaud my initiative." The headache throbbed beneath her forehead. "If he doesn't, I'll use my powers of persuasion to convince him to be patient."

"Hugh thinks you have control issues." With the lightest touch, her sister made soothing circles on Meade's back. "He says you can't enjoy anything unless you're in charge. You're up, you're down, happy, sad—you'll never even out until you stop micromanaging everything."

"He thinks I'm a control freak?"

"He does."

"Frankly, I'm hurt. I'm an accomplished businesswoman, but I don't insist on taking charge."

"Face it. You're a five-star general conquering the business world. If anyone gets in your way, you shoot to kill. Metaphorically speaking."

"Hugh said that?"

"Sure did."

"What do *you* think?"

Birdie stilled. "I think I should stop lying to you. Hugh doesn't think you're too ambitious. I do."

The admission broke the tension festering between them.

Playing along, Meade removed her heels. "What else do you think?" She crawled onto the bed to lay side-by-side with her sister.

"Don't give me a heart attack. Since when do you value my opinion?"

"Since forever. Go on. Hit me with the truth. I can take it."

The invitation put mischief in Birdie's remarkable violet eyes. "You're sure? Last chance to change your mind."

"I'm sure."

"Let's see. You're strung too tight. You're so well-manicured you've clipped your creativity down to a nub. Who cares about perfection? Life is messy. It's fun playing in the mud. You love Hector? I'll lay odds you've never told him because it isn't proper or it's too soon or some other dumb reason. Who gives a shit about protocol?"

"Birdie!"

A further chastisement stuck in her throat. Tears blinded her, the unbidden, hot tears that were the providence of childhood. They were similar to the tears shed at age five when the fat sausages of her fingers prevented her crayons from coloring inside the lines. Or the tears of sheer gratitude, like those shed when she won the gymnastics competition in junior high or aced a geometry test after weeks of drawing polygons and memorizing theorems.

No, she didn't like the messy aspects of life, like the call from Liberty's chief of police when her mother's body washed up on Lake Erie's shore; the unpredictable and ghastly events that followed, the glory of *Vivid's* first years of profitability passing without celebration as she began to comprehend the permanency of her father's depression, how it was as real as the unspoken heartache they shared.

A tissue appeared before her nose. Taking it, she dabbed at her eyes. "Birdie, where were you when I was growing up?" She took the pillow her sister offered and gratefully lowered her head. "You could've taught me to enjoy risks."

"I would've tried."

"I hate them. I hate being unprepared. Bad stuff happens when you're not on guard."

"Can't keep watch all the time."

160

"I think you can." A fallacy she wanted to believe. "If you'd been around, I would've learned courage."

"No way. You would've said I was too young to teach you anything. You were already a teenager before I perfected the art of talking back. Almost ten years between us. You would've beaten the crap out of me."

"I wasn't a hitter." Shoulder to shoulder, she took Birdie's hand and twined their fingers together. "I would've dressed you up like a baby doll. I had so many. Every kind of doll imaginable."

"Me? Dressed like a pretty princess? I would've run away."

"I would've caught you. If you'd behaved, I might have considered dressing you in a neon blue frock." She squeezed her sister's hand. "Even if it was fashion suicide."

"Yeah. Right." Birdie rolled onto her side, her gaze uncomfortably attentive. "About Dad. Are you glad he's helping to grow *Vivid?*"

Tough question and she wasn't sure how to answer. "Did you know about the purchase?"

"Not a clue. How much did he spend?"

"More than three million."

"Wow. Guess he's serious about the expansion. And you?"

"Naturally I'm happy. Thrilled."

"Meade, don't ever play cards. You have a lousy poker face."

"Fine. I'm also nervous. I wasn't planning to put *Vivid* front and center. Not now. I think Hector will find a permanent job in Ohio. I want to give our relationship time to evolve."

"Evolution, huh? How scientific. You sound like Darwin."

"I sound like a pragmatic woman. Birdie, I'm nearly middle-aged. Set in my ways. Hector is too, probably more than he thinks. I can't presume we'll have a successful marriage on the basis of a few months dating. We need time."

"Have you told him you're leaving for Atlanta in the morning?"

"I'll mention the trip, but no details. I won't be entirely convinced this is a good move until I've negotiated with Nels Norling. I also need to think about increasing payroll quickly, stocking the new facility . . . there's much to consider."

Later, at dinner, she gave Hector the most cursory details about the trip. Leaving out the true developments in her career wasn't her best moment, but she needed time to think it through. Despite her father's generosity, she refused to alter *Vivid's* business plan without doing her own homework.

While Hector rummaged around his kitchen, she made a mental note to call her accountant. At the least, she should've mentioned the real estate transaction before leaving the office today.

At Hector's urging, Glade agreed to join them for dinner. Tossing ginger and garlic into a wok, Hector pointed her toward the cupboard where dishes were stored. They shooed an exhausted Meade to the table.

"How are you doing with names?" she asked as Glade carried dishes over. With her due date less than two months away, she'd been trying to decide.

"I'm still stuck." She swiped a frizzy tendril from her brow. "Got any ideas?"

Hector put in, "Ask Blossom. She's made a list of names for Mary's baby."

Meade dragged a second chair near and put her feet up. "Don't listen to him, Glade. The names Blossom has in mind are silly. Not one is appropriate. Besides, I think Mary has settled on Lily for a girl and Anthony Jr. for a boy."

Hector added chicken to the wok and splashed in soy sauce. "Anthony Jr.? That'll get confusing."

"They'll call him Tony."

"Good call." He stirred then threw in vegetables. "I like Lily. It goes with Blossom."

Glade asked, "Meade, what's your middle name?"

"Natasha. From my mother's side. She was part Russian. It was her grandmother's name."

Glade placed napkins and silverware on the table. "Natasha. It's pretty."

"I think so."

"Do you mind if I use it for my daughter? I want her to be like you. Smart and successful."

A stunning request. Meade opened her mouth. Nothing came out.

Unplugging the wok, Hector took his sweet time placing the stir-fry into a serving bowl. Try as he might to hide his reaction,

Meade caught the pleasure on his face.

She felt something deeper than mere amusement. Glade wanted the baby to be like her? As if she were a role model? It was an honor, one she didn't expect.

Finding a measure of composure, she said, "I thought you'd decided not to peek at the ultrasounds. If you have a boy, you'll need a different name."

"I couldn't resist looking. I'm having a girl." Ruddy spots, the dreaded hives, invaded her neck. "If you don't want me to use your family name—"

"Nothing would make me happier. Thank you for thinking of me."

Rising, she threw off her natural reticence and gathered the girl into her arms, a difficult proposition with the baby twitching between them.

Twitching.

With a grin, Glade rolled her shirt up several inches. Beneath the veiny skin of her protruding belly, a limb—it looked like a foot—grazed across before disappearing. Spellbound Meade lowered her palm in hopes it would happen again. Her heart pounded out joy as the baby roused beneath her restive fingers in a fluid sweep of movement. Delight surged through her. With it came a rush of emotion as profound as the child's announcement she was awake, demanding center stage and their undivided attention.

In that instant Meade forged an unbreakable connection with the fussy, energetic baby, a child she had yet to meet, an infant conceived out of wedlock and carried all the way from West Virginia to a better life in Ohio. Natasha.

Her name was Natasha, and Meade already loved her.

Chapter 11

On television, the twin boys, toddlers with ebony skin, and curls spiraling from their skulls in an adorable profusion, took hold of the tablecloth. With a grunt of combined effort, they pulled mightily. Down came dishes, glasses and a Siamese cat with the good sense to vault over their heads to escape.

The resulting crescendo of sound—not to mention the cat's hissing rage—loosened the medical bag in Mary's grasp. It hit the floor with a *plunk.* Blossom, seated Indian style before the tube, didn't notice.

Sweeping up the bag, Mary strode into the living room.

"What on earth are you watching?"

"A reality show. *Trouble with Toddlers.* Kids my age send in video."

"They film younger sibs instead of babysitting them properly?" Onscreen, the tots toddled out of view with the grace of drunken sailors. "Not exactly responsible behavior. I don't approve."

"You should've come home five minutes ago. The last clip will give me nightmares. A peewee took a plastic hammer to her brother's computer. You wouldn't think a crappy kid toy could do damage, but it did."

"The young man *filmed* his sister instead of stopping her?"

Blossom looked at her like she'd taken stupid pills. "No way. He was at football practice. His bratty younger brother filmed it."

"Still irresponsible. Who puts shows like this on TV?"

"Marketing execs, who else? This stuff is great for ratings." Her stepdaughter's expression became grim. "Should I worry about a troublesome toddler? I mean, will we need to keep him on a tight leash?" She stared pointedly at Mary's still slender waist. "Or her?"

"For your sake, I hope you're joking. If I find Sweetcakes' leash wrapped around the baby's ankle, you're in for it." Mary placed her medical bag on the coffee table and sat on the couch. "To answer your question—yes, we'll need to take care once the baby starts to crawl. We'll baby-proof the house."

"Sounds like a lot of work."

"Count on it. You'll help."

"Okay . . . on one condition. You'll keep the troublesome tot out of my bedroom. It's a no-fly zone. A sacred shrine. If a peewee gets pudding on my clothes or messes with my computer, I will *not* be happy."

The truculent outburst took Mary aback. "I thought you were excited about having a peewee to boss around. Someone to fake out about the Easter bunny and Santa Claus. You're not exactly sending out a happiness vibe." More like primal fear.

"I am excited. Or was."

"And now?"

"I'm nurturing my inner capitalist. I don't want anyone trashing my stuff."

"Too late for a change of heart, *muchacha.* The train has left the station."

"Can we call it back?"

"In your dreams."

"Okay. So we're in this for the long haul." Blossom whistled, and her golden retriever bounded into the room. From beneath Sweetcakes' wagging tail and wet licks of devotion, she added, "I won't need chamomile tea to help me sleep or years of therapy if you'll make one guarantee. Give birth to an angel, one of those kids who minds her own business and never trashes her sister's stuff. Or a little guy who follows me around in an adoring silence and keeps his mitts to himself. Can I get something in writing?"

"No can do, but you can have this." Mary withdrew the two index cards from her medical bag. On each she'd used glue to write the name in cursive. Then she'd covered her handiwork with glitter snatched from Blossom's art supplies. At her medical practice, the art project had left a sparkly trail of blue and pink across her office. Handing over the cards, she added, "Hang them on the Christmas tree. While you're at it, take down the other names."

Struggling out from beneath the dog, Blossom read the shimmering names.

"Lily. Tony." With impatience she flapped the cards. Flecks of glitter drifted down on Sweetcakes. "Really? These are the names? They're boring."

"Your father loves Anthony Junior. If I give birth to a boy, we'll call him Tony."

"Dad would like Tony. Men are egomaniacs."

"He's nothing of the sort. Lily is also his suggestion. It goes beautifully with your name, which is lovely. Feminine."

The compliment didn't banish her stepdaughter's distress. "Here's a nightmare scenario. What if you have two girls in a row? Will you name the second one Rose? Or Gardenia?" She wrinkled her nose. "I can't deal with Gardenia. It's an old ladies' name. Theodora and Ethel Lynn will be the only people who hang around with the kid."

Playfully Mary swatted her toward the dining room. "I don't like Gardenia, but Rose is nice. Assuming I have two girls in a row."

"Do we vote during your second pregnancy? Seeing that we ignored parliamentary procedures this time around?"

"No."

"Tyrant." Blossom began removing cards from the mini Christmas tree.

Beneath the drooping branches, Mary spied a small package. The gift was tastefully wrapped in striped paper of silver and mint green. "Who sent this?" she asked.

"Mrs. Jackowski. She stopped by around noon."

Stella Jackowski lived several doors down. Over the years the retired bookkeeper had babysat many of the children on the street, Blossom included. Most of those kids were now older, leaving room in her schedule.

Originally Mary planned to talk to Stella about a weekly babysitting schedule after the second trimester. Why wait? All of

Liberty knew about the pregnancy. It was a good bet Stella wondered if her services were needed.

"I'll be right back," she told Blossom.

All the way down North Street, the welcoming arms of the maple and oak trees rustled in the summer breeze. The sweet aroma of barbecue reached Mary and she wondered who was cooking out on this perfect summer evening; the Corleys with their brood of rambunctious boys or the Blanchards with their dozen or so grandchildren, all of whom lived nearby.

In an open field between houses a gaggle of children was playing baseball, their voices as bright as the cloudless blue sky. Contentment settled on Mary, a sense of being at peace in her picturesque neighborhood, a nearly perfect world she'd add to next spring with the birth of Lily or Anthony Jr.—Tony.

Stella was on her knees weeding the flowerbed in the front of her compact brick house.

She was rather like her home, a sturdy woman with plain features and a shock of white hair. Her grey eyes revealed intelligence and a hearty sense of humor beloved by every child on the street. At Halloween she went all out, dressing like a witch with a charmingly oversized black hat and decorating her residence with cobwebs, bubbling cauldrons and a soundtrack of wicked cackling.

Dropping a wilted dandelion into the bucket by her knees, she asked, "Did you like the gift? I left it with Blossom at lunchtime."

Mary settled on her front steps. "I haven't opened it yet. Thanks in advance."

"If you're curious, it's not a sleeper. From what I hear, you already have too many."

"I also have too many tiny knit hats and baby booties."

"Ethel Lynn's knitting circle?"

"I think they purchased all the yarn at the craft store."

Stella removed her gardening gloves and joined Mary on the steps. "I'm sorry your secret was blabbed all over town. I know how much you value your privacy."

"My privacy is long gone." Stella's eyes grew warm with understanding, encouraging her to add, "Don't tell my husband, but I've discovered I'm becoming superstitious. It's silly. I'm a doctor, for heaven's sake. The gifts and phone calls, walking down the street and having people stop to offer congratulations—it seems . . ."

When she was too embarrassed to continue, Stella supplied, "Like you're tempting fate?"

"Yes. Exactly." Mary placed her hand protectively on her abdomen. Why her medical knowledge didn't lend confidence was hard to fathom. "I didn't expect to react like some of my patients, the first-time mothers who call their obstetricians at all hours and worry needlessly. I'm only a few weeks along, and everything's fine. I'm in good health. The ideal candidate for an uneventful pregnancy."

"Mary, this is your first child. Your reaction is normal."

"You think so?"

Stella looked off at the shadows gathering on her lawn. "When my younger sister had her first? Someone blabbed at the office where she worked. Similar to what happened to you—a million gifts, and she wasn't yet through the first trimester. She refused every gift. Said it was bad luck."

"Bad luck," Mary repeated. Unaccountably, she shivered.

"At the time I laughed, but I *did* understand. No woman is prepared for the promise of new life to disappear tragically. We all fear miscarriage. Don't let anyone tell you different." She patted Mary's knee. "If you're wondering, my nephew was born without complications. Today he's a strapping tax attorney in Dayton."

"I'm glad."

"Is that why you stopped by? For an opinion on whether or not to return your gifts?"

"I was hoping to talk to you about babysitting next spring."

The comment barely out, Stella clapped her hands with glee. She disappeared inside the house, leaving Mary in a state of confusion. Returning, she handed over a neatly penned list.

A schedule.

"I hope you don't mind if I keep Thursdays for myself," she said. "I'm absolutely hooked on my swim aerobics class. I assume the weekends aren't a problem either? Anthony mentioned you'll no longer keep Saturday hours once your due date approaches."

"Sometime after the first of the year. I'm not sure when I'll reinstate weekend hours for patients. Not right away, certainly."

"Good for you. Give yourself time to recuperate, and enjoy your bundle of joy."

Mary scanned the dates with relief. Monday, Tuesday, Wednesday and Friday—her conscientious neighbor planned to babysit each afternoon until 6 PM.

"Stella, I can't thank you enough. This is a huge help. You don't mind four days a week?"

"Don't be silly! I love newborns. You needn't worry about the baby when you're busy with patients." In a businesslike tone, she negotiated a wage far lower than Mary was prepared to pay. Wrapping up, she added, "I'm thrilled for you both. Anthony was a single father for too long, and dear Blossom! She waited a long time for you to come into her life. Nothing makes me happier than to see your family grow. Now, relax. I'm here if you need anything."

On a second flurry of thanks, Mary started for home. With Stella now on board, she *did* feel better. Anthony could rearrange his schedule to handle Thursdays, leaving Mary with early mornings, evenings and the weekend to care for her child. It was a workable plan. If Blossom wished to participate, her help would be welcome. However, if she proved unreliable or too busy with high school activities, they'd manage fine without her.

The crack of a ball against a bat lifted Mary's attention to the street, to the silver Toyota speeding toward her.

With horror she noticed the boy, his attention riveted on the ball high in the air. He rushed into the road, and danger. Icy fear swept down her spine. She called out.

The warning was lost beneath the Toyota's blaring horn. The boy stopped mere inches from the car's fender.

The Toyota sped off. Without a hint he understood the peril he'd survived, the boy zeroed in on the ball rolling across the Corley's front lawn. At a loping gait, he fetched the prize and returned to the game.

Mary realized she was panting.

For reasons too mysterious to comprehend, the sensation pulled her out of the present moment, and flung her back to the first year of her residency at Cincinnati General. To a day buried beneath the sediment of her busy life, the final hour of a grueling shift working the ER. It was near midnight.

The three-year-old boy didn't arrive by ambulance. He arrived, blue-faced and near death, in the arms of his teenage mother. Why she waited so long to seek medical help for a son laboring mightily to draw a breath was a frustrating unknown, and Mary worked with desperate futility. She couldn't save the child drowning in his own bodily fluids, the delicate alveoli of his lungs filled with pus and mucus from a bout of pneumonia that would've been treatable with antibiotics ten, twelve hours sooner.

Now the long-ago death, the senseless losing of a child during her residency, scarred Mary's heart with a grief so profound, it seemed she'd once again lost the boy.

A doctor understood how easily the thread of life snapped. She'd lost patients since, to accident, disease or foolish life choices. No one was immune to life's gamble. A morbid truth certainly, yet she rarely allowed the knowledge to preclude her from celebrating the far more frequent successes: the teenager saved after a three-car pileup, the two-pack a day smoker who survived open heart surgery, the construction worker who walked again after a fall that should've brought his life to an abrupt and pitiful close.

Still, no one was immune.

On a sharp intake of breath, she mouthed a silent prayer.

The celebrated owner of the Norling department store chain reminded Meade of a restless sea captain.

Nels Norling was a huge, short-tempered man with piercing blue eyes and the swagger of a person grown accustomed to having his every wish granted and his orders followed assiduously. His silver-studded brows were as thick as caterpillars; the royal blue tie at his throat was askew. He was in constant motion, fielding calls from suppliers in London and Manila while hurtling one of his minions from the office on the strength of his booming voice, and demanding his secretary find *a damn blueberry muffin* to go with the coffee that, he, on taking a sip decided wasn't hot enough.

The secretary returned with a steaming mug and an oversized muffin. Nels drew still and noticed Meade.

His expression opened like clouds parting on a blistering sun.

"Meade Williams. Hello." He gestured toward the upholstered chair before his desk. "If you'd been much later, I would've needed to reschedule."

She was ten minutes early.

"I appreciate your time," she said, waiting until he was seated before doing the same. Snapping open her briefcase, she withdrew the proposal she'd drawn up for adding *Vivid's* product line to the chain's seventeen stores.

Before the hour was out she'd deftly taken charge of the conversation, impressing Nels with the success of her company's products in Ohio's larger department stores and exclusive boutiques.

After a lengthy conversation with her accountant last night—a conversation that left her convinced this was the correct time to expand her company—she was prepared to strike a deal advantageous to *Vivid.*

As Nels nodded with approval, she produced samples of bath salts and soaps milled by family operations in France, and lotions he sniffed with interest, his brows wriggling in approval of the soothing lavender blends and heady rose fragrances. He rubbed a lotion of Ylang Ylang and Eucalyptus between his massive finger and thumb, nodding in agreement to the suggested inventory to begin their arrangement next year, once *Vivid's* new Atlanta distributorship was up and running.

After concluding their business, she took a taxi to her new southern office. The mothballed department store was intimidatingly large, an endless sea of open spaces once brimming with clothing for sale by Atlanta's premier retailer. The cosmetics department, the building's central hub, would need to be torn out.

On the second floor the suite of offices wore miles of burnt orange shag carpeting and peeling wallpaper in a variety of outdated styles. Many of the offices were dreary, windowless cubicles, and she wondered how many walls would need to come down.

Like the gift of the property itself, her father planned to assume the expense of renovations. It was as if the altercation at Birdie's wedding reception had spurred him to bequeath a stunning inheritance before his death, a notion she didn't find reassuring.

Despite her father's depression and his reliance on her, she couldn't bear the thought of losing him. Shaking off the troublesome thought, she formed another: putting her father in charge of the renovations, through phone calls and videoconferencing with the architect in Atlanta, would give him something positive to do.

On the ride to the hotel, she called Hector. After they hung up, she noticed her headache returning and, with it, a stronger wave of nausea. The taxi glided to a halt before the hotel and, apologizing, she asked the driver to take her to a drugstore instead.

Rarely did illness pose a problem on business trips. Meade prided herself on a constitution ready to vault time zones and the stamina to endure days of little sleep. Walking the drugstore's aisles she selected a bottle of aspirin then, changing her mind, approached the pharmacist.

After listening to the list of symptoms the woman asked, "Are you pregnant? If you are, there are drugs you shouldn't take to alleviate a cold or a virus."

The question sent Meade's stomach into free-fall.

When *was* her last period?

Having abstained from relationships since her mid-thirties, she'd become lax at timing her menses. In truth she'd never been regular. Stress, travel, and changes in diet—often her periods were off by more than a week. Add in the rigorous exercise she'd always favored, and she could go well over a month without the inconvenience of tampons and maxi pads.

However, she hadn't abstained.

In May she'd shared one night of intimacy with Hector. One night only, but they hadn't used protection.

On autopilot, she thanked the pharmacist. A numbing wave of disbelief accompanied her up the feminine products aisle. She reached for the cheery pink box. A pregnancy test.

Alone in her hotel room, she ordered a salad and mineral water from room service. After the light meal, she showered and pulled the nightgown over her head. Night fell across Atlanta, a velvet patchwork embedded with twinkling lights.

At 9:10 P.M. she padded across the suite rolling her neck to release the tension. Then she found the courage to read the pink carton's directions.

The results were dismayingly prompt. Beneath her feet, the earth shifted on its axis.

She was pregnant.

Chapter 12

Meade left Atlanta with the troubling sensation she was standing outside her skin.

She conducted business at *Vivid* in a trance her staff misread as intense concentration. In the early evening she went out on the boat with her father and Hector for a picnic-style dinner of roast beef sandwiches and potato chips.

Landon applauded her success in landing the Norling account. Hector, though he didn't question her, seemed cognizant of her changed attitude: without reproach, he watched the sandwich he'd lovingly prepared become a shredded mountain of bread. Only slivers of beef reached her mouth. Since returning from Georgia, she craved protein with the zeal of a starving carnivore—meat, eggs, even a scoop of vanilla ice cream she'd surreptitiously downed before meeting the men on the dock.

At noon the following day, she wrangled an appointment with her gynecologist.

Dr. Wendy Smythson confirmed Meade was well into her first trimester. In retrospect, the stunning fact should've been obvious. She hadn't missed a period—she'd missed *two*.

How did a woman with the intelligence to manage a company and a staff of fifty miss the most predictable phases of her body? What deep-seated and dimwitted negligence allowed it? There was no comfort in the doctor's reminder that Meade's periods were never easily timed, that travel and the habit of rigorous exercise altered a woman's menses. Long distance runners often skipped periods. Women nearing middle age became irregular or endured menstrual cycles too close together. The notion all women enjoyed a predictable cycle was a fallacy.

Waving off the reassurances, Meade demanded the dreadful list of possible complications, including the odds of miscarriage or Down's Syndrome. Facts, no matter how difficult to digest, were pieces of usable knowledge much preferred to the doctor's softly issued questions, her circling around from sturdy, solid facts to the final query empowered with a force sure to stir any woman's heart.

Do you want this baby?

Later, on the bustling street, Meade found herself striding past *Vivid's* chrome and glass façade. She walked the city for hours. What she wanted was an explanation sure to break through the wall of disbelief numbing her brain.

How did a mature woman who'd gone years without intimacy become pregnant after one, singular night of pleasure?

Many women—much younger women—struggled to achieve this basic human accomplishment, the securing of the seed of the man they loved and bringing forth new life. Couples five, ten years younger than Meade jammed infertility clinics, couples desperate to form their love into life's finest creation; a baby.

How had she managed the impossible in the space of several unforgettable hours as she clung to Hector on the moonlit beach?

Do you want this baby?

She held a deep suspicion of unpredictable events. Her world was ordered, precise.

Children were capricious, each born with a unique temperament. How would she cope? She didn't think fast on her feet, she studied and practiced and carried through with sheer grit.

Do you want this baby?

She did, with a shocking firmness of resolve. She would have this child.

Like her mother before her, the celebrated and shallow Cat Seavers, she would raise one heir with access to every comfort and opportunity wealth afforded; the pick of private schools and music lessons and weekends at the country club with the tennis pro.

Unlike her mother, Meade wouldn't squander the opportunity to build a true relationship with her child. She wouldn't waste years, as Cat had done, flitting from one illicit affair to the next, and doing the rounds of couture shows in France and Italy purchasing gowns she wore once or not at all.

Meade had charted a different life, a better life. Though she didn't possess a flexible personality, she would learn to bend. She would curve the arc of her days around the child nestled inside her womb.

And Hector? He must be told quickly. The sense of possession she felt didn't preclude her deep-rooted ethics from leading her to a central truth. The baby was his too.

He would ask to marry her. They were in love, and he was a responsible man.

Finishing the walk, she doubled back to *Vivid*. She passed the building and went directly to her car. Shutting off her cell, she drove to her father's estate with a new, equally demanding question swirling through her mind.

Did she wish to marry Hector?

No. Not like this. Not with the pregnancy prodding them up the aisle like a pitchfork.

Why take the risk? Too many marriages ended in divorce, the unions hasty or ill-advised. They were like Hector's mistakes in his twenties. Or the union was fraudulent, like the farce Meade's parents enacted before her mother's death.

Meade was determined to have a solid, enduring partnership or none at all. On the material level, the baby was already cared for. Her wealth assured it. In less tangible ways? Whether she married Hector or not, he would love his child. He would provide a father's affection. Not for a moment did she question his fidelity.

If they married at a future date, the choice would be mutual and freely made. Never would their child confront an ugly fact of a union sealed in haste. Nor would they risk dissolution because they hadn't taken care to build a sturdy foundation before tying the knot.

Returning to the estate, she let hunger lure her to the

kitchen. On the center island, burgundy colored cherries spilled in tempting profusion. One by one, Reenie dropped them into a colander. At her elbow, the small pile of bruised fruit she'd discarded was growing.

No doubt she'd purchased the fruit from one of the local farms earlier today. The cherries looked impossibly fresh, and her mouth watered. Meade swiped a handful. It dawned she was craving something other than protein. Gobbling them down, she reached for more.

Reenie looked up from her task. "Goodness, did you skip lunch? I can make a sandwich if you'd like. Chicken or egg salad. This week your father asked for both."

"Finish your task. I'll eat later." Primly, she spit a mouthful of pits into a napkin. "Where's my father?"

"Polishing half of the plants in the greenhouse with banana peels."

"You're kidding."

"Don't laugh. The peels are like furniture polish for plant stock. The palm tree looks gorgeous."

Since purchasing the Atlanta real estate, he'd been more energetic than usual. "And Glade? Where is she?"

"Hiding in her room."

"Didn't she work today?"

"Until early afternoon. Finney thought she looked tired, and sent her home. She's been holed up in her room ever since."

Most likely she was doing her level best to avoid Meade's father. They were still practically strangers, a situation Meade should have rectified weeks ago. Doing so was increasingly difficult, what with Glade's part-time job at The Second Chance and her tutoring lessons with Hector at his RV. Most days she cleared out before Landon shuffled down the stairwell in a surly mood that didn't abate until he'd quaffed his second cup of coffee. Was it any wonder the girl had grown adept at avoiding the temperamental master of the house?

Guessing her thoughts, Reenie said, "Don't bother mending a fence that isn't broken. Your father hasn't made a fuss about Glade. Not one complaint. He hardly mentions her at all. They stay out of each other's hair."

"It isn't right."

"Meade, I'm grateful Glade is here. Does it matter if your father treats her like a guest?"

"At the least he should acknowledge her. I'm ashamed of his behavior."

"He's old. Try to remember that. This is his home, and he wasn't consulted about having a pregnant teenager take up residence for months on end. Glade understands the situation. She'll manage. Believe me, your father is a saint compared to most people."

Reenie gave the colander an angry shake. Droplets of waters spun out like bullets released from a Gatling gun. The burst of anger seemed to catch her off-guard and she sat the colander down, the metal base rattling. She laid her hands flat on the counter.

"Reenie?" Meade went to her. "What is it?"

The housekeeper glanced at the doorway leading to the basement. Whatever was troubling her, she didn't want Glade to hear. With trepidation Meade watched her pull open a drawer brimming with odds and ends. Packets of out-of-date flower seeds fought for space beside spools of thread and an odd assortment of discolored silverware. From beneath a heart-shaped cookie cutter and a pair of scissors, she withdrew a white envelope.

The cursive was instantly recognizable. Reenie's cramped penmanship wove across the envelope in neat lines. An official stamp in red ink partially hid the mailing address.

RETURN TO SENDER.

With cold fingers, Meade took the envelope.

It was addressed to Glade's mother in West Virginia. Putting it all together, she gasped. "Her mother left without a forwarding address?"

Reenie nodded grimly. "Phone's disconnected too. I've checked with the rest of my family—they think she found a new job in another town."

"What about her house, the kids, their school—"

"She was renting a trailer half the size of the fancy RV Hector has parked beside the *Liberty Post.* She wouldn't think twice about walking away. Not for the right job."

"She left without telling anyone where she was going?"

"From what I gather."

"I don't understand. Who picks up and goes without leaving a forwarding address?"

The puzzlement in her voice put a weary smile on Reenie's face.

"People who don't have anything rooting them to a place. Meade, you don't understand poor, the kind of poor that means you don't put on the heat until winter piles snowdrifts on your doorstep, and a living wage comes by rarely. If my niece found a better job, she left in a hurry because she didn't want to lose the chance. She doesn't have a man. She's probably staying with a woman friend, someone who also has kids. If need be, they'll pack their children five to a bed until they earn enough to rent a decent apartment."

The explanation closed Meade's throat. What hardships did people endure simply to survive? Softly she asked, "When did she leave?"

"Last week. Packed her kids in the truck and drove off."

She recalled Glade's arrival in May, the sorrow Reenie soothed away if only for one night and the meager belongings stuffed into a garbage bag.

"Glade did the same, walked away from a familiar life."

"Glade's a child. Children make reckless choices. You hope they learn from their mistakes. You hope they don't hurt themselves too often." Reenie's voice was hoarse as she added, "I don't condone my niece's behavior, but she probably thought it was necessary. I hope she found something good."

"Should we tell Glade?"

"Not yet. My niece will turn up eventually. She'll get word to someone. Might take a while." The housekeeper turned the damp berries into a bowl and patted them dry. "Glade's now well and truly on her own. Running off from her mother, getting mixed up with a man who probably threw her out on the street—how can we add to her worries? She's got new friends here, a chance at a good life. Let's not spoil it."

The teenager who'd renounced her family was now equally abandoned. Inside Meade anger blended with pity.

"You're right," she agreed. "Now isn't the time. Later, perhaps. Or she'll try to contact her mother and discover she can't. We'll talk to her then."

"Why don't you sit with her a while? Unless you're hurrying out to see Hector."

"We're meeting later. He's helping Hugh paint the baby's room."

"They're painting with Birdie nearby? It isn't wise."

"She's not breathing paint fumes. They've banished her to the newsroom and opened every window in the apartment." The housekeeper took the news with a sharp nod of satisfaction, but Meade sensed she was troubled by something further. Capturing Reenie's skittering gaze, she asked. "Is there something in particular I should discuss with Glade?"

"Babies," Reenie said simply.

A whirlwind of emotion went through Meade. Like her young houseguest, she too would become a mother. *I'm having a baby.* Yet again the astonishing fact rushed her mind, vaulting her heart and striking her dumb with a heavenly euphoria. With effort, she smoothed the joy from her features.

"Poor Glade," Reenie was saying, "I think she's finally got it through her head that babies don't come without a great deal of pain."

"Reenie, she's received lots of good advice. I've personally chatted with her several times, and her obstetrician and Mary have too."

"Doesn't matter how often three adult women explain. Glade's now bigger than a barn. Little Natasha is kicking up a storm. You know as well as I do how uncomfortable the last months of pregnancy are for a woman."

She didn't possess firsthand knowledge. Not yet. Anxiety spilled through her.

"I should've insisted she take a birthing class. There were several offered in the area." The suggestion had been turned down. "Delia would've made room in her schedule to go as Glade's partner. Or I would've found a way. Doesn't matter— Glade isn't interested."

"There's nothing you can do about a teenager's natural stubbornness. Well, now she's scared. Ticking off the weeks until her due date and uncomfortable most of the time. Why don't you sit with her for a while? You're sensible to a fault. You'll soothe her worries."

In the servants' quarters, the girl's bedroom was no longer given over to a messy wallpaper of photos pulled from fashion magazines. To be sure, some of the photos were still in evidence, the stick-thin women cavorting in sheer gowns or vibrant lingerie, their thick-lashed eyes dismissive as they surveyed the cramped environs.

Taped on top of many of the photos were new and more sedate images of mothers cradling children. A few images were of blissfully expectant women or clips of the perfect nursery, a crib netted with lace as fine as gossamer and the walls stenciled with bunny rabbits or papered in tiny rosebuds.

Like the offer of birthing classes, Glade had refused a baby shower out of embarrassment or sheer obstinacy. Nonetheless gifts were arriving. Near the rocking chair Meade had recently purchased for her, a growing stack of baby clothing, blankets and toys lay amidst a nest of wrapping paper and ribbon. Meade's poodle Melbourne lay asleep in the mess.

For its part, the bed resembled a desk. All manner of index cards, written in Hector's bold hand, formed a circle around the pensive girl. On her swollen thighs was a book.

At Meade's entrance, she set the book aside.

"I can't concentrate," she admitted.

"Time for a break? You do look tired."

"Tell Hector. He never lets up. He thinks I should already have this stuff memorized." She ruffled the book's pages. "Politics and Citizenship. Boring. Why do I need to learn this stuff for the GED? Who *cares* how many people are in the House of Representatives?"

"Educated voters are the backbone of a democracy."

"If you say so."

Meade noticed the Raggedy Ann stuffed beneath the pillow. Withdrawing the doll from its hiding place, she asked, "How's Natasha today?"

Glade scooted to the bed's headboard and leaned back with a sigh. "Moving around like a kid on a jungle gym. Bouncing on my spine, my kidneys, my bladder—I'm going to the bathroom more often than an old lady."

"Soon you'll bounce her on your knee."

Chewing it over, Glade took the Raggedy Ann by the hair and gave it a shake. "How am I supposed to get something this big out of my body? Even if they give me something for the pain, it won't be enough. It'll hurt." She squeezed the doll's middle as if gauging the volume of a baby in transit, a slippery, impatient life thrusting its way into the world. She startled Meade by adding, "I never should've slept with him. It was dumb. Or I should've asked him to use . . . you know."

"A condom?"

She rushed on. "I didn't think I'd get caught. I knew how babies are made—who doesn't? I thought I was lucky. I'd mess around and nothing would happen. Lots of girls do. It's not like everyone ends up like this."

She lifted her belly an inch, jiggling the generous orb. Frustration welled on her face, and the fear Reenie had mentioned. She *was* afraid. Stone cold terrified of giving birth.

Before Meade found the opportunity to offer comfort, she plunged on. "I didn't even tell him. Stupid, right? He'll have a daughter, but he'll never see Natasha. He won't even know she exists."

As it should be, Meade thought.

Natasha would have a hard enough time as the child of an unwed mother. Did she need an abusive father? It was better if the child never met him, whoever he was. Meade was sure of it.

Carefully she said, "You don't think he should know, do you?" The question was met with a stony silence, prodding her to add, "Glade, you're eighteen years old. The best years of your life are ahead of you. I'm not saying you'll have an easy time as a single mother, but you will have help. I'll help you. Delia too. Many people, in fact. Someday you'll look back on this phase with pride. You were brave—brave enough to keep Natasha and build a future for her. You'll find a job you enjoy. One day, you'll find the right man too."

"Who'd want an ugly girl lugging around a baby?"

"You aren't ugly." Meade smoothed her hand down the girl's back. "You're a very attractive young woman. Would you like to spend an afternoon at the salon? We'll go together."

"You spend too much on me."

"Only because I enjoy it so."

"Did you mean it about a guy? I'll find someone?"

"One day you will. I'm sure of it." She squeezed Glade's hand. "Look at Anthony and Mary. For a long time, Anthony was a single father. His wife left when Blossom was a toddler. Now he has Mary. Believe me, she loves Blossom like her own child. In every way that matters Blossom *is* her child."

"I like Blossom," Glade murmured with grudging acceptance of the advice Meade offered. "Mary isn't her real Mom? I thought she was."

"Mary wed Blossom's dad last year. As for 'real' or not, don't let Mary catch you making a similar statement. Any woman devoted to raising a child is a real mother."

In the nest of torn wrapping paper, Melbourne stirred. Shaking off the remnants of sleep, the dog spotted Meade. His tail beat the floor in a drumbeat of love.

She whistled, and he trotted over. Scooping him up, she ruffled his soft ears.

"Are you seeing Hector tonight?" Glade asked.

She checked her watch. "I should leave soon."

"Thanks for talking." With renewed energy, Glade returned the book to her lap. Her nose deep in the pages, she added, "I feel better."

⁂

Bobbing the paintbrush like a baton, Theodora said, "Go on and thank me, Hector. Your days on the unemployment line are over. I've got it all worked out."

They were standing in the newly-painted nursery surveying their handiwork. Hugh, on his knees, was taking a last swipe at the baseboard with the grass green paint.

He smirked at Hector. "Run for cover, pal. Once Theodora gets an idea stuck in her head, wild stallions can't dislodge it. Look at me. Thanks to her meddling, I'm the proud owner of the *Post.*"

"What are you fussing about?" The paintbrush morphed into a weapon she used to flick paint at Hugh. He ducked, but not before several droplets landed in his hair. "Running the *Post* makes you happier than a pig in shit."

"Not today, it doesn't. Birdie's downstairs grousing about the lead story for tomorrow's edition. I still haven't written it."

"Bitch, bitch, bitch."

"I'm not complaining. Okay, I am. But only because I've been praying to a baseboard for over an hour. I'm sick of crawling around on my knees."

"Spiffing up the nursery makes your wife happy. Now, send her over the moon with joy by writing the article." After he left, Theodora tossed the brush into the empty paint can and approached Hector. She drew herself up tall. Given her petite stature, the effort got her to nearly five feet in height. "Well?" she demanded. "Do you want to hear my plan or not?"

He folded the plastic sheeting they'd used to protect the carpeting. "Have you found something in marketing or sales? Either works. I'll begin winding down my hours at the *Post* soon." Hugh had found a part-time bookkeeper, and Hector promised to continue pitching in on weekends if needed. "I don't mind commuting. Strike that. I'd prefer a short commute. I don't want anything cutting into my evening hours with Meade."

"The job doesn't require a long commute."

"Good pay?"

"It won't make you rich, but what do you care? It'll keep you in Liberty to woo Meade. You'll also help a sight more people than you would as a salesman."

He was intrigued. "Go on. I'm listening."

"We're opening a youth center."

"We?"

"All right, *you're* opening the center. I'm too old for such nonsense. I've already talked to Mayor Ryan about taking over the basement of the courthouse. Plenty of room once we clear out the junk."

"I don't know the first thing about running a youth center. You need someone with a background in administration or social work."

"Take a few online college courses to improve your skills. People do it all the time."

"I'm not qualified."

"Hogwash. You have a talent for working with the young." From the hallway she dragged in the garbage can. Together they

185

cleaned up the nursery. "Aren't you helping Glade with her studies? Didn't you help boys in Philadelphia in the Big Brothers program? What more experience do you need?"

"Those were volunteer jobs. I didn't run Big Brothers. I pitched in a few hours a week."

"You tutor Glade practically every day." She stomped her foot. "Damn it, Hector. You've got a knack with kids, and Jeffordsville County needs your help. Do you have any idea how many girls there are like Glade? Getting pregnant, dropping out of school—do you wonder why so many of our youths get mixed up in drugs? Oh, Liberty looks pretty as a picture, but you aren't seeing the *entire* picture. We have folks in Jeffordsville County with barely a pot to piss in, and children running wild. If you won't help them, who will?"

Her soliloquy aimed well at his sense of responsibility for young people in general and the less fortunate in particular. He *did* care about kids like Glade making poor choices because they lacked guidance or options or plain common sense. Helping her achieve the basic dream of a high school education gave him a sense of accomplishment. In many ways, the same desire to help had informed his choice to marry two women who'd both survived traffic accidents that should've taken their lives.

Theodora was correct. A purely mercenary drive to achieve wealth wasn't part of his calculus. Of all the jobs he'd held, the entire lot, the most enjoyable work centered on giving back and doing something worthwhile.

When it seemed flames would shoot from the top of Theodora's head, he said, "Let me think it over. Get your ideas together, and we'll talk. No guarantees, all right?"

As she nodded in agreement, Meade popped her head into the doorway.

"Hey, there." She regarded Hector then noticed Theodora. "Should I come back in a minute?"

Theodora waved off the suggestion. "He's all yours." She wagged a finger before his nose. "Think about my idea. If I don't steer you to success, who will? Don't disappoint me, son."

She stalked off, leaving a heavy silence in her wake.

Breaking it, Meade asked, "What was she talking about?"

"Don't ask." He took her by the shoulders and turned her at

186

angles to survey the freshly painted room. "What do you think?"

"You did a beautiful job."

"There's more. Birdie found a crib."

"For the baby?"

"It's too small for Hugh. If he throws a tantrum, he'll have to sleep on the couch."

The light banter went right over Meade. She stared at him like a waif in need of a morsel.

"What's wrong?" he asked. "You look like you've had a bad reading from one of those carnival psychics. My aunts, in Philly? They've got a thing about getting those readings then worrying about it afterwards."

Another misfire in the humor department. Meade, usually composed, went red. Not the fetching blush of a girl accepting a compliment, no; she turned the color of a ripe tomato rotting in the sun. The air she gulped shuddered from her throat clear down to her waist.

The reaction threw Hector. Why was she upset? Taking a wild guess, he said, "I'm sure Birdie has the receipt for the crib. She'll take it back."

"Why would she return it?"

"If you bought her one."

"Oh. Right." Meade spat out a laugh. "I didn't buy a crib." She dragged her eyes from his curious gaze and peered out the window, flung open to air out the room. Racing to a new topic, she said, "I just saw Glade. Her nerves are stretched thin enough to snap. The Raggedy Ann—why, it must be smaller than Natasha. Don't you think? She was holding the doll end-to-end, trying to visualize what it'll be like."

"To go through labor?" She gave a chipper nod and he scratched his head. The ordeals of womanhood weren't something he wished to contemplate. If nature had put men in charge of propagating the species, the planet would be devoid of humanity within a generation. "Did you reassure her? About getting through labor, I mean."

"We talked for twenty minutes like a mother to her expectant daughter."

"She relies on you."

"Isn't it odd? I am like a mother to her. Middle-aged Meade.

Business maven and fairy godmother to luckless girls." Another laugh, more forced than the last, and she added, "When Natasha comes, it'll be like I'm a grandmother."

"You don't look like any grandmother I know."

Missing the compliment, she rolled tension from her shoulders. "Mind if we take a walk?"

He wanted dinner. Clearly Meade needed something else.

"Sure. Let's go for a stroll." He followed her down to the newsroom.

They'd explore Liberty Square's center green. After, he'd take her to The Second Chance. It wasn't like he'd cook tonight. Not after catching up on the *Post's* bills earlier today and painting a nursery.

He was fishing the car keys from his pocket when Meade surprised him again by sweeping through the newsroom past her sister, Hugh, Theodora and three of Hugh's newbies without so much as a glance. Her gait accelerating, she raced out the door. He picked up his feet and ran.

She went right past his car, into the overgrown field beside the *Post*, a blanket of green flung clear to the horizon. She stomped over a clump of wild garlic, releasing savory bombs of scent. On she went, into grass higher than her knees, and he was thankful she'd had the foresight to wear jeans. Her hair bounced as she strode forward with chin raised and eyes planted on an imaginary destination. She was marching to Camelot and he was her over-taxed Sir Lancelot. Wheezing, he caught up with her.

He captured her by the wrist. "What's the hurry? I'm not up to a marathon this late in the day."

"What?" Her eyes were placid pools of blue. They seemed a contradiction to the forced march she'd put them on.

"Must we run? An afternoon of painting did me in. I'm beat." The desperation in his voice barely slowed her stride.

"Hector, there's something we need to discuss."

"I get that."

"Don't be upset."

"Meade, I'm crazy about you. Nothing you say will upset me. We should always be honest with each other."

"Good. Great. I can't bear for you to see this as an obligation. We're doing well together. Let's not spoil it. We take each day as it comes. No pressure."

"Sure. No pressure."

The relief flooding his gut sprouted perspiration on his temples. For a nerve-wracking moment, he'd thought she was ending their relationship. Recalling Theodora's bizarre proposal, he wondered if he shouldn't consider the job. Running a youth center was a respectable occupation. It would demonstrate to Meade his intention to make Liberty his home.

She ground to a halt, and he nearly toppled over her. "Let me be clear," she said. "I don't expect anything from you."

Not the most promising turn in the conversation, but he remained calm. "I want you to have expectations. I plan to meet every one."

"Fine, fine. We take our time. There's no reason to rush. We have all the time in the world."

A bee landed on her hair. He swatted it away. "Great. Nothing changes."

Why would it? As far as he was concerned, they were both in love. He was in deeper, sure. In time, she'd fall just as hard. She'd reach the conclusion he'd wrestled with for weeks—they were meant to be together.

She was a planner. She needed time to get used to the idea of marriage.

Which, obviously, wasn't the problem.

Finally he hit upon it. Thanks to her father's largess, she was moving up the schedule for *Vivid's* expansion, opening the new facility faster than anticipated. She was concerned the change would affect their relationship. It wouldn't. He didn't like the idea of more travel in her schedule, but he'd manage.

Careful not to reveal his disappointment, he said, "Don't worry about Atlanta. I back your ambitions one hundred percent. I'll keep busy while you're traveling. If the renovations for the new distribution center require you to stay in Georgia for weeks at a stretch, I'll fly down on weekends. We'll work it out."

"Right." She rubbed her eyes like a child rising from daydreams. "The new warehouse. I do need to think about it."

"What?"

Another bee landed, drawn by her perfume. He drove it off. Then he shooed a mosquito hovering by her neck. If he didn't get her out of here, she'd be eaten alive.

"Nels is sending the contracts," she murmured to herself. "Will he agree to a delay? He won't like it. Then again, I shouldn't commit to a hectic schedule until I'm sure how I'll feel."

Lost, Hector asked, "You're delaying the opening of the Atlanta office?"

"Until I'm sure how I'll manage."

He pulled her to a stop. "Manage what?" When she refused to look at him, he caressed her cheek to calm her. She didn't resist when he took her chin, turning it slightly to mesh her troubled gaze with his. "Meade, *what* are you managing?"

"I'm pregnant."

If a Neanderthal had leapt from the long grass and clubbed him on the skull, Hector couldn't have been more dazed. "Run that by me again."

The invitation to reveal all uncorked Meade in a bubbly rush. "It's physically impossible," she stammered. "Kids like Glade get pregnant from one-night stands, not mature women on the brink of middle age. Do you have any idea how much three of my friends paid for *in vitro?* Thousands. Tens of thousands. The oldest is thirty-eight, and she thinks making a baby is harder than pushing a two-ton boulder up Mount Everest. She's still not pregnant. No one gets pregnant at age forty without a team of specialists and the kind of stupid luck that rarely strikes."

Stupidly, he replied, "We didn't have a one-night stand."

"My apologies." She followed the prim comment with a goofy smile. "It was the best night of my life."

"Guess again. I have better tricks in store."

A belly laugh erupted from her throat. "I believe you."

"What do we do now?"

"Go on like before."

"Sure." Not the answer he would've preferred. "Like nothing has changed. Makes perfect sense."

Except it didn't. Woozy, he dropped his ass on the ground.

"Hector!"

Knees drawn to his chest, he sucked air in and out. Clammy perspiration sprouted on his chest. Meade was pregnant. They were pregnant.

They were having a baby.

"Hector, are you all right? Say something!"

The plea was a distant echo beneath the thoughts thundering through his head. He'd become a father outside the respectable bonds of marriage. The child's mother—the woman he loved—was more apt to expand her company overnight than rush into marriage. Hector cradled his head in his hands. Were his parents rolling in their graves?

"Having a baby isn't the end of the world." She crouched beside him, her perfume drawing more bees. "Don't be afraid."

Now it was his turn to laugh. "Meade, I'm not afraid. I'm overjoyed. I want our baby. You want it too, right?"

"More than anything."

"He should have my name. He's not a Williams. He's a Levendakis."

There. He'd said it. He'd bypassed his shock and brought them to the crux of the issue. On rubbery legs, he rose. Then he dug deep in his gut.

He dug until he found the moral imperative that layered steel on his voice. "You aren't Glade. Our baby has two parents, two rational, mature adults to care for him. Now, I understand you're not ready for marriage—"

"I'm not!"

"Well, I am. I've been ready since our one night together even if I haven't let myself hope too much. I knew you required a long courtship. Which would've been fine." He hesitated. "This changes everything."

"Hector, we've just started dating."

"Like hell."

"We need more time. Think of all the topics a couple should discuss before making a commitment. It's no different than a business negotiation. Actually it's quite similar."

"We're talking about our future, not articles of incorporation. You're carrying our child." A terrible fear bore down on him. "Do you love me?"

He'd never asked. Too soon, too forward—he wasn't sure why he'd held off. Now he needed the truth.

She looked like she'd been slapped. "Hector, please. I've never married and you've married too often. Let's not hurry in before we're ready."

191

"Meade, do you?" The tears pooling in her eyes made him sick with shame. Why push her like this? Unable to stop himself, he added, "Because I love you—more than anything except the baby you're carrying, whom I'll love just as much. I'm sorry I haven't told you until now. Do you understand? Whether you're ready to hear it or not, I *will* spend my life with you. I don't blame you for wondering if a man twice-divorced has staying power. I'll spend the rest of my life proving I do, each and every day. You won't regret our marriage. I love you."

The power of his affection knocked against her, shuddering through her limbs. Tears rolled down her cheeks. "I love you too," she whispered, her voice as thin as dreams. "I do. But please don't rush me. There's so much I have to grow accustomed to, and I'm scared."

"Don't be scared."

Hugging her tight, he rocked her until their hearts beat in rhythm and his eyes burned with an off pouring of grief. What if he'd lost her? What if she'd admitted she didn't love him?

She did. For now, it was enough.

Mary smiled at the sight. In the grocery store's produce section, Birdie was standing pineapples inside her shopping cart one after the other.

Mary nudged her husband. He looked up from the locally sourced tomatoes he was comparing.

Anthony grinned. "Think Birdie's planning a party?" he asked. "Pineapple ambrosia for twenty?"

Mary, with a doctor's intuition, came to a different conclusion. Wheeling her cart over, she made a quick tally. "Six pineapples." She eyed Birdie's rounded belly. "Is the baby tired of peaches?"

"Since last week. Now we've moved on to tropical fruits. I think mangoes are up next."

"At least you aren't craving pickles and peanut butter."

"Are you?"

"Not on your life. I've never liked pickles."

"She thinks they're too salty," Anthony said, joining them.

Birdie patted her precious baby bump. "He can't get enough

192

of tropical flavors. Or she can't."

"You didn't check the ultrasound for the baby's sex?" Mary assumed she would.

Approaching, Hugh said, "Don't launch us back into battle. I was all for knowing the baby's sex. Birdie changed her mind. She thinks staying in the dark is more of an adventure. Sicko."

Birdie put another pineapple into the cart. "Flow with it, dear. I like the mystery of not knowing if I'm carrying a boy or a girl. Like waiting to unwrap a present."

"You're wasting your time. News flash—we're having a girl." To Mary and Anthony, he explained, "Our mystery guest is a polite kicker. Never goes overboard like Glade's baby, throwing itself around like a kid on a trampoline. I'm betting we'll have a dainty princess."

"For the record, Glade is having a girl." Mary reconsidered. "An *energetic* girl. Your dainty girl may in fact be a boy with a quiet temperament. Ever consider that?"

"I'll be the father of a geek? A boy with more books than baseballs?"

"Guess you'll have to wait to find out."

A giddy delight glazed Hugh's features. "A studious kid works for me. He'll start writing for the *Post* before he hits junior high. He'll be like Blossom, but without the detention slips." He withdrew three pineapples from the shopping cart beneath Birdie's howls of protest and led her toward the meat department saying, "How about salmon for dinner? It's the perfect brain food for my geeky son."

"Or daughter," Mary called after them, laughing. She turned to discover Anthony missing. Where was he?

She spied him at the end of the produce department. He picked up a carton of blackberries.

"Lily adores berries." He placed them in the cart, his nose lifted like a beagle's. "Where's corn on the cob? I think it's Tony's favorite."

If this was a deranged form of baby-love, she couldn't complain. "If you're wishing on a star for twins, guess what. I'm emotionally prepared for *one* baby. Twins are out of the question"

"I know we aren't having twins." He guided her away from

the cart and lowered her hands to her slender waist. To her astonishment, he bent slightly and told her tummy, "Grow big and strong. We love you. We can't wait to meet you."

"Anthony, what are you doing?" By the potatoes, a white-haired matron bobbed her shoulders back and forth like a kid waiting for ice cream. Evidently the profession of love had made her day. "Let me go. You're causing a scene."

He noticed the ears of corn piled high in the next aisle. "This way, matey." When she drew the cart to a stop, allowing him to toss in several ears of corn, he added, "Hugh got me thinking about how we're acting about Lily or Tony. We aren't far into this game, and we talk *about* the baby, never *to* the baby. We should. Shows the kid we love him."

"Or her."

"Right. We should include him in our conversations since, you know, he's with us all the time."

"Or her."

"Or her. I love Lily. I hope she likes frilly stuff. When Blossom was a peewee, she was a tomboy. I always found worms in her pockets. Wonder what it's like to raise a daughter who'll wear a dress once in a while. And bows in her hair. Pink ones."

"Or a son who'll play catch with Dad. He'll be the star pitcher in high school."

"Or he'll play the violin. Imagine that. I've never known anyone who played the violin. We'll get him lessons."

"Or her."

"Right."

On tiptoes, she kissed his cheek. "News flash," she said, aping Hugh's oft-used phrase. "You're a little nuts. It's your most endearing quality. Oh. And I love you. So does Lily."

"Or Tony."

"Him too."

They finished shopping. Anthony selected a variety of foods for their mystery guest, his mood light and playful. By the time they carried the bags up the back steps to the house, Mary was convinced the tiny life growing inside her was listening to their repartee with approval. Not that she believed the fetus would develop rudimentary hearing before the eighteenth week of pregnancy. But still.

Overhead, muffled voices drifted through the second floor. Sweetcakes' lively barking followed.

She closed the refrigerator door. "I thought we were having a quiet Sunday afternoon. What's Blossom doing upstairs?"

Anthony patted her tummy. "Don't worry, kiddo. If your big sister is up to no good, I'll bring a stop to it."

Chuckling, Mary followed him out of the kitchen.

At the top of the stairs, the bathroom door was closed. The toilet flushed. Snoops, their daughter's best friend, stepped out. Behind purple-framed glasses, her eyes widened as she caught sight of them trudging up the stairwell. She locked herself back in.

"This is not good," Mary said.

Anthony shrugged. "Don't jump to conclusions. The stress isn't good for Tony."

"Or Lily."

"Right."

The old Victorian mansion boasted many unfinished rooms, including a small bedroom right beside Blossom's. Recently Mary and Anthony had been debating whether to turn the room into the nursery, or use another unfinished and much larger room a stone's throw from the master suite.

The decision was made without their consent.

Inside the small bedroom, two ladders, a level, rulers, rollers, and an old table hauled in from the garage, took up much of the space. Blossom was on the ladder. Glade and Delia were grunting with effort, helping her decorate the walls with the most ridiculous wallpaper.

Lemony yellow paper with purple baby elephants. The elephants sported wings, like angels.

Elephant angels. Mary cringed.

Anthony, an old pro at parenting, turned on the cheer. "Hey. This is nice." He bent to Mary's stomach. "What do you think, Lily? Isn't this great? Tony, do you like elephants?"

Mary pushed him away. Turning to the girls, she demanded, "What are you doing? Blossom, who gave you permission to design the baby's nursery!"

The sulky comment froze the trio. Blossom, teetering on the ladder, slapped her palms against the wall to stop the last sheet of paper from sliding off. Delia slunk behind the much larger Glade, who waved them into the room.

Glade proved her powers of observation were faulty by saying, "Don't you love it? We wanted to finish before you got home. A surprise, you know? Geez, wallpapering is a lot of work. We thought we'd finish a lot faster than this. Isn't the design sweet? We got the wallpaper online. Blossom let me pick it out."

The wallpaper was dreadful.

The girls were designing a nursery for a baby born in a theme park. Or a child raised in the circus. If they were planning to trim the window in purple paint, Mary knew she'd weep.

When the ability to speak eluded her, Anthony said, "Nice job, ladies. You've done us proud. I never would've thought of elephants."

Blossom, trembling on the ladder, said, "You aren't mad?"

Sweetcakes nosed Anthony, and he gave the dog a scratch behind the ears. "No way. I like elephants."

Delia put in, "We let Glade pick out the design since she's the expert." Anthony tipped his head to the side, and she clarified, "Because she's pregnant."

"Good thinking. Right, Mary?"

Miraculously her voice returned. "It's beautiful," she got out. "Exactly what I wanted."

The pronouncement coated Glade's features with happiness. "I was sure you'd love it! I almost went with the giraffe wallpaper—it looked so soft and dreamy—but I thought you'd like the elephants better. They're so cute, I want to kiss them! I'll show you the site where we got the paper. You can get a matching quilt for the crib, and a rug too. The rug only has the elephants on the border, but it's nice. Let me know when you're ready to shop 'til you drop."

The chatter drawing to a stop, she looked to Mary for thanks. Or, God forbid, gratitude. Mary swallowed against the dry spaces of her throat.

She slumped against the doorjamb. "I can't wait."

Chapter 13

While it was common knowledge in Liberty that Theodora cherished Birdie, her once-lost kin, it was equally true the elderly matriarch loved her 1960s Cadillac with a frenzied devotion. The impeccably restored car led every parade in the county. When it was parked before The Second Chance, its crotchety owner dining inside the restaurant on Finney's good eats, local kids stayed clear of the bumper. They never leaned against a polished door or so much as touched the gleaming rear beauty panel. People said the Saturday night special tucked in Theodora's satchel was loaded with rock salt, but no one knew for sure.

Given his appreciation for American ingenuity and tailfin design, Hector played along like everyone else. He never brought food into the Cadillac. Like every other man in town deemed worthy of a ride, he suffered the indignity of having the petite driver relegate him to the passenger seat. If Theodora ignored speed limits with cackling delight, sending the car aloft for perilous seconds on country roads, it was the price of admission into her car—and her good graces.

But today, he didn't care about her feelings. He didn't care much about anything. There were times when life knocked a man to his knees.

Next spring he'd become a father. He couldn't pass out cigars in a spirit of celebration over the upcoming arrival of his firstborn. He couldn't call his sister in Philadelphia with the news, or grab a barstool with Hugh and compare fatherhood notes at the local tavern. For now, Meade was keeping the pregnancy a secret. No one, not even her closest friend, Mary, was yet privy to what should've been a joyous announcement.

Which was why, on a day like today, sitting in the driver's seat was imperative for a man with his fair share of testosterone.

His resolve firm, he strode across the *Post's* parking lot and nipped the keys from Theodora's hand.

He slid in behind the wheel. "I'm driving."

By the time she wiped the incredulity from her face, he was buckled in.

She stomped her foot. "My Cadillac doesn't fancy anyone but me."

"I don't care what your Cadillac likes. Get in."

"Lord and Jezebel! Are you ordering me around? Why, I should take you out behind the barn and knock some sense into you." She jabbed a finger at the *Post*, conveniently housed in a red barn. "If you've got any brains in your head, you'll get out of my vehicle right quick."

"Tick tock." He jammed the key in the ignition. "Coming?"

Irritation sizzled up her spine. "What do you think you're doing?" Rushing the car, she clawed for the keys. He rolled up the window.

Through the glass, he said, "I'm feeling testy. I need to drive. Get in, or I'm leaving without you."

Backing up the warning, he brought the engine to life. On a howl, she wrenched open the passenger door and threw herself inside. He was out of the lot before the door clicked shut.

"Hector Levendakis, are you trying to meet your Maker?" She fumbled with her buckskin satchel, growling and throwing spittle on the dashboard.

He took the satchel and tossed it in the backseat. "I'm not ready to meet the Big Guy in the Sky." He paused as she swiveled to stare at the satchel. When she whipped back around in a failed attempt to scorch him with contempt, he added, "Give it a rest. By the way, here's another surprise. We're not going to the courthouse as planned."

He'd already investigated the basement, her proposed location for Liberty's new youth center. It was a no-go. The center needed to serve kids at night, after the courthouse closed, as well as during the day.

"Where in the blazes are we going? I told Mayor Ryan we'd meet in her office."

"I canceled the appointment." He'd also tapped Hugh's investigative skills to research youth centers in general and Jeffordsville County's teenage population in particular. Twenty-somethings too, and the statistics were troubling. "Here's a fun fact. Nationally, teen pregnancies and drug addiction are down slightly, but the numbers aren't good. There's also a growing problem between the haves and have-nots. Too many kids from disadvantaged homes don't go to trade school or college. They tough it out in slave wage jobs and start families too soon. Or they turn to drugs. Some end up incarcerated."

The speech wicked the fury from Theodora's eyes. With a muttered oath, she buckled herself in. "Is this your way of saying you'll help me get a youth center off the ground?"

"And run it, on one condition."

"Which is?"

"I choose the location. The courthouse is no good. Police at the entrance, the hours of operation—kids who've been in trouble need a place where they're comfortable hanging out."

"You've given this some thought."

"I need a permanent job. Getting a youth center up and running won't be easy, but I would like to help kids like Glade."

"Still tutoring her?"

"Constantly. I'm no expert, but I'd guess she reads at a sixth grade level. Nowhere near as well as a kid like Blossom. A pity."

"There are lots of kids like Glade in the county."

"Exactly. The center can provide after school activities, leadership camps with local business owners, sessions at night for kids trying to finish high school or get on track to enter trade school or a four-year university—I've been researching programs in larger cities like Columbus. We'll need qualified staff. There are enough adults in Liberty to fill the slots, assuming the town's more successful adults will volunteer. You'll need to pressure Mayor Ryan for funding. Several of the social workers at Jobs & Family Services are keen to help if you get the mayor on board."

"Consider it done."

He slid a sidelong glance. "We also need wealthy benefactors. I'm counting on you to donate. Perhaps you'll reach out to other like-minded families in the county."

"Happy to help." She gave a sharp nod, her gaze softening. "Mind telling me why you're testy? A spat with Meade?"

"We're getting along fine. She's back in Atlanta. Comes home tomorrow."

"You mind all her travel?"

"Necessary evil to open the new distributorship." He wasn't sure how much rest a pregnant woman required. Meade was lucky if she got five hours a night. Not enough, surely.

"So why the foul mood?" she pressed. He veered her beloved Cadillac too close to the curb and she shouted, "Mind the road!"

Straightening the car out, he collected his thoughts. "I know she loves me," he said. "I'm not worried about when or if we'll marry. At some point, she'll decide we've dated long enough. We'll set a date."

"She's particular about following cockamamie rules she invents for herself."

"I get it. She follows steps in order. A to B to C. She's a linear thinker. We'll marry, we'll be happy—we'll love our jobs and each other. If we were, say, to have a kid, it wouldn't be a problem. I'll organize the youth center around our child's schedule. When Meade travels, we'll hire in help. It's not like money's a problem. Meade's got it covered."

"Son, don't start wishing on a star. At Meade's age, her ovaries are as shriveled as raisins."

"Could be," he hedged. Theodora was dead wrong, but he couldn't elaborate. Meade would decide when to reveal her pregnancy.

"Then what's made you as sour as rotten grapes?"

The question brought a memory to the surface.

Months ago, during the conversation by the lake, what had Landon said? *You may lack confidence in your abilities, but you strike me as a man with solid instincts.* Falling in love with Meade had given him more confidence in his instincts—more confidence in himself.

During the moments when he held her in his arms, he glimpsed the life they'd build together, a better life than he'd

200

have if she'd never walked into his life. But the dream wasn't enough. His solidly male instincts were taking a beating. What good was he if he didn't assume the role of provider for his wife and the child they'd soon bring into the world? Meade wasn't his, not yet, and her wealth promised to swaddle their child in comfort beyond what he could offer.

His role in their lives seemed secondary at best. At worst, it was unnecessary.

On a dull wave of heartache, he asked, "Theodora, do women need men?"

Nothing heroic about the query, and the wavering quality of his voice gave her pause.

"Do they?" he persisted.

She heaved out a sigh. "Does the earth need the sky? We aren't meant to spend our days alone. Even an independent woman like Meade needs someone to love. Oh, she'll never be much of a nester if you catch my drift. She won't bake brownies on Sundays or greet you at the door when you come home from work. If you want her, you'll have to take her on her own terms."

"I can deal with the terms if they stop changing. I'm never sure what deal I've struck."

"You mean Atlanta?"

"And Paris. She flies overseas in October, I guess. An annual buying trip."

Theodora gave a grunt of sympathy. "More travel than you anticipated. Hard to romance a woman when she's always packing her carry-on."

"I miss her when she leaves." The admission took a jab at his self-respect. As did the smile creeping across Theodora's face. "You don't have to look so amused. I didn't expect to take her travel schedule this hard."

"Go with her. I'm sure she'd like the company."

She'd offered to take him on this latest trip to Georgia. He'd declined out of pride more than anything else. "I can't follow her around like a private secretary," he admitted. "If we're going to make our relationship work, I need my own sphere of influence. I'm keeping busy."

"Good for you. A man willing to ride on his woman's coattails might as well hand her the family jewels. Carve out your own path, son. If you miss her while she's away, why, rest assured she misses you too. I've seen the way she looks at you. Loves you more than anything. Find your own way, and everything will work out."

The advice did little to lighten his mood. Half a mile from The Square, he steered the car onto Miller Road, a tree lined stretch once solely residential but now seeded with small businesses amidst the single-family homes. A graphic design firm shared a cottage-style house with an accountant. Several doors down, the owner of the consignment shop had set out a wrought iron patio set and a rack of women's sunhats on a tidy square of lawn. In between, the homes were owned by families proud to have achieved a basic promise of The American Dream. Flowerbeds of simple marigolds or petunias were neatly tended, and each small house was freshly painted or in the process of receiving other improvements.

At the end of the street, the acreage fanned out before a low slung brick building with a FOR SALE sign in front.

Theodora got out of the Cadillac, her palm open. After Hector returned the keys to her cherished Cadillac, she said, "This place was Liberty's original bowling alley. Built before you were born. When the new bowling alley opened closer to The Square, a mechanic took this place over."

"What happened to him?"

"Retired, about two years ago. It's been vacant ever since."

"I think it's perfect for our needs."

"What's the asking price?"

He told her then added, "Mayor Ryan has funds from Parks & Recreation she's willing to donate for the purchase. Most of the churches and the synagogue will also pitch in. I'm hoping you will too. Heck, I'm counting on it. The local Girl Scouts promised to hold fundraisers, and several women's groups will host events. I'm waiting to hear back from The Boy Scouts. A number of men's groups are also willing to help, both with funding and running programs."

"You've been busy."

Working on the youth center kept his mind off the pregnancy and his frustration waiting for Meade to come around and marry him. He hadn't officially dropped down on bended knee to propose—why bother? When she was ready to settle down, she'd tell him.

Like it or not, his child wouldn't enter the world bearing the Levendakis name. The prospect made him a failure in ways he preferred not to contemplate.

A tan BMW glided to a halt before the building, and he set his personal troubles aside. "I asked the realtor to meet us," he said, taking Theodora's arm. "Care to look inside?"

She hooked her arm through his. "I would like a tour before opening my checkbook," she agreed.

Spreading out the blanket for their impromptu picnic, Hector asked, "Are you happy with the design for the renovations?"

With admirable resourcefulness, he'd discovered the tranquil spot by the gurgling waters of the Chagrin River. Ten miles outside Liberty, the isolated meadow was in the park system that formed an emerald necklace around northeast Ohio. Birds twittered in the fir trees. A rabbit hopped out of the forest to feast on a patch of clover.

From the picnic basket Meade withdrew two bottles of water. "I like the design Gavin Abrams is putting together," she said of the architect hired by her father. "The building is twice the size of what I'll need initially to open the southern distributorship. Gavin has it well thought out. We'll renovate half of the space this year. At a later date, we'll finish the rest. There's no sense spending the money until I secure more clients in Georgia and the surrounding states. Norling's stores are just the beginning."

"When do you fly back down?"

"Next week," she supplied, hating the way her reply thinned his mouth. Hector never complained about the demands on her schedule, but his disappointment was plain enough. "Just for one day. I'll fly back the following afternoon."

"Find time to talk to Glade. After the baby is born, she's thinking about getting an apartment with Delia and one of Delia's friends. Three young women pooling their resources with a newborn in tow."

"They can't be serious. Glade's eighteen years old and will need help with the baby. Help from mature adults—not two young women with busy social lives."

Hector took a sip of water then set the bottle aside. "She's bored, Meade. The job at The Second Chance is working out. Finney's willing to give her a flexible schedule. Part-time, with more hours whenever Glade is ready. If Glade lives in town it'll be easier for her to work and find a babysitter."

"There's a woman on Mary's street who watches children in her home." Meade couldn't recall the woman's name. Older, retired, she had an impeccable reputation. "For years she's watched children, including infants. Mary plans to use her services once her baby arrives."

"There, you see? Glade has a good reason for wanting to live in town. Not that I think an apartment with Delia makes sense. I wish we could find her a room to rent in a house with older adults."

"Ethel Lynn's home is within walking distance of The Second Chance. She has spare bedrooms."

Hector shook his head. "Not Ethel Lynn—too high strung. Having a baby under her roof won't work out."

"I can't think of anyone else I trust." She'd hate to see Glade leave the estate, but the girl's needs were understandable. Living twenty minutes outside Liberty was a hardship. Thinking of something else, she added, "I need to buy her a car."

"Can she drive?"

"She has a license. I have no idea if her skills are up to snuff. Who knows when she was last behind the wheel?"

"Odds are, they aren't. After she passes the GED, I'll take her out on the road. New drivers need lots of practice." He smiled. "Best if we take this one step at a time."

The suggestion reassured. Hector may have drifted through too many careers, but he was a caring man. He'd taken to Glade— taken to Liberty—with full dedication. Did he miss Philadelphia's faster pace, the city's energy and the friends left behind? Occasionally he mentioned his sister and extended relatives but not often, not as often as he talked about Birdie and Hugh, the steady growth of the *Liberty Post* and the newbies still learning their jobs. He chatted with Finney whenever he met Theodora at the restaurant for lunch or dinner. Between the two women, he was privy to more town gossip than Meade. In fact, his romance with Meade had smoothed the hard edges of her relationships with both women, neither of whom had ever thought much of her. Or perhaps it was Meade who was changing, her personality blooming like a tight bud brought into the sunlight and nourished with the proper quantities of love and acceptance. Whenever Hector was near, a lightness of spirit unfurled inside her.

Drawing her from her thoughts, he reclined on the blanket and waggled his brows. A welcome invitation, and she joined him eagerly. Face to face, he draped his arm across her hip.

"We've locked up the purchase of the old bowling alley," he said before she might question the sudden intimacy. In three months of dating, they'd traded nothing but kisses ripe with longing. "Some of the men from The Rotary Club volunteered to help with carpentry. We're building three rooms to use for classrooms and presentations."

"What about the bowling alley's lanes? Are you tearing them out?"

"We're cleaning up five lanes and removing the rest."

"Why keep five?" she asked, acutely aware of his hand gliding across the indentation of her waist.

"We'll keep a few lanes so kids can bowl for free. I'd like to bring in a pool table, maybe two. The youth center will offer counseling and coursework, but also provide a safe place to socialize. I'm thinking about asking teens to drop their smartphones at the door. If they can't text nonstop, who knows? They might learn the art of conversation."

"What about the twenty-somethings?"

"Too much of an imposition. They're adults. I can't hold their technology hostage."

"I'll donate the pool tables." If he continued awakening her senses with his roving touch, she'd pay to refurbish the bowling lanes too.

"I hoped you'd offer to help." He toyed with a lock of hair by her cheek, his soft brown eyes growing softer still. "How's the morning sickness? You haven't mentioned it in days."

"Same old, same old."

"Getting worse?"

"Some days. It's miserable. I've stopped taking appointments before 11 A.M. If this keeps up, my employees will become suspicious before I make an announcement."

"You aren't worried about your employees." Hector rested his hand at the base of her neck, his lips a breath away from hers. "Landon's the problem. Once you tell your father, he'll ask the obvious question."

"Why we don't marry?" He would ask. More likely, he'd demand an explanation as to why they hadn't set a date.

"Can you blame him? He'll expect me to make an honest woman of you. Tell him I'm waiting at the altar whenever you're ready to mosey up the aisle."

"Mosey." She chuckled. "You're spending too much time with Theodora. It's something she'd say."

"Don't get me thinking about Theodora. It'll throw me off my game."

"What game are you playing?" She'd gladly play along.

He kissed her lightly. Then he shocked her by unbuttoning her blouse with single-minded focus, his gaze latching on the lacy edge of her bra. Heat fanned across her skin.

"What are you doing?" she blustered. He seared her collarbone with a kiss, and she gasped.

Guiding her onto her back, he planted his palms on either side of her face. "Making love to you." He paused for effect. "Slowly and thoroughly."

"I thought you were planning to court me properly."

"Change of plans. It's crossed my mind you may not understand the depths of my devotion. A demonstration is in order."

Dizzy, she draped her arms around his shoulders. "Don't keep me waiting."

At the tree line a doe stepped from the forest's gloom to nibble the clover growing thick in the field. The doe was untroubled by the soft moans and tender endearments rising from the grass as the larks and the cardinals twittered in the trees.

❧

They made love until the crickets sang a hearty chorus in the meadow and dying bands of gold slanted through the fir trees. Hector wrapped the blanket around them, bundling them in a tight cocoon. Purple martins took to the sky, swooping and arcing high to feast on clouds of mosquitoes.

In the untouched picnic basket, Meade's smartphone rang. She untangled herself from the blanket.

It was Glade. Listening to the girl's rapid-fire explanation, Meade snatched up the clothing tossed across the blanket. Following her cue, Hector dressed quickly.

"We'll be right there," she assured the girl. Snapping the phone shut, she regarded Hector. "Glade's in labor."

"How long?"

"Since this morning." She wrenched the blanket out from under him, sending him stumbling onto the grass. "Who goes into labor at 6 A.M. and waits until 8 P.M. to tell anyone?"

"A teenager who'd rather see her friends than spend the night in pain. Can't blame her for a last grab at denial." He fetched the picnic basket. "Take a deep breath. You won't do her any favors if she sees you're anxious. Relax. We'll get her to the hospital on time."

During the drive to the estate, they took a call from an agitated Reenie and another from an increasingly frightened Glade. They also tracked down Glade's obstetrician. As luck would have it, she'd finished a delivery an hour ago and was in the hospital cafeteria eating dinner.

Before Hector parked in front of the mansion, Meade leapt to the pavement. She vaulted up the steps with her pulse ringing like church bells.

In the foyer Glade and Reenie huddled together.

Glade's shoulders rose to her ears on the fearsome wave of a contraction. "I don't like this. It didn't hurt real bad until right before I called you."

A lock of hair swam in the perspiration glossing her brow. Brushing it back, Meade said, "Everything will be fine. Your OB is waiting at the hospital." To Reenie, she asked, "Are you timing the contractions?"

The housekeeper flinched. "Oh, dear. The contractions. I forgot to time them." Blinking rapidly, she reached for the suitcase at Glade's feet. "I did pack her things. Should I go with you?"

"Do you mind staying here? If Daddy needs anything, he'll be upset if we've all left."

Glade doubled over. "Ouch! I really felt that one!"

Hector dashed inside. In his haste, he let go of the doorknob. The door cracked against the wall before swinging back and slamming shut.

"What are we waiting for?" he demanded, jumping as his smartphone rang. He spun in a circle, stared at Meade's bag then fished his cell out of the back pocket of his jeans. "Yeah. Yeah, it's me. No, we've got it covered. Glade's doctor is there. Another delivery, right." Pulling the phone from his lips, he told Meade, "I called Mary."

"Tell her she doesn't have to go in."

"Got it."

"Oww! That really hurt! How much worse will this get?"

On the mansion's second floor, the pounding of feet grew loud. A pounding like elephants, a furious stampede.

Muttering curses, Meade's father rounded the corner. At the top of the grand staircase, he ground to a halt. His hair stood on end and his eyes blazed.

A sensation of doom clenched Meade's stomach.

After months of skirting past Glade in a sulk, all the silent looks like daggers and churlish spells of pouting, he was now livid. Of all the times to lose his temper—he'd chosen precisely the worst moment. There wasn't time to placate him, not with Glade clutching her belly and whimpering with fear.

"What is all this racket?" he bellowed. "I can't hear myself think!"

Meade flew toward the stairwell. "Daddy, we're leaving. The house will be quiet in a moment."

"I want it quiet *now!* Doors slamming, people shouting—I'm not running a saloon. If a man can't have peace and quiet in his own . . ."

His rage careened into a dark, deathly silence. The void left behind altered the molecules suspended between him and the chastised group watching from below. The moment froze.

Fear shivered across Meade's skin. But her father looked

most surprised of all.

His mouth drooped on a slurred, incomprehensible word. Staggering, he clutched for the rail. The support was frighteningly out of reach of his tall, and now unwieldy, body.

He collapsed to the floor.

Chapter 14

Bawling lustily, Natasha Reenie Wilson was born seven minutes after her mother was rushed into the maternity ward. She weighed a strapping nine pounds, seven ounces.

Three stories below in the ER, Landon Williams received a life-saving injection of tPA, *tissue plasminogen activator,* to break up the blood clot causing his stroke. Once he was stabilized, he was transferred to the cerebrovascular unit on the fifth floor.

Soon the baby nuzzled contently at her mother's breast. Landon's prognosis was unknown.

Tired of wearing tracks in the Williams' kitchen floor, Mary stretched her arms over her head. "May I have an iced water?" She joined Reenie at the kitchen's center island.

The housekeeper plunked ice in a glass, her face drawn and the grey tendrils on her scalp in disarray. Mary suspected she hadn't slept in days.

In the servants' quarters below, Blossom and Delia were keeping Glade and her energetic baby company. For her part, Natasha entertained her female adorers with the fidgeting of dimpled hands and the squirming of plump legs. All morning long she'd given her lungs a workout with periods of ear-curdling tears. Her pudgy cheeks and red lips made the transgressions easy to forgive. Her eyes—when they weren't shut tight with teary agitation—were a most fetching shade of marine blue.

Sipping the water, Mary gave the housekeeper an appraising look. "Reenie, you don't have to wait with me. Why don't you lie down? You look like you need a nap."

Reenie followed her back to the table. "Don't try to dissuade me from my duty. They'll be here any moment."

"It might be another hour."

The last time Mary had checked, Meade was completing the discharge paperwork and chatting with the full-time nurse who'd met her at the hospital for the ride home. The man came highly recommended from the visiting nurse service.

"Doesn't matter if it's another two hours. I couldn't sleep if God Himself demanded it." The housekeeper attempted a smile. She failed miserably. "Such a heartbreaking situation. I'm not sure who I'm more worried about, Meade or Mr. Williams. Meade, I think."

Her concern was understandable. Since her father's stroke, Meade had only left the hospital for short stints at work. Each night she curled in a chair by her father's hospital bed; in the morning she patiently fed him and kept up a cheery stream of conversation. When Landon tried to respond, his eyes first glowing with frustration before dulling with fear, she patted the perspiration from his brow and feathered her hand over his receding hairline until his face grew peaceful.

No one better understood Landon's pride or his need for propriety, and Meade shooed the nurses from the room in the early evening to give her father a sponge bath and gently wash his feet. She insisted a male nurse was in charge to take her father to the toilet.

Birdie also visited and so did Theodora, but Landon relied on his older daughter. He was frightened by the decline in his health, his right arm motionless at his side and his mouth drooping from the ravages of the stroke. He cried easily.

Drawing from her musings, Mary said, "Don't fret too much over Meade. She's a strong woman. She'll come through this in one piece."

"Mr. Williams is lucky to have her. She's never let him down, not in all the years I've known her."

"He's lucky he got to the hospital in time. A blood clot can be deadly."

"It breaks my heart to see how hard he's been trying to speak. Will he regain the ability?"

"Too soon to tell. Once he receives therapy, we'll have a better idea." Privately Mary was more concerned about his cognitive functioning. He was experiencing a delay in responding to cues, and was having trouble focusing his attention for more than short periods.

"When will therapy start?"

"Next week, if he's up to it. If not, we'll wait. He's still very weak."

Blossom appeared at the top of the stairwell. In her arms, the sleeping baby nestled in a pink blanket.

"I'm holding her the right way," she said before Mary could protest.

Mary patted the chair beside hers. "Do my nerves a service and sit down, please." She checked to ensure Blossom was supporting Natasha's head properly. Satisfied, she added, "You're doing a great job."

The compliment brightened Blossom's eyes. "I love how she smells. Clean and really sweet." She nuzzled the baby's cheek. "She's yummy."

"Babies usually are."

She kissed Natasha's tiny nose. "I can't wait until our baby comes. I wish you'd hurry."

Reenie said, "Don't rush your mother. She'll have her baby in due time."

"Spring is too far away."

Mary quirked a brow. "Babies don't stay small and cuddly. They become troublesome toddlers. Your love affair might be a short fling."

Reenie looked from one to the other. "Troublesome toddlers?"

"It's a show Blossom likes. Teenagers shoot video of siblings during the worst of toddler behavior."

"I'm done watching the show." Blossom rubbed her nose across Natasha's creamy brow. "Babies are addictive. I want to keep this one. She's so cute."

Mary took the baby and started for the servants' quarters.

"Let's get this beauty back to her mother. Glade probably wonders if you've kidnapped her pride and joy."

She returned in time to hear a car door slam outside. In the foyer, Meade's voice was followed by the clatter of the wheelchair. Mary went with Reenie to greet them.

The male nurse, a swarthy giant with limpid eyes the color of sand, drew the wheelchair to a stop in the center of the foyer. Reenie murmured something to Landon. He looked dazed, the folds of skin surrounding his eyes carved in deep grooves of distress. Behind the wheelchair, Meade and Birdie chatted in quiet voices.

Mary urged the sisters toward the library. "We'll take it from here," she said, motioning to Reenie. The nurse had already lifted Landon from the wheelchair for the climb to the second floor.

Meade wasn't easily put off. "I'd better go with you."

Birdie took her by the hand and forcibly pulled her toward the library. "No, you don't. Let Mary handle this. Daddy's in capable hands."

Within minutes Landon was settled in his bedroom. Reenie, ever thoughtful, showed the nurse the oversized rocking chair. Mary checked Landon's pulse and temperature. Both were normal, and she patted his arm as his eyes drifted shut. Excusing herself, she went downstairs.

In the library, Birdie was reclined on the couch with her ankles crossed. Meade was spinning through messages on her smartphone.

"Where's Hector?" Mary assumed he'd meet them at the house.

Meade appeared too engrossed in her task to reply. Birdie said: "He offered to come home with us. Meade argued with him at the hospital."

Meade stalked to the bar and stared at the bottles lined up on the glass shelves. "Don't exaggerate. We weren't arguing."

"You were, and you hurt his feelings. He's only trying to help."

"He has a meeting with Mayor Ryan. It's more important." Out of habit, Meade took down the vodka and a martini glass. "The mayor has suggestions for the youth center she wants to share with him."

"He would've rescheduled. He wanted to be here when we brought Daddy home."

Meade studied the bottle of vodka then returned it to the shelf. "What I'd give for a martini."

The comment put Mary on alert. Something was wrong. "Go ahead and have a drink," she said, sliding onto a barstool. "You've certainly earned it."

"I can't."

"Why not?"

On the couch, Birdie reclined fully and kicked off her tennis shoes. "Have you sworn off Hector *and* booze?" she asked tartly. "Putting yourself in a convent won't help Daddy. Why don't you loosen up?"

"Stop baiting me."

"I will, in a moment." Birdie pounded a throw pillow into submission and stuck it behind her head. "First, I want to know why you're pushing Hector away. You've been snitty to him since Daddy's stroke. I've never seen him this blue. Are you on the outs?"

"It's none of your business."

Needing to intercede, Mary hopped off the barstool and went to Meade. Looping her arm around her friend's waist, she led her to the couch opposite of Birdie.

After they were both seated, Mary said, "Talk to us." She threw a warning look at Birdie. "No one is attacking you. We're asking why you're upset."

Briefly Meade closed her eyes. "I should've known."

Mary patted her knee. "Known what?"

"How sick Daddy was. I feel like . . . it's hard to explain. I guess I feel negligent in some basic way. Why didn't I do something, take him for a check-up or notice he wasn't feeling well? He's my responsibility. I've been too wrapped up in my own life." She heaved out a breath thick with regret. "I let him down."

"A stroke isn't a predictable event. There's nothing you could've done."

"I don't believe that."

The pain etched in the comment erased the irritation from

Birdie's face. In a contrite voice, she said, "Geez, sis. Is that why you're taking it out on Hector? You think you failed Daddy?"

Not the most diplomatic comment, and Meade grimaced. "I was having enough trouble juggling a romance with the demands of my job," she admitted. "Now Daddy's ill, seriously ill, and we have a long road ahead. He needs me, Birdie. He loves you too, but he doesn't expect you to take care of him. It's different for me."

"You've brought in a nurse, and he has Reenie too. You don't have to do everything."

"I need to supervise them, ensure he's well cared for."

"Supervise." Birdie drew out the word with distaste. "Do you ever give yourself a break? Leave Reenie in charge tonight and go to Hector. Make love for hours in his RV. Forget your troubles and stay over. Wake up in his arms."

Mary put in, "They've decided to wait for intimacy."

"We didn't wait."

The disclosure put all eyes on Meade. Her expression churning, she dropped her hands to her lap. She wasn't comfortable revealing the most private details of her life, certainly not with her younger sister. They'd only been acquainted for one, short year. While they'd grown closer, they rarely shared confidences. They didn't share the rapport Meade enjoyed with Mary.

At last Meade said, "We made love the day of Daddy's stroke." At Mary's surprise, she added, "Yes, I remember what we talked about at your office. I didn't initiate, I swear. It was Hector's idea. I thought we were having a picnic like usual. He changed the agenda."

Birdie scrambled into a sitting position. "And?"

"It was wonderful."

"Talk about mixed signals. You go the distance then push him away. What's he supposed to think?"

"Birdie, I have no idea. I can't think about Hector when Daddy is in such bad shape. What am I supposed to do? Plan a wedding between Daddy's visits to physical therapy? What about my career? Next Wednesday I'm scheduled to fly to Atlanta. I'm meeting with the architect and vetting construction companies. My life is more complicated than yours. Why can't you understand?"

Birdie huffed at the barb, but Mary's attention hung on the impassioned speech. "Would you like to marry?" she asked. "Hector does care for you deeply. If you want my opinion, you're perfectly suited for each other."

Confusion lowered Meade's gaze to her lap. For nearly a week, she'd kept a vigil at the hospital, praying her father's condition would improve. During the rare hours when she left his side, she visited Glade and Natasha. Or she rushed to the office to keep her staff from drowning in work. The opportunity to process the idyllic moments spent with Hector on the day of the picnic . . . when would she have found time to probe the contents of her heart? She'd reveled in a short, sweet hour of bliss. Ever since, she'd been consumed by responsibilities.

Mary, waiting for a reply, bumped her shoulder against Meade's. A playful gesture, and Birdie, waiting on tenterhooks, said, "Answer the question, sis. Are you thinking about marriage?"

"No. Yes. I should." She nearly blurted the truth about her pregnancy. She didn't dare. Not while her emotions were in turmoil. Deftly she said, "We might wed next year, after Daddy's better and I've opened the Atlanta office."

Birdie swatted the response like a pesky fly. "Oh, please. You're stalling. You love Hector. Set a date. While you're at it, apologize to him. Do it in something lacey. Men like see-through nighties."

"I don't own a see-through nighty."

"This far into a relationship, it's probably a sin if you don't. Let's go shopping tomorrow. You'll buy something sexy, and Hector will forgive you for treating him badly."

"Birdie, I'm too old for the sex kitten routine."

Her sister threw her hands into the air. "That's the problem. You think you're old. You're not."

Meade's smartphone rang. Reading the number, she groaned. "It's Nels, in Atlanta. I can't deal with him right now. He wants the numbers on house brand moisturizer and bath salts. I haven't worked them up." She flung the cell phone back into her purse.

"Don't talk to him at all," Birdie said. "Forget about Atlanta's premier department store. *Vivid* has enough accounts in Ohio. You don't need an astrologer to see the stars are *not* aligned for an expansion. While you're at it, sell the building in Atlanta."

"I can't! Daddy went to a lot of expense purchasing the property."

"Think he cares now? He's ill. He won't improve without you egging him on. He'll hate it when you travel, and there's France to consider. You have to go this fall, right? A buying trip for next spring's orders? Marry Hector, take care of Daddy, and slow down on *Vivid's* expansion. It was a good idea at the time. Now it's just plain stupid."

"She has a point," Mary put in.

She did, but Meade refused to agree.

In Hector's estimation, success in romance was never guaranteed. Sometimes life got in the way, setting up roadblocks and detour signs, making the journey's end hard to reach. Other times, two people fell in love but they didn't navigate well together; they disagreed about whether to take the highway, saving time, or a meandering route to waste time. There was no telling how it all would work out, not in the early stages of a relationship and maybe never. Couples reached their destination if they were endowed with a special fuel, determination or dedication or an ungrounded trust in their powers of navigation no matter how often they lost sight of love's signposts.

Hector knew he'd been lost plenty of times. Somehow he always found his way. He'd failed at two marriages. He wasn't doing much better with Meade, but he didn't dwell on his disappointment. In the week since her father's release from the hospital, Meade rarely called and begged off most evenings. A pessimist might entertain thoughts of breaking it off, but Hector liked to think he walked on the sunny side of the street. Soon Meade's pregnancy would begin to show, and she'd have no choice but to announce the baby's paternity.

The reality of her situation—an expectant mother, with a loving man waiting in the wings—was sure to melt her resistance to the idea of marriage.

There were other reasons to avoid wallowing in self-pity.

For the first time in his life, he was encountering success in his professional life.

Through a combination of county funds, Theodora's largesse, and donations from churches and private citizens alike, the town of Liberty completed the purchase of the old bowling alley.

The youth center was on its way.

As news spread, townspeople visited the center to donate time to renovate the building and volunteer to run programs. The high school PTO held a fundraiser to outfit the computer lab. Gangly Timmy Dever, the junior high basketball team's point guard, took it upon himself to go door-to-door, raising funds for sports equipment, including a basketball hoop that Hector gladly hung on the side of the building. At The Second Chance Grill, Finney stuck a basket by the cash register with one of Blossom's homemade posters requesting donations. Her efforts and the poster, a glittery mess with a snapshot of the youth center glued to the center, raised enough cash for the purchase of art supplies, used desks and a new couch Hector bought on clearance.

Meade continued to beg off on dates, but he was rarely lonely. The town was rooting for the center's success. Their support made each day satisfying.

This morning he found Anthony and Blossom waiting outside the center. They were trading jokes and sugaring up with a box of donuts. A variety of sledgehammers and a bag of white masks were at their feet.

Hector unlocked the front door. "You're not letting the kid swing a sledgehammer, are you? She might take out a kneecap."

"She's my cleanup crew. Some of her friends will stop by to help. Might as well keep them all busy during the last weeks of summer vacation."

Blossom shrugged. "Slave labor. What can I do?"

Hector grinned. "Start by helping me wash down the kitchen while your father tears out the wall by the bowling lanes. It won't be much of a hardship, promise."

Anthony tousled her curls. "You'll survive, amiga." To Hector, he said, "Delia's father and some of the guys in his bowling league will come by this afternoon to frame in the computer lab and the art room. Expect them by four 'o clock."

"Are they bringing supplies? I got a donation of paint and particleboard, but nothing else."

"They'll bring lumber. They all pitched in to cover the cost."

"Sounds great."

They parted ways. Blossom followed Hector to the kitchen.

The room was a simple affair with a large grill in decent shape and an oven they planned to remove. It was beyond ancient. The cupboards were spotless, thanks to one of the local Girl Scout Troops. They'd left behind paper products and a box of thin mint cookies.

Blossom picked up a neatly typed sheet on the counter. "Hector, what's this?"

"The volunteer list." Everyone from the high school art teacher to a local CPA had volunteered to run after school and evening programs. "We'll start with programs for kids your age and older."

"What about little kids?"

"Maybe someday. For now, the center will target older kids and young adults."

"Delia says you'll have a class on budgeting money. She wants to take it."

"Starting in October."

"Will you have a class to teach kids like me how to babysit infants? No one lets me hold Natasha for more than five minutes. Glade looks at me like I'm wearing a ski mask and Natasha is the loot. Mom's worse. She acts like I'll drop the baby. If I get certification, they'll relax."

Adding a basic childcare class wasn't a bad idea. "Planning to become an expert before your mother has her baby?"

"I should be able to hold the peewee, right? It's only fair."

"I'll see if I can put something together." He tweaked her nose. "Are we chatting or working? Why don't you wash down the counters? I'll scrub the grill."

Soon the scent of lavender wafted through the kitchen, compliments of the organic cleaner someone had donated. They'd nearly finished washing down the kitchen when Theodora marched in with a sack of sandwiches and a jug of her homemade lemonade. Hector's stomach rumbled. Since Meade's disappearance from his dinner table, he rarely cooked. Most of the time, he forgot to eat.

"How was rehab?" He knew Landon was scheduled to begin therapy today.

"Cancelled." She took two sandwiches and handed them to Blossom. "Take these to your father, will you?"

Blossom left, and he tossed the rag into the bucket of soapy water at his feet. Worry dampened his mood. Theodora needed to speak to him in private. Whatever the topic, it was too upsetting for a child's ears.

She confirmed his worst suspicions. "Landon's health is declining." In the cupboard she found a bag of Styrofoam cups. Opening the bag, she poured them each a glass of lemonade. "Yesterday he went back to the hospital for more tests."

He drank then set the cup aside. "Are they worried about another stroke?"

"I don't believe so. The tests were fine. Mary is sending him home this afternoon."

"It's probably nothing. He'll start rehab in a few days."

"I don't think so. When folks reach a certain age, nothing has to go wrong to make them give up. They plain run out of steam. Some do their best to run out. A hard choice, but they make it."

"Not Landon. He's got Meade and Birdie. It's not like he's alone."

"Hells bells. You act like a man's love for his daughters will keep him standing. I know Landon better than anyone, and you're wrong. Looking in his eyes, why, I can read his mind plainly."

The turn of conversation was upsetting. Hector didn't like the gravelly fear in Theodora's voice or the way her eyes flitted like sparrows rousted by a predator.

"What are you trying to say?" he asked.

"The stroke stole most of what Landon took for granted, freedom of movement and his ability to spout off whenever he pleases. He knows there isn't a physical therapist on earth that can give him back everything he's lost. He'll never be the man he was."

"He'll have a good life regardless."

"Hector, some people don't agree to life's bargain. They live on their own terms, or they don't live at all."

Sorrow bolted through her expression like an electric current, twitching the muscles around her mouth and convulsing the wrinkles of her brow. She was no less proud than Landon, maybe prouder. Yet the strength of her personality couldn't withstand the grief swimming in her eyes. She wasn't the sort of woman who looked kindly on tears—she was more apt to threaten your ass with buckshot than reveal her more vulnerable nature—but her love for Landon was too great, their friendship hard-worn and solid. If anyone understood Landon's intentions, it was Theodora.

With misgiving, Hector turned her words over in his mind. Was death seeking Landon?

Was he willingly running toward it?

Chapter 15

"**W**hat do you think, Daddy? Nice, yes?"

Meade placed the pot of miniature roses on the nightstand. They were called Rainbow's End. The buttery yellow petals were tinged with fiery orange, the leaves a rich profusion of emerald. The cultivar was one of Landon's favorites, a prolific bloomer removed from the greenhouse and carried upstairs like so many other plants, the cheery pots of roses and the larger, leafy houseplants he'd nurtured to jungle-size before his stroke.

For days now, the winding staircase and the upstairs hallway wore a dusting of potting soil from Meade's travels between the vigorous life greening downstairs and the shadowed, unspeakable danger permeating her father's bedroom.

Life and death, light and dark—she traveled uncomfortably between opposite realms. Each day Landon's skin became greyer while she, why, she was like the plants festooned throughout the bedroom, bursting with life. Was the baby growing inside her a miniature version of herself, or more like Hector? Or a blend of their physical attributes and personalities, a play of opposites like the energies mixing in the bedroom, the scent of grief easy to ignore beneath the fragrance of the tiny rosebuds bobbing by her father's sunken cheeks and the damp aroma of the pothos tumbling across the dresser.

Landon had given up on trying to speak. The malformed syllables dropping from his lips were too great an embarrassment. He was too weak to write on the notepad she'd left on the blanket. They'd resorted to the most basic form of communication, eye movements and squeezing fingertips to convey agreement or disagreement. Birdie, when she visited, quickly grew frustrated by her inability to understand her father's needs. Meade never wavered. She understood when he was tired or needed company, when he'd had enough of the chicken soup Reenie made by the gallon, preferring instead to listen to his older daughter's one-sided conversation about *Vivid* and Hector's progress with the youth center.

Time and again Meade nearly revealed she was pregnant. Doing so seemed unfair. The topic was too light amidst her dark thoughts about the awful possibility of planning a funeral and saying goodbye to the father she loved.

"It's pretty, yes?" she said of the rose. She wasn't ready for goodbyes. Her father squeezed her fingers and she added, "I ground up eggshells in the food processor and mixed them in the soil. Just like you do. I left a mess all over Reenie's kitchen."

Another light pressing of her fingers. *Good.*

With care she lifted his head and plumped the pillows. His eyes closed with pleasure before opening again to alight on her face with a child's eager curiosity. No, she wasn't ready. He must improve. Get out of bed, get on with life. He was ten years younger than Theodora. His death would be yet another event out of order, like the baby curled in her womb as she stood on the edge of middle age, like the younger sister she would've spoiled if she'd known of Birdie's existence when they were children. She should've met Hector before her career leafed out and she tended a garden of opportunities, the multi-million dollar deals and the company's expansion. Out of order, all of it, and she felt unmoored from her feelings, unsure if she still trusted her heart or understood her deepest needs.

"Daddy, I met with Nels yesterday." She drew a breath for courage then added, "I returned the contracts. He was upset, naturally. You see, it's not the right time for *Vivid* to enter the southern states. I can't give the expansion the proper focus. I've cut back on my hours at the office."

Against her palm, her father's hand grew limp. *I'm disappointed.*

She hurried on. "Hector doesn't know yet, but he'll be happy. He hates when I travel. I have no choice on the Paris trip in October, but I'm staying put until then. It's almost September, and I need to organize. If I don't, how will I know what to buy from my French suppliers? I hated to disappoint Nels, but I must take care of my established customers here in Ohio. They're the core of *Vivid's* business model. They come first."

Her rationale wasn't readily accepted. Closing his eyes, Landon turned his face away.

She left him brooding and went downstairs. Mary was at the bottom of the stairwell typing a text message.

She shook her head with frustration. "Blossom is driving me batty. She says she needs intel on the baby's sex for a stenciling project. As if I'd tell her even if I knew."

"Explain it to her."

"Impossible. She's convinced I have magical powers and must know if I'm having a boy or a girl. Why can't the new school year begin a.s.a.p? Kids have too much free time."

"What is the stenciling project?"

Mary plowed her hand through her glossy chestnut hair. "For the nursery. You know, the nursery I'm supposed to use that's decorated like a carnival ride? Blossom wants to stencil the baby's name in a border across the top of the elephant wallpaper. Lily or Tony, all over the place. Next she'll want to cover the door in glitter. She's on a binge with anything sparkly."

Meade was glad for the momentary respite from worry. "Why not take her shopping for new school clothes?" she asked lightly. "Get her mind off the baby."

"Good advice. I think I will." Mary glanced up the stairwell. "How is he?"

"Upset." She explained about her decision to halt work in Atlanta. Finishing, she said, "Birdie was correct—now isn't the proper time. Daddy needs me, and I want to be there for him. As for the expansion, I told the architect we might resume work on the building next spring."

With a doctor's practiced calm, Mary nailed down the topic they'd been avoiding. "Meade, I'm concerned your father may only have a few more months. He's not improving. His health is declining."

"A temporary setback." She thought of the sensation she encountered in his bedroom, the frightening notion death crouched unseen in the corner, calmly and without mercy, waiting for her to turn away, waiting to take her beloved father. Tamping down the fear, she straightened her spine. "No one bounces back quickly from a stroke. We should stay positive."

"Did the nurse get him up and moving today?"

"I'm not sure. Daddy hasn't come downstairs if that's what you mean."

"Is he relying on a bedpan or walking to the bathroom? Preferably it's the latter."

The familiar heaviness settled on Meade's shoulders. Not once had she asked the nurse, a quiet, gentle giant, for specifics on the daily routine. Admittedly, she'd been afraid to do so. After a lengthy pause, she said, "I think he's using the bedpan most of the time."

"His vitals are within the acceptable range. He should be improving. I'd suggest more tests, but they won't tell me anything new."

"What can you do to help?"

"Not much, I'm sorry to say. Medical outcomes are influenced by desire. Healing takes work, and Landon isn't motivated to heal. He needs to walk—outside, if you can manage it. The fresh air would do him good. If you get him moving, we'll begin working with the physical therapist. Your father may not regain full mobility, but he's decreasing the odds of any improvement by remaining bedridden. Starting small, say, ten minutes of walking a day, would be a good start."

As she went over the options, talking more for her own edification than anything else, Meade narrowed her attention. Shadows, as faint a blue as a butterfly's wings, formed half circles beneath Mary's eyes. Her coloring, usually a warm pink, was off.

"Are you ill?" Meade asked suddenly. She wasn't sure why she'd ask. The moment she did, ice pricked her skin.

Mary stopped talking midsentence. "I'm not sure," she admitted. "I haven't felt right all afternoon."

"Then why are you here? It's after six o'clock. Go home to your husband and crazy daughter. You need the rest."

"I will, after I check your father."

Oddly, the hairs on the back of Meade's neck prickled. "I wish you'd go now," she said, trying to make light of her concern. "Are you running a temperature? Perhaps we should check."

"It's a summer bug. No temp—I'm sure. Whatever it is, I promise not to infect your father." She kissed Meade on the cheek and started up the stairwell. "I'll be out of here in ten minutes, promise." On the landing, she glanced down and grinned. "Don't wait to show me out. There's someone else you ought to see. Honestly, you should schedule a hearing test."

Meade was about to ask for a further explanation when she heard Hector's voice in the distance. He was singing a lullaby.

Excusing herself, she walked through the dining room and out to the patio, washed golden by the setting sun. Hector was seated with Natasha held firmly between his hands, dangling happily in the air. The baby's deep blue eyes were riveted on his face.

"Hector." He turned, surprised, and she laughed. "Where's Glade?"

"Reenie and Delia took her to the movies. You're looking at the babysitter." He angled the baby into the crook of his right arm with the finesse of an experienced grandmother. "What are you doing here? I thought you were in Atlanta."

"Cancelled."

"Tomorrow then?"

She told him about her decision. He listened passively, his attention returning to the baby gurgling in his arms. She wondered at how much she'd hurt him by staying away, staying close to her father instead.

Unlike Mary, with butterfly wings of fatigue beneath her eyes and a yellowish cast to her skin, Hector was ruddy with good health, his skin bronzed and his eyes bright. The heartache she'd caused him wasn't powerful enough to affect his health; certainly not in the way a lifetime of temper tantrums had caused her father to have a stroke and the demands of caring for patients had worn down Mary.

Had her absence hurt him at all? He looked vital and strong, his profile caught by the setting sun, the bands of gold filtering across the mouth she missed kissing. Usually she was adept at compartmentalizing her emotions, but her muscles were weary from the long day and the heat passing through her ribcage was too intense, fanning down to her thighs then upward, until her neck and her ears were hot with the yearning she'd diligently suppressed.

"You're good with babies," she heard herself say. Natasha remained fixed on Hector's face like a traveler drawn to the North Star. "You'll have to teach me."

"With our baby?" he asked, and she detected a note of forgiveness in the phrase, *our baby,* forgiveness she didn't deserve. "I doubt it. You'll be a natural."

"Guess again. I have no experience with children."

"Doesn't matter. You're precise by nature. You'll learn without trying." He carried Natasha to the end of the patio, to the wicker love seat. Enough room for two, and he motioned her over. After she sat beside him, he asked, "Have you held her?"

The flames scorching her ears tickled her cheeks. "Will you consider me gutless if I admit I haven't?" Every day she spent long minutes cooing over Natasha, but she'd managed to avoid holding the baby. Glade hadn't called her on it, and Reenie hadn't either.

"Meade, you're unbelievable. She won't break." As if to demonstrate, he lifted Natasha above his head.

"Be careful!"

"I won't drop her." He tipped the baby forward and kissed her forehead. Natasha's lashes fluttered. "Ready to try? It's simple."

"I'm not sure I'm ready." For the baby, for him—for the child inside her, taking shape from the most precious threads of her unspoken dreams and Hector's love.

"Meade, you *are* gutless. C'mon. You can do this."

"Why are you always confident in my abilities?"

"Habit." He rubbed noses with the baby, an Eskimo kiss. "Keep her neck supported and place your other hand under her bottom. Like this." He demonstrated, turning the baby in his capable hands. "You see? Nothing to it."

"Sure."

He handed Natasha off.

Breathless, Meade settled the baby against her breast, the gesture automatic. A soft mewling floated from Natasha's mouth.

She seemed intent on burrowing into Meade's breast.

"She's hungry." Hector checked his watch. "Good thing Glade will be home soon."

The comment disappeared beneath the quiet enveloping them. Natasha's scent was slightly sweet and immensely satisfying, like the aroma of vanilla rising off cake fresh from the oven. She was surprisingly sturdy, a compact bundle of flesh softer than calfskin and more alluring than starlight. The heat consuming Meade left her skin, sinking deep inside her to form a molten core beneath her rib cage, a thrumming core of awareness and wonder. Was this how a woman fell in love with her child? Was Glade similarly besotted the instant she first held Natasha?

One breath, one touch, and the bond sealed.

The library's grandfather clock chimed the midnight hour.

Glade had taken the baby and retired for the night. Reenie had gone too. She'd turned off the lights with the exception of a lamp in the foyer and the library's overhead spotlights, which she'd dimmed. In Hector's lap, Meade hovered at the edge of sleep. Her chest rose and fell on the edge of dreams.

He stole a glance at his watch. Time to take his leave. Resisting, he drew his fingers across her cheek and through the locks framing her face.

Her bombshell regarding Atlanta rolled through his thoughts. If she'd halted the expansion, it meant only one thing. She believed her father's weakening condition warranted her full attention.

Like Theodora, she doubted he'd recover.

Was Landon dying? Was he *choosing* to die? The notion was repugnant, an insult to Hector's most fiercely held ideals. Landon had every reason to live: respect in the community, financial security and, most important of all, the devotion and love of his adult daughters. Not a perfect life, not without a woman to share his days, but it was a good life nonetheless.

The possibility of a funeral was a cruel turn of events for Birdie and Meade. A splintering pain cascaded through him. Especially Meade.

"Hector, what is it?"

He hadn't realized she was watching him. "I thought you were asleep."

"I was."

"Should I leave?"

"Not without telling me what's wrong. You look terribly sad."

"I was thinking about Birdie." Revealing a portion of the truth seemed the best gambit. "This Christmas, she'll have three stockings on the mantle. Gifts for a newborn under the tree, Hugh baking cookies—maybe he'll trust her to ice them."

"Christmas is so far away," she murmured, sitting up. She rubbed her forehead as if banishing an unwelcome thought. "None of us may feel much holiday cheer. If Daddy continues to decline . . ."

She didn't finish, but her thoughts were clear enough. If her father continued to decline, they'd plan a funeral long before the holiday season. Landon would die without seeing either of his grandchildren. They'd grow up without knowing him.

Grief bowed her shoulders, and Hector clasped her hand. Softly he asked, "Have you told him you're pregnant?"

"Not yet. Soon." A sea of anguish threatened to pull them both under, and she tightened her hold on his fingers. "Hector, I can't think about a wedding when I might need to plan a funeral. I can't think about anything but helping my father regain his health. I don't want to lose him."

"You won't," Hector said, hating the false promise. But he hated the fear in her eyes more.

"Are you angry?"

"About waiting? Not even a little. At least you're thinking about our future. A step in the right direction."

"It is."

"Should we get engaged?"

She glanced at him with the charm of an imp. "Can you afford a ring?"

"No."

"Good. I don't care about diamonds. When we take the leap, meet me at the altar with a simple gold band."

"You're letting me off easy."

"Who wouldn't? You're the most patient man in the world."

"Only because I love you. I hope you know how much."

"I do." They were still holding hands as she helped him to his feet. "Don't leave just yet. Let's go upstairs."

The suggestion was startling. "What if someone hears us?" he asked, sorely tempted.

"Everyone's asleep." She brushed his lips with a kiss. "No one will hear a thing."

They'd make love until dawn overtook them, and propriety sent him home. "Then let's go," he replied.

Chapter 16

The pain seized Mary in the shower.

A second wave of agony, and she shut her eyes. Curls of mist rose past her nose. She tried to inhale slowly, tried to keep her wits. Drawing on her medical training, she subdued her roiling emotions.

Her heart pounding, she made herself look. The water streaming down her thighs mixed with the blood swirling in a tragic circle to the drain.

Anthony drove her to the hospital white knuckled and grim. A shelf of black clouds was overtaking the sky, and the air smelled like rain. The cramps hadn't stopped. She tried to ignore the uncomfortable sensation.

She tried to ignore everything she'd lost.

The following morning, she found Anthony at the kitchen table with Blossom. Anthony's coffee had gone cold and Blossom's bowl of cereal was untouched. By unspoken agreement they spent a silent Sunday at the house, the sorrow hidden beneath the busywork each found as a refuge.

Seated at her computer, Mary spent hours sifting through photographs from their smartphones, sending some images to the drugstore to be made into physical copies for a family album. Others were archived on the computer's hard drive, a mindless task that took her far away from the heartache.

At dusk, she was grateful when Blossom and Anthony left for dinner at The Second Chance; they knew not to ask if Mary wanted to join them.

On Monday, Anthony suggested she take the day off. Mary refused. Life didn't stop for a private loss and she assured them that she was fine. Collecting her medical bag and her purse, she announced she'd walk to the office.

In the waiting room, conversation hummed like bees. It would be an especially busy day. Sprinkled in with the typical caseload were eight or ten mothers waiting with children for the physicals required for the upcoming school year's athletic programs. Delia Molek was the first patient of the day, her head congested and her eyes red. Mary told her not to wait tables at The Second Chance until her sinus infection cleared up.

It was bad luck that Ethel Lynn Percible was the day's second patient. One of the women in her knitting circle worked at the hospital, and Ethel Lynn already had her suspicions. After posing a number of roundabout questions, she'd ferreted out the facts.

Just as the town had once celebrated Mary's pregnancy, the people of Liberty now mourned. Handwritten notes appeared in the Perini's mailbox. On the street, passersby made a point of acknowledging Mary with a tip of the head or a smile rife with sadness. Stella Jackowski, who'd planned to babysit next spring, sent over dinner for five days in a row, everything from chicken and rice to a steak fajita concoction that Blossom adored.

Finney, who wasn't put off by the sorrow refracting off Mary or her refusal to stop in to restaurant, began appearing outside the house on North Street each morning at 8:30 A.M. She was a bulldog of an escort, guarding her charge from curious stares and the well-meant comments of sympathy the townspeople wished to offer. If anyone tried to stop Mary during the short walk to Liberty Square, the cook's expression smoldered like trout left too long in her skillet. The cook, understanding the depths of Mary's unvoiced misery, made no attempt at conversation.

Which was a great comfort. The companionable silence allowed Mary's thoughts to scatter in the dappled shade. The maple trees were still vibrant with summer growth. Only a few leaves wore a trim of gold. Apple trees, the pride of Ohio, wagged limbs heavy with fruit.

On the seventh day after the miscarriage, the small

Christmas tree disappeared from the dining room table. Anthony was still at the Gas & Go finishing an oil change and tire rotation. Sweetcakes dozed on the living room rug, her intrepid owner missing. Mary went upstairs and peered into Blossom's empty bedroom. The Christmas tree was stuffed in the corner beside the dresser. The cards proudly made for Lily and Tony were missing.

The door to the nursery was closed.

There was no doubt—Blossom wasn't inside. They'd all been avoiding the nursery, and the stolen promises the cheery space represented. Where was she?

In the kitchen, the window behind the table was open. Air streamed inside, crisp with the first hint of autumn. Mary padded to the window and peered out.

The long rectangle of grass was shaggy and in need of a cut. Like most of the household chores, the mowing had gone unattended while they grieved. Far into the yard, darkness lapped at the trees like the tide coming in. The night's first fireflies were out, dotting the shadows with light that spun between the trees, a glowing, revolving universe. Nearer, by the bed of roses bordering the south side of the lot, Blossom was on her knees.

In her fist, the garden trowel moved quickly, rounding the edges of the small hole she'd made in the grass. The task completed, she tossed the trowel aside.

Blossom turned the cards over in her hands. The dying sun caught on the glittery surface of each card, sending diamonds of light across her damp cheeks. Leaning back on her heels, she shut her eyes tight. Her lips moved on a silent prayer.

When she'd finished, she gave the cards to the brown earth.

September crept in like a visitor barely noticed by the members of the Williams household.

At her father's elbow, Meade squeezed the excess water from the cloth. The scent of French lavender cascaded across the bed as she smoothed the cloth over the furrowed lines of his face and then his eyelids, which were drawn shut with sleep. Lavender water, rose water, an infusion of mint from Reenie's herb garden—all the fragrances Landon adored arrived in the bedroom, one after the next. Initially the practice was meant to revive the man growing thinner by the day, to encourage him to rise from the semi-conscious stupor in which he was trapped. The strategy had proved unsuccessful but Meade continued, and the scents of living things became a shield against the sickly, sour odor clinging to the bedroom.

Beneath her loving ministrations, Landon released a rattling breath.

It was late. Meade had sent the nurse to the kitchen for strong coffee, and insisted Reenie and Glade go to bed. Hector had also gone, taking an exhausted Theodora with him. Only Birdie remained.

In an unspoken agreement, the two sisters now shared a nightly vigil by their father's bedside. Everyday concerns were shucked off. Birdie rarely visited the *Post,* leaving Hugh to handle the staff and the daily rush of deadlines. At *Vivid,* two of Meade's assistants now shared junior management duties. She'd restricted her work to several hours in the afternoon as her obligation to her dying father took precedence.

She dipped the cloth back into the lavender water.

There was no accounting for life's jarring shifts and sudden turns. One minute her father was a vital, healthy man and the next he was stripped of the energy and the fire that had carried him through decades. Beneath the blanket, his body appeared skeletal, his pelvic bones jutting out and his thighs shorn of much-needed muscle. During the rare moments when he reached consciousness his eyes were dull and flat, no longer revealing the sharp intelligence Meade had always admired and, now that it was gone, she understood she'd relied upon. Since early adulthood she'd been Landon's caretaker, his patient and quietly suffering child. But he'd also been her advisor and companion, a trusted confidante eager to celebrate her success as *Vivid* grew from the germ of an idea into a multimillion-dollar business.

On the opposite side of the bed, Birdie stroked his forearm. She was deep in thought, her inimitable violet eyes smoky with anguish.

Meade reached across and patted her hand. "You've been here since morning. Why not go home?" Instinct warned their father wouldn't last the night, but it seemed an unnecessary cruelty to expect Birdie to stay and watch him die.

Birdie's eyes snapped. "Do you think I'd leave you here alone? I'm staying, and that's final."

Her desire to share the burden warmed Meade with gratitude. "At least take a break. Go downstairs, stretch your legs."

"I could use something to eat."

She never stopped eating. Well into the second trimester of pregnancy, she'd acquired the nonstop snacking habits of an adolescent boy. "Reenie has fruit salad in the fridge," Meade said. "She also made chicken."

Birdie eased herself from the chair. "I won't be long." Yawning, she rubbed her spine. "Want anything?"

"I'm not hungry."

Tiptoeing out, her sister made a point of leaving the door ajar. It was yet another demonstration she wouldn't leave Meade alone during these terrible hours. Despite her sadness, Meade was comforted. They *were* becoming sisters in the truest sense. The tragedy befalling them had bound them close.

 The sound of footfalls retreated down the hallway. The quiet returning, Meade leaned close to her father's ear. She'd stalled long enough.

"Daddy, I don't know if you can hear me." The anguish locked in her heart rushed out. "I can't bear to think of losing you. You're stubborn, and you won't stay—why won't you stay for Birdie and me? Why must you go when I'm not ready, when there's so much I need to share with you?"

Her forehead throbbed. She couldn't breathe, the rush of emotion clogging her nose. Yet she pushed herself on.

"Daddy, I need you to stay." She clasped his hands. His fingers were as cold as marble. She rubbed them to impart her warmth into the dying flesh. "I'm having a baby. Can you hear me? Next spring I'm having a baby, and I want you to live to see my child. I want you to walk me down the aisle like you did with Birdie, escort me to the man I'll love for the rest of my life." Grief drummed at her breast, but so did happiness, the purity of which brought a gurgling laugh from her throat. "Who knows? Maybe good fortune will strike twice, and I'll have a second child—

another grandchild for you to hold. Anything is possible if you put wings to your dreams. Daddy, won't you stay? I need you to see how happy I'll be with Hector and our children."

The words rushed over her father as if he were a rock in the riverbed of her confession, untouched and unmoved. She felt his pulse. It was slow, weak. Was he listening? Did he understand she was miraculously pregnant? In every way that mattered, it appeared he was already gone. The bitter likelihood increased her sobs.

Afterward, she dried her face. No good would come of allowing Birdie to see her overwrought. She went to the rocking chair by the window, and looked around for her purse. Where had she placed it? Finally she located it in the shadows behind the chair. Lightheaded, she dug out a compact of powder and lipstick, and fixed her make-up.

Two stories below, moon glow danced in the garden. Meade pressed her fingers to the glass. Take a walk? Doing so would clear her head. Help her prepare—help her find the strength to comfort her sister when the worst minutes arrived. She was certain the dawn, only a few hours off, would arrive on the heels of death.

"Meade."

She spun around.

In the doorway, Birdie shook like leaves caught in a summer gust. How long had she been standing there?

She approached slowly, pausing at the foot of their father's bed. "Why didn't you tell me you're pregnant?" Hurt swam in her eyes.

Meade looked away, embarrassed. "I wasn't ready to tell anyone."

"Meade, *why?* Don't you trust me?"

"It has nothing to do with trust." A shudder rocked her ribcage. Weakness followed, and she sank into the rocking chair. "I couldn't tell you—tell anyone—until I decided a course of action. I wasn't prepared to become a single mother, and I can't bring myself to rush into marriage. I needed time for my own counsel."

"Naturally."

"Birdie, please don't be angry."

"I'm not angry," she shot back. "I get it. You travel solo. It's habit. I used to think you were brave. I don't now. You're a coward. You don't have the courage to let anyone get too close. You're afraid if you're vulnerable, you'll risk getting hurt."

The accusation stung, but Meade got to her feet. Her sister's feelings of betrayal were justified. There was no logical reason to hide the pregnancy. There had been countless opportunities to share the news. Even if no one else was apprised of the situation, why keep the truth from Birdie?

Glancing at their father's sleeping form, Meade lowered her voice to a whisper. "I didn't mean to hurt you. Honestly, I didn't. I'm not used to bringing anyone into my confidence."

"Except Mary."

"I didn't tell her."

The admission squelched the ire on Birdie's face. "You didn't?"

"I told Hector because it was the right thing to do. I should've told you too. It was a mistake. Can you forgive me? Forgive your foolish, bumbling sister?" Meade came forward, her eyes brimming. She placed her hand on Birdie's precious baby bump. "We're family, Birdie. Our children will grow up together. They'll have everything we were denied—each other."

"You'll stop shutting me out?"

"I will."

"It's not fair. What have I ever done to make you doubt me?"

"Nothing."

"You have to let people in, Meade. Especially the people who care about you the most."

"I know, sweetie. I'll do better."

Satisfied, Birdie offered the shadow of a smile. Then she turned mournful eyes to the bed. "I feel cheated. I've only known Daddy for a year. Not enough time." She took Meade's hand, seeking strength. "Should I get the nurse? He's drinking coffee in the library, trying to keep his eyes open."

"Don't bother. We'll manage together. You and me—sisters."

Her expression fluid, Birdie fell into Meade's arms.

On a dreary Thursday in September, Landon was buried at

All Soul's Cemetery.

The sky spit droplets, but the mourners were spared an all-out downpour as final prayers were said over the casket. Many townspeople attended, and the brisk wind bit at the women's calves and the children's cheeks. A queue of cars waited to ferry the mourners to the Williams estate. Reenie and a staff hired in for the day had prepared a buffet in the ballroom where, a few short months ago, Birdie and Hugh had celebrated the beginning of their life together.

In the grand foyer, Meade greeted mourners in a fog of exhaustion and grief. Birdie stood at her side, her generous figure wrapped in a steel grey dress and her face void of makeup. The heated conversation on the night of Landon's death seemed forgotten, and Meade was grateful her sister had forgiven her. She vowed never to hurt Birdie again.

The din emanating from the ballroom grew in volume as the last mourners arrived to pay their respects. The sky remained overcast but the threat of rain diminished, and people spilled onto the patio in back. Meade smiled as Hector appeared.

"Have either of you seen Theodora?" he asked. "I couldn't find her in the crowd."

"Isn't she with Hugh?" Birdie lowered her voice. "She's taking Daddy's death hard. She shouldn't be alone."

"She's not with Hugh."

Mary came out of the library. "Theodora went for a walk alone," she supplied. "I saw her heading toward the boathouse." She looked to Meade. "Why don't we go down to fetch her?"

Nodding, Meade brushed her fingers across Birdie's wrist. "Come with us?"

Birdie agreed, and the three women started off. The circular driveway before the mansion was crammed with cars three deep. Wending their way past, they strolled across the damp grass. The late afternoon gloom painted the gardens in shades of ash, and the golden heads of the Black-eyed Susans drooped nearly to the ground. Rounding a stand of boxwood, Meade cast an appraising glance at Mary. Birdie did the same.

The sympathy in their eyes brought Mary to a standstill. "Let's not do this, all right? I don't need to talk about it." She rubbed her arms, a futile attempt to banish the agony Meade knew she felt. "Blossom is taking this hardest. Anthony and I will muddle through. We always do."

Meade heard herself ask, "Have you talked to Blossom?"

"I tried. How do you explain first trimester risk of miscarriage to a thirteen year old? A woman can lose her baby and never know she was pregnant. There are always risks. Oh, we assured her next year we'll try again. When I'm ready. Anthony and I agreed not to tell her until I'm well into the second trimester."

"Sensible."

"I hate seeing Blossom like this. Just heartbroken. Glade is helping drive away her blues. She's invited Blossom over to play with Natasha twice in the last week. It's something."

"How are *you* managing?" Meade asked.

Mary shrugged. "Keeping busy helps. I'm a doctor, well-versed in life and death situations."

"That doesn't make it easier."

"Maybe not." Mary kicked a stone from the path. "The odd part? The pregnancy never seemed real. I couldn't tell Anthony. He wouldn't have understood. From the beginning I felt like . . . I don't know. Like I shouldn't hope too much."

The comment surprised Meade. Her experience was the opposite. From the onset she'd experienced the uncanny sensation she knew the baby she was carrying. A girl sure to inherit Birdie's matchless violet eyes. The baby would grow into a woman more headstrong than Meade, but with Hector's compassion woven through her personality.

Fanciful dreams, but she believed every one.

Dismissing her musings, she said to Mary, "I'm sorry about your miscarriage. My heart goes out to you."

"Mine too," Birdie put in.

Mary sent a look rife with compassion. "As mine does for both of you. I'm sorry you lost your father. I wish I could've done more."

"You did everything possible," Meade assured her as they continued walking toward the lake. "Daddy never tried to bounce back from the stroke. He felt it was his time. We have to accept it."

Seagulls swooped through the blustery wind. The lake flung

angry waves toward the overcast skies, the waters churning and throwing foam. At the lake's edge, Theodora was tossing aside her shoes and hitching up her severe black skirt. Boldly she waded into the surf.

Birdie was the first to reach the sand. "Hey! You aren't thinking of diving in, are you?" she shouted. "You'll freeze!"

The admonishment brought a cackle from Theodora. "What are you fretting about? Do I look like I'm dressed for a swim? If I were thinking about doing laps, I would've put on proper gear." She regarded Meade and Mary, giggling and pulling off their shoes. "That's the spirit. The water's fine. I wish I did have my bathing gear. I'm so fidgety—so blazing mad—a swim would do me good."

Meade understood the sentiment. She felt similarly agitated, the grief in her bosom residing uncomfortably beside the anger. What sense was there in being furious at her father? He was gone. Besides, it wasn't uncommon for the elderly to give up, to refuse to fight for another day of life. It wasn't uncommon for a man to surrender. He hadn't abandoned her any more than he'd abandoned Birdie. Had he drifted out of their lives comforted by the knowledge they now had each other, and the men they chose to love?

The waves smacking at her knees, Meade fought for balance. "Do you want to talk about it?" she asked Theodora.

"What's there to say? Landon was a stubborn mule. He led a good life, and left us on his own terms. It was an honor to know him. Of course, I'll miss him," she added, and the admission convulsed the muscles beside her weathered lips. Sorrow careened through her eyes. Warding it off, she told Meade, "I'm proud of you, child."

They'd never been close, and the compliment raised Meade's brows. "You are? Why?"

"What a damn fool question. Didn't you take care of that cantankerous old hoot for more years than I care to count? Did a fine job, too." A devilish light entered her dark eyes. "It's a wonder you didn't lose your mind."

"He was my father. I never would've let him down."

Birdie waded in. "If I fall over, someone rescue me. I'm a lousy swimmer."

Theodora chuckled. "Ask Meade to do the honors. Once when she was a bitty thing, she swam out in these waters all the way to the horizon. Barely five years old at the time. Gave me the sort of fright a woman never forgets."

Mary followed them into the churning waves. She held her arms out, nearly slipped, and giggled. Grinning, Meade helped her steady her feet.

"What did Meade do?" Mary asked.

"The bitty thing, why, she got into a tiff with her mother right before a banquet and ran out to the beach. No one saw her leave the mansion."

"Except you?"

"Exactly."

Eddies of water swirled around Meade's ankles. "Theodora, I don't recall swimming the lake by myself, certainly not as a young child."

"Think, child. You swam to catch the moon. Fast as lightning."

"I don't—" A wave slapped into her knees.

The shock of cold water jogged the memory long hidden in her mind. She recalled the moon rising in the sky and the much warmer waters of July.

Startled, she said, "Do you mean the night I swam with my father in the moonlight? I was young. Getting ready to enter kindergarten, I think."

Theodora snorted. "Not with your father. You swam with me. I saw you cutting through the waves, and stripped right out of my evening gown. Didn't think I'd be doing laps in my fancy lingerie, but there you have it. I thought you'd drown before I got to you."

The story was disconcerting. "Was I drowning?"

"Hell, no. You were swimming like a dolphin. Swimming with the angriest look on your face, like you'd beat the water if it didn't give way. When I asked what the blazes you were doing, you said you were running away from Cat."

Running away from her mother. Naturally. When *hadn't* she been intent on escaping her indomitable mother?

A gust of wind nearly blew Meade back. Finding her center of gravity, she pushed long tendrils of hair from her eyes. She was entranced by Theodora's story. "Why was I angry at my mother?"

"The silliest thing. She found you sitting in your father's closet, shining his shoes for the ball."

"Why did she care if I shined his shoes?"

Theodora laughed with derision. "Lordy, I can't believe you're asking. Why, your mother was livid. Thought you were behaving like one of the servants. Hiding in the closet, shining your father's shoes—she didn't understand how much you needed to please him. My, how he loved you. Every time Cat threw a barb, he'd lavish you with praise."

Meade's heart ached. "I do remember Daddy's praise." And her mother's hard criticism.

"You wanted to help him get ready for the banquet. It wasn't like you could get within ten feet of Cat when she was readying for a hundred guests. Her suite of rooms was off limits to everyone but her private maid, the hairdresser and the rest of her retinue."

Birdie, equally taken with the story, said to Meade, "You've been caring for Daddy your whole life."

A vestige of the lonely child inside Meade stirred. "I suppose I have."

"I'll miss him as much as you will, but I can't help but wonder. What will you do, now that you're free?"

What indeed?

Forty years old was late to begin one's life, yet a surge of excitement rushed through her. The light emotion lessened the grief burdening her, and she gazed at the overcast sky with defiance. Her heart's calling seemed instilled with special power, and the sun poked out from behind the muddy edge of a cloud to laser the tumultuous waters with a knife's edge of gold. It was gone as quickly as it appeared.

When their calves were icy to the touch, the women waded back to shore. The temperature was dropping fast, and a scattering of red maple leaves danced along the shore. There were towels in the beach house, and Meade led the women inside to dry off.

Absently Mary picked through the tackle, and the other odds and ends cluttered on the table. "You didn't answer the question." She smiled at Meade. "What will you do now?"

Untangling the knots in her hair, Meade shrugged. "Spend more time with Hector and less at work. What's it like to put in forty hours, and no more? I have no idea. I'd like to find out."

"Send me the memo when you do. I'd like to learn."

"You're a doctor. Take charge of your schedule. Stop taking new patients."

Theodora found a chair and dropped into it. "Don't listen to her, Mary. You're Liberty's only physician. How can you turn people away?"

"I can't."

"Good to hear." The hem of Theodora's skirt was waterlogged, and she squeezed large droplets onto the floor. When she'd finished, she gave Mary an appraising look. "I've got a suggestion. I hope you'll hear me out."

Finding a chair, Birdie dragged it close. "Now you're in for it. Once Theodora gets an idea in her head, there's no arguing with her."

"It's all right, Birdie." Mary cleared some of the tackle out of the way and hopped onto the table.

Theodora grunted. "I'm not twisting arms today. I'm too upset. Mary's a kind woman, isn't she? Reasonable. When doesn't she look out for the less fortunate? Anthony, too. Why, he changes the oil in Finney's car every three months and never asks for a dime. He knows she's stretched thin living on a waitress's wages."

"Delia's car too," Mary admitted. "It's the least we can do. The Second Chance wouldn't stay afloat without them. The restaurant may never provide my family much in the way of income, but I'm happy to keep it open. I like knowing I've created jobs in town." Swinging her legs like a schoolgirl, she regarded Theodora. "Now, what's your suggestion?"

"If memory serves, there are six bedrooms in your home."

"Seven, if you count the attic." Mary laughed. "We'll never finish renovating the house. There's room enough for three families. Thank God Anthony loves weekend projects."

Birdie folded her hands on her belly. "He's not the only one. Didn't Glade and Delia help Blossom fix up the nursery?"

Mention of the nursery sent emotion filtering through

Mary's features. Containing it, she said, "An understatement. They went on a mad decorating binge. Glade chose the wallpaper, cartoon elephants with angel wings. The most ridiculous thing you've ever seen. No one but a teenager like Glade would think the room was appropriate for—"

Halting in midsentence, she leaned back on her palms. Her legs stopped chasing the air. A surge of expectancy swirled around her—

Swirled around them all.

Meade, leaning against the wall, looked up. She met Mary's astonished gaze.

Theodora, as usual, was onto something.

Chapter 17

Birdie came across the Perini's front porch with arms outstretched. "You're here, finally! I've been dying to hold Natasha. Time to share, sis."

"Must I give her up?" Meade pressed her lips to the baby's petal-soft brow. "She's been in my arms for all of ten seconds. I'm not ready to give her up."

"Like it or not, you're sharing."

"No."

"Yes." Laughing, Birdie waved to Glade and Hector. They were pulling bags from the back seat of his car. Taking the baby, she asked, "How was moving day?"

"For Reenie? Suffice it to say she's not happy. She'll miss having Glade underfoot."

"Tell her to come into town for a visit whenever she likes. This really is for the best. Glade can walk to work at The Second Chance, and have all the help she needs with Natasha. Plus Blossom's thrilled over the prospect of a little one in the house."

"So are Mary and Anthony."

"This doesn't make up for their loss, but they do seem better. It's as if helping Glade is helping them too."

"I'm sure it is." The aroma of charbroiled steak reached Meade's nostrils. Switching topics, she said, "I've had nothing to eat since we started packing this morning. Please tell me Finney is manning the grill."

"She promised to have lunch ready whenever we finish

unpacking the nursery. Mary and Anthony are upstairs preparing the rooms with Blossom."

It was a lovely Sunday at September's end. All along North Street the maple trees blazed crimson and orange. The whirr of a lawn mower split the air, and a few kids were across the street tossing a football. From the windows on the second floor of the Perini's house, lighthearted banter drifted down.

Like her younger sister, Meade was still grieving the loss of their father. The sadness struck at unpredictable moments. While chatting with clients at *Vivid* or enjoying an evening stroll with Hector, the sense of loss seemed overwhelming. Some days were worse than others, and the blues were so enervating she struggled to forestall the tears. Yet since this morning, she'd felt nothing but joy while helping Glade pack for the move into Liberty.

Even though Glade was now a parent, she was still very much a teenager in need of companionship, something she'd receive in abundance residing in town. Anthony and Mary had agreed to give her a bedroom for her own use, and the cartoon-themed nursery for Natasha, rent-free. After one year, they'd discuss whether she was prepared to live independently with her child.

Meade's cell buzzed. With satisfaction, she read the caller ID. For the last three days, she'd been trying to reach the mayor of Atlanta. She was tired of leaving messages with his secretary.

The mayor got right down to business. "Miss Williams, I understand you'd like to make a donation to the great city of Atlanta?"

She explained about the department store her father had purchased for *Vivid's* expansion. Finishing, she added, "I've decided not to expand my company, and won't need the facility. The neighborhood where the building is located . . . is there a youth center?"

Her query met with a long silence. Finally the mayor said, "As much as we appreciate your generosity, we can't turn a mothballed department store into a youth center. It's too large."

"No, but you can take the proceeds from the sale, build a center and fund it for the next decade."

Atlanta's mayor was still thanking her when Hector reached

the front porch. Finishing the call, she tucked the cell into the back pocket of her jeans.

Hector tossed a garbage bag filled with Glade's clothes into her arms. "You made the donation?" He held the door open for her.

"Sure did."

"I'm proud of you."

"Me too."

"Does this mean you'll have more time in your schedule?" He grinned devilishly. "If so, how 'bout penciling me in for the next fifty years?"

She chuckled. "Consider it done." Midway up the stairwell, she heard the front door bang. Glade, carrying three bags, dumped one in the foyer. Meade called to her, "This isn't a marathon. Drag one bag up at a time. Leave the heavier stuff for the men. What good is brute strength if it isn't put to good use on moving day?"

Inside the nursery, Anthony and Mary were on their backs halfway beneath the crib. A toolbox sat between them.

Hector peered under. "Safety check," he explained to Meade. He kicked at Mary's pink tennis shoes. "Come on out. I'll help Anthony secure the beast. We'll have every bolt tightened a.s.a.p."

They traded places, and Meade helped Mary to her feet. Glade came into the room dragging a bag torn in several spots from the march up the stairwell.

Glade trailed her hand across the crib's dainty white railing. "This is beautiful. Natasha will love it." She noticed the comforter inside, which matched the elephant wallpaper she'd selected weeks ago. "You bought it! Oh, Mary—it's perfect."

"The rug is on its way," Mary replied. "It was on back order. We'll have it by the end of the week."

"You bought the rug too? The one with elephant angels on the border?"

"The very one."

Glade pulled Mary close and spun in a dizzy circle. "Thank you!" Letting go, she rushed back out. "Let me get Natasha. She's got to see this!"

"Wait until the new mother sees her own room," Meade said

249

to Mary. "Last night Hector and I went on a shopping spree. New bedspread, sheets, curtains—the works. We also found a floor-to-ceiling bulletin board to spare your walls. Just in case Glade decides to paper the place with photos from fashion mags."

Mary looked positively relieved. "I owe you one. I remember filling nail holes in my first apartment. It took hours . . . and I used toothpaste."

"You didn't."

"I hope the landlord never found out." She bent, to check Anthony's progress. "Are you done or what? The women need the room. We have to unpack the baby's things before moving this party to Glade's room."

For the next hour, Meade and Mary organized the two bedrooms. Fuzzy sleepers were folded and stowed in the nursery's dresser. The closet in Glade's room was filled with shirts, the magazines she loved and the few dresses she owned. Blue jeans found their way into her dresser, and the women made up the twin-sized bed with the linens Meade had purchased—a tie-died pattern in vivid purple, pink and blue.

After they'd finished, they followed the savory aroma of Finney's good eats to the backyard. Sweetcakes ran in circles as Blossom heaped a plate with steak and all the trimmings. Natasha was in Birdie's arms, fast asleep. Anthony and Glade were jokingly throwing elbows and jockeying for position in front of Finney.

Mary went to join them, and Meade cast her attention across the crowd. Where was Hector?

She found him deep in the yard, appreciating the sun dipping low in the sky. "Hey, you," she murmured, slipping beneath his arm. "Aren't you famished? If we don't get in line, the last steak will disappear."

"I think Finney will take pity on us and hide a steak. We'll split it."

"All right."

He glanced at the trees to their left, rustling in bands of crimson. "I can't believe summer's gone. Before you know it, we'll be handing out Halloween candy."

"From your RV?" It sounded charming.

"The youth center, silly. I'll have the place open by then." His

250

brows lowered. "I nearly forgot. The Rotary Club is dropping off more supplies tonight. I'll need to sort through the stuff."

"I'll help."

"You have to work in the morning."

"I'll go in late. The two assistants I've been grooming? Turns out they're pretty good. I don't mind delegating more of my workload to them."

"And here you didn't think you were flexible," Hector joked, turning her to face him. Placing his hand on her abdomen, he nodded toward the others. "When are we making an announcement? I don't care if we wait to set a date, but I would like my bragging rights."

"You're incorrigible."

"Nope. Just a man in love."

He gave her a hungering kiss. His hand remained lightly caressing her belly, giving rise to the quivering connection with the baby they'd created, the precious life they'd bring together into the world.

Quivering.

On a gasp, Meade broke off the kiss. Beneath Hector's fingers, a slow, rolling sensation built in her abdomen. It curled through her, an expression of life, a feeling like nothing she'd ever before experienced.

"Hector. The baby. I can feel the baby moving!"

His eyes glazed with shock and delight. "You're sure?"

For proof, she held his hand firmly against her skin. The movement began again, stronger now—

Strong enough to carry his shout of joy across the sun-drenched grass.

Dear Reader: If you enjoyed Four Wishes and posted a review, please contact me at christinenolfi@gmail.com for a special gift. I truly appreciate the kindness. Please write "Review Posted" in the subject line of your email.

The books in The Liberty Series work as stand-alone novels you may enjoy in any order. Look for the other books in the series: Treasure Me, Second Chance Grill and The Impossible Wish. Other novels outside this series: The Dream You Make and The Tree of Everlasting Knowledge.

You'll also find me at christinenolfi.com or please visit my Facebook Author Page. On Twitter: @christinenolfi

⁂

About the Author

Award-winning author **Christine Nolfi** provides readers with heartwarming and inspiring fiction. Her 2011 debut *Treasure Me* is a Next Generation Indie Awards finalist. The Midwest Book Review lists many of her novels as "highly recommended" and her books have enjoyed bestseller status on both Amazon and Barnes & Noble. She has also written the manual for writers *Reviews Sell Books.*

Please visit her at
www.christinenolfi.com

Follow her on Twitter at
@christinenolfi

Also by Christine Nolfi

Treasure Me

Second Chance Grill

The Impossible Wish

The Tree of Everlasting Knowledge

The Dream You Make

Reviews Sell Books

Made in the USA
Lexington, KY
22 May 2015